— THE —
PAWN

L.J. JONES

Trilogy Christian Publishers
A Wholly Owned Subsidiary of Trinity Broadcasting Network
2442 Michelle Drive
Tustin, CA 92780

Copyright © 2020 by L.J. Jones

All Scripture quotations, unless otherwise noted, taken from THE HOLY BIBLE, NEW INTERNATIONAL VERSION®, NIV® Copyright © 1973, 1978, 1984, 2011 by Biblica, Inc.® Used by permission. All rights reserved worldwide.

Scripture quotations marked (KJV) taken from *The Holy Bible, King James Version.* Cambridge Edition: 1769.

All rights reserved, including the right to reproduce this book or portions thereof in any form whatsoever.

For information, address Trilogy Christian Publishing
Rights Department, 2442 Michelle Drive, Tustin, Ca 92780.
Trilogy Christian Publishing/ TBN and colophon are trademarks of Trinity Broadcasting Network.

For information about special discounts for bulk purchases, please contact Trilogy Christian Publishing.

Manufactured in the United States of America

Trilogy Disclaimer: The views and content expressed in this book are those of the author and may not necessarily reflect the views and doctrine of Trilogy Christian Publishing or the Trinity Broadcasting Network.

10 9 8 7 6 5 4 3 2 1

Library of Congress Cataloging-in-Publication Data is available.

ISBN 978-1-64088-377-2 (Print Book)
ISBN 978-1-64088-378-9 (ebook)

My childhood was somewhat like a chess game
Rob taught me how to play but then showed no mercy
He planned his moves in advance and
snatched my pieces with ease
Cunning, manipulative, and powerful
Winning was impossible
I was too young
My pawns were scattered throughout
Some broken
Some buried
Some burnt
Some turned into ashes
Until…

The last pawn that
Brings forth God's radiant light into
The detestable darkness
Remains courageously standing

Preface

This book depicts graphic descriptions relating to barbaric acts of child abuse for sadistic purposes. These are factual accounts which may be unfathomable for some to imagine and downright disturbing. For others, you may be able to identify with the trauma, which may bring up your own suppressed memories. But hopefully, you can realize you're not alone. We are bound together for one ultimate purpose—to rise above our circumstances. In order to grasp the concept of my spiritual awakening, "coming full circle" (so to speak) and discovering the revelation uncovered along the journey, it will be worth reading in its entirety. Hopefully you can visualize my personal transformation which, in turn, ignites hope and inspiration for all who read this memoir. I've experienced relentless heartache reliving the nightmares of my childhood many times over while writing this book the past several years. However, it's fully worth the discovery that I've experienced, called to share with humanity and bring hope to a hurting population. It's ironic—I wouldn't have chosen this painful path for myself, but now I'm grateful it was chosen for me. Well, most of it.

I need to mention that I realize this book may not resonate with everyone, and that is completely understandable. I wrote this geared specifically toward those individuals who can relate or identify with the horrific cycle. The purpose is to show God's unfailing love in my own life so it can be used as an illustration for each and every one of us—no matter how dark our pasts may have been.

Disclaimer: I have tried to recreate events and dialogue from my memories of them. In order to maintain anonymity in some instances, I have changed the names of individuals and places that I felt necessary.

This is my story.

I always wondered why the powers that be—often referred to as the Higher Power, the Universe, our Creator, and God (which I now prefer)—allowed such an unworthy, defective, drug-addicted soul like mine a second chance at life. Okay, countless chances.

I didn't consider these chances to be divine interventions by any means. I called those bizarre situations "coincidences," leaving absolutely no room for the spiritual aspect. Maybe I was agnostic. I just couldn't put a label on my beliefs. I tended to have a one-track mind, a my-way-or-the-highway kind of thinking until my near-death experience broadly expanded me to consider spiritual possibilities, although not instantly. Slow learner, perhaps.

Inspired by the book title, even though I didn't understand the shattered pieces of my broken life at the time, I later realized that each fallen pawn (symbolically speaking) in my journey represented a painful part of me that *survived* and *healed* enough to share my story with you.

My intention is not to share my experiences to show how I was singled out for abuse or to unravel a spool for pity. I am presenting a string of events that have a running thread of truth that others may identify and cut the ties, leaving behind that one thread of hope and healing. I had to consciously alter my worldly perception if I wanted to survive. My young adulthood was riddled with drug abuse, domestic violence, loss of self, and an absolute disregard for God. Two steps forward, one step back had been my process. I'm far from perfect but have come to believe that somehow my story may be used for the greater good rather than merely serving a helpless victim.

My prayer is that through my challenges, other individuals will find compassion, understanding of themselves, self-acceptance, and forgiveness. No matter what unfortunate circumstances you may have encountered, you will begin to know God, experience His mercy, love, and share many stories of triumph for all to witness. Rise above the challenges and unify together.

> *But those who trust in the Lord will find new strength. They will soar high on wings like eagles. They will run and not grow weary. They will walk and not be faint. (Isaiah 40:31 NLT)*

I literally died that night, I thought to myself. I reflect on what should have been a woman's precious moment in time, which turned out to be the worst day of my life. Now I'm about to reveal the one part of my past that I've tried relentlessly to cover up from these people for years.

Shame and guilt no longer have power over me—I acknowledge this to myself then exhale a prolonged, deep breath.

I sit behind a fold-up table alongside my former esteemed colleague and fellow recovering addict, admiring the newly renovated Hiram Johnson State Building in San Francisco. My hands are folded in a prayer position perched on the table as I fix my eyes on the poster board that reads, "September 21, 2007," with a familiar name listed as one of the primary speakers for this conference.

Staring at my name, displayed on the metal stand, along with three others near the door entry, I shook with amazement. *Wow—that's me*, I affirm, shaking my head with disbelief.

For a moment, I acknowledge all the challenges that I have overcome, and I am filled with gratitude. I offer a silent prayer for courage and give thanks for this opportunity to give back. At last, my long-awaited redemption has somehow arrived in a spiritual kind of way.

I gaze out to the audience, feeling a bit jittery and nervous about the upcoming expectations and potential judgments of some. *It's going to be okay. I'm okay. Just like the song Lisa used to sing to me.* I move my arms across my stomach as if I am wrapped in an invisible security blanket. *I feel safe now.* I know there are various occupations present (Children's and Family Social Service workers, MFTs, MDs, RNs, substance abuse counselors, and community outreach workers). Dry mouth suddenly sets in.

The audience's eyes are straight ahead. The professionals occupy the seats that were empty just a few seconds ago. The early birds flip through the itinerary while the others glance up at the projector screen that hangs from the ceiling just above my head. Then a few latecomers scurry in at the last minute.

I smile at Dr. Saffier, who soon will be introduced as the Addiction Medicine Specialist, our main facilitator and presenter for today's training event. He's testing the projector to prevent any technical difficulty of the video he had constructed of my tragic life story years prior. He smiles in return and nods with confirmation that *he's ready*. I affirm and take a sip of water.

I'm ready.

Pinch of Reality

Twenty years earlier...

I literally died that night. All I knew was—the one day that was supposed to be a woman's precious moment in time turned out to be one of the worst days of my life.

When I entered through those double sliding-glass hospital doors that chilly Thursday evening in November 1988, I had little knowledge that I was about to become the property of the county hospital—more psychologically than in the literal sense. By the reaction from the medical staff, I assumed the neon-orange sticker on my chart signified something awful, along with the big red "warning" label stuck on the front of my file. Behind the nurse's station, "induce labor" was thrown out there as if I had no rights and had just enlisted into the army.

"I see that the last time you were seen at the clinic was a couple months ago," the nurse commented as she walked up to my bedside flipping through the medical chart. She quickly looked behind her and gave the other nurses a quick yet unusual nod.

Understandably, the charge nurse considered my pregnancy "high risk" due to my lack of prenatal care. Apparently, I showed symptoms of toxemia, had elevated blood pressure, water-retentive swollen feet, and appeared to be under the influence of narcotics. These conditions reinforced her decision to start the inducing process without my consent. She was noticeably suspicious that I was under the influence of something because her entourage of three nurses came in my room, turned off the lights, and shone the flashlight directly into my eyeballs the way those trained police officers check for a DUI. They began huddling in the corner as if they were three Inspector Gadgets, nodding their heads and whispering as if they were contemplating a bust. The intensity of my nervousness escalated as I watched their every move suspiciously. Normally, reading body language wasn't one of my strengths, but it didn't take a genius to figure out what was about to happen. I started violently screaming at the nurses, "I'm not ready for the baby!" Blankets flew across the room off my feet. Then I realized what was soon to follow—the rubber tubes.

In a panic, two nurses rushed to my side and forced my shoulders back to the mattress in an attempt to calm me down and control the situation. Before I knew it, a syringe was injected into the IV by the other nurse, and within no time, that dreaded labor began. Five hours later, my newborn son was swept away from my arms. Within seconds, beneath me, I felt excessive warm fluids that raged from my bottom area as if a main artery had burst. I had hemorrhaged and gone into septic shock when my blood pressure vastly plummeted. In these deadly danger zones, vital organs start to fail. All the monitors beeped at the same time, and I saw sweat vividly dripping from the bushy brow of an olive-skinned nurse, or maybe a nurse practitioner, since there was a shortage of physicians that night—unsure why the doctor was unavailable. Her hair was drawn back in a ponytail. I stared directly into her teary, intensely bloodshot eyes, and we both knew death was knocking at my door. From her facial expression, eyeballs bulged, she appeared to be just as petrified as I was, sweating profusely. I knowingly looked at her straight in the eye and said, "I'm dying…here I go." She began nodding in agreement, although she continued to fight for my life, furiously shuffling the medical equipment and spewing out medical terminology I didn't understand over an intercom.

Suddenly I felt like my body was rising. I had giant eyes—meaning, my peripheral vision was heightened—and I was looking down at myself from a different point of view, helplessly lying in that hospital bed. My lower body was vastly covered in blood. The nurses ran in and out, scrambling around frantically, pushing different buttons, grabbing packets of medication with one hand, and squeezing my hand with the other. I had been in this position before when I was a little girl, being tortured by my step-grandmother for wetting the bed. I had the ability to leave my body when the pain was too intense. It became automatic for me. But this experience was much different.

Then it happened. I was no longer going up; I was falling in a narrow tunnel of darkness. I felt like I was slipping down into a steep tunnel with wretched souls being held behind thick bars trying to grab me. Looking back at this reminds me of the movie *Ghost*, when the evil from the underground goes up and snatches the punished soul to its final destination. I knew I was headed to somewhere awful, the dark side, because I could see no rays of light in sight. It looked more like the black abyss. I was petrified to die. Luckily for me, I didn't meet who or what was standing at the end of the tunnel to greet me for my eternal departure that day, although I was soon to get an unexpected visit from an unwanted stranger.

When I woke up midmorning, my head was spinning. I was feeling disoriented and groggy from the side effects of the mag-sulfate drip running through my veins to reduce the high-blood pressure, and who knows what else was counteracting my fluctuating blood flow. The room looked blurry, and the strong disinfectant aroma made my stomach a bit queasy. I could hear the classic tongue-rolling dialect from individuals speaking Spanish at the same time just a few feet away. Although I couldn't interpret what was being said, I could sense by their laughter that they were ecstatic with their new family addition.

On my side of the room, there were the same red-blinking monitors above my head, an annoying beeping sound in my ear, and surprisingly, no family members in sight. *Where is everybody?* Kicking the blankets off my feet, I struggled out of bed and secured my hospital gown from flying open by scrunching the backend together.

Still feeling weak and wobbly from giving birth the night before, I gripped the IV pole with my right hand to keep my balance. I slowly pushed my way through the hallway, feeling somewhat uncomfortable that the menstrual pad I was wearing felt like a diaper—they're triple times the size of a store-bought pad.

Just ahead, I observed a young female down the hall whom I flagged down. She reminded me of a playful character from a Disney flick. The young volunteer wore a candy-striped apron with a matching red-white boat hat. Her outfit was what caught my attention. Growing up, my mother had always taught all five of us girls how to coordinate our clothes to match. She'd tell us never to wear checkered shirts with striped pants and always match the colors. She'd go on to say, "But you can wear any color with black because black goes with just about anything." That always stuck with me. (Unfortunately, today's fashion—not so cool. As a matter of fact, a youngster told me recently, it's "flat-out not cool." Oh boy, times have changed.)

I guess because I felt so screwed up on the inside, it was important for me to look halfway presentable on the outside, or so I thought.

"Can you help me?" I asked. "Do you know directions to the nursery?"

"Yes. Make a right at the corner, and you'll run right into it," she politely responded with a pleasant smile on her face, pointing me in the right direction. "By the way, would you like a newspaper this morning?" she offered as she straightened the disorganized magazine piles on the cart just perfectly to her liking.

"No, thank you," I responded. I didn't want to admit I was a horrible reader, assigned to the slow readers' group in elementary school. I had a hard time with comprehension and wasn't concerned with current events. Besides, I thought newspapers were for old people.

"Candy canes?" I asked.

"Sorry. Newspapers, magazines, and coffee."

Approaching the nursery, I stopped at the huge square window for excited sightseers and gazed around for the blue name tag announcing, "Dustin—Baby Boy." I observed each baby nicely tucked in a wraparound blanket, and I started counting in my head: one, two, three through eighteen. Wow, a lot of babies had been born, but my son's name tag was nowhere in the room. As I looked around further, I could see one nurse cuddling an infant the old-fashioned way—bottle feeding on a worn-out wooden rocking chair. Another nurse was near the incubators checking a little heartbeat.

Where could he be?

An older nurse saw the worrisome look on my face, opened the door, and asked, "Which one is yours?"

"I don't see him anywhere," I responded, somewhat hysterical.

"What is your child's name?" she asked.

"Dustin Raymond, born last night."

She dropped her chin into her chest and looked at me wide-eyed with heavy bags under her eyes and dark circles like she had worked a triple shift.

"Oh, oh," she said. She then scratched her head and rapidly uttered, "Apparently, your son was having complications earlier this morning, so we are running some tests."

"What's wrong with him?" I asked.

"Like I said, we are running tests." Her answer was short and abrasive. I suggest you go back to your room and try getting some rest. Someone will be in to speak with you as soon as tests come back and we have more information."

Is she completely out of her mind? Who can possibly get some rest after hearing that? It looks as if she's the one who needs to put those bags to rest, or maybe take a suggestion for a soothing-cucumber facial day. Obviously, with her snobby, snotty attitude, she needs to retire.

I guess I was a bit defensive and deeply hurt, which brought out the worst in me during an extremely vulnerable moment—which, by the way, wasn't hard to do.

My negative thoughts were racing faster by the minute, and the what-if syndrome was taking its toll on my nerves. I began pacing back and forth from the main hallway to the designated smoking area like I was in the "crazy" ward. By this point, I didn't care if my backend was hanging out or not. A couple of hours later, minus almost a half pack of Kools, I crawled back into my bed and pulled the covers over my head to hide the tears from the other family coming in and out of the room. A few minutes later, I could hear a female voice humming nursery rhymes, the sound of the rollers coming around the corner, and the echo of a hungry infant getting closer and closer. My upper body instantly sprung up; a stirring butterfly feeling started to develop in my stomach with excitement to finally meet my son. I sat there and watched the basinet roll directly past me and into the roommate's area on the other side of the blue draped curtain.

The butterfly feeling I usually get when I'm excited about something instantly turned into anxiety, which I get more often than I want to admit (I guess it runs in the family, according to my mother, along with nervous breakdowns, depression, and the biggie—addictions of many kinds). What a contrast—goosebumps to cold chills within a few seconds.

"She wants her mama," the nurse asserted exuberantly. The room began to fill with *oohs and awww*s from the Hispanic family thrilled about their new family addition, kind of like a celebration of the firstborn generation had just taken place. I had mixed emotions. Although I felt happy for the family, at the same time, I felt empty inside. With no family members around me to distract me, I was beginning to dwell on the last words I heard from my baby's father, Jason, that his wish might come true. He yelled, "I hope you and the baby both die!" after a heated argument just before leaving to the hospital.

How could he say something so cruel to the person he supposedly loved? This kind of reminded me of those conflicting words I've heard after a beating, "I'm doing this because I love you," or "This hurts me more than it hurts you." What's the message here? If I'm not getting beat, I'm not loved? What a stupid statement.

The afternoon shift change began. A different nurse, holding a medical chart, came in to check my vital signs. She placed the blood-pressure wrap around my arm and stared at her watch. "I hear you gave us quite a scare last night, Ms. Lorrie, according to my colleagues." She stood there upright then exhaled exhaustedly like she couldn't wait to go home. "Oh boy, it appears that your blood pressure is up and down."

She stuck a syringe into one of the small tubes taped to my hand. Although my mind was filled with worry and a hazy fog of confusion lingered, her statement jogged my somewhat obscured memory of the ordeal the night before.

I was deliberately trying to recall what she meant by that as my eyes were blinking rapidly like I had something stuck in my eye. If I had fully remembered, I would have ripped all the tubes off my body like a madwoman, refusing any more medication to be injected into my body. Before I knew it, the medication took hold, and my memory fell asleep along with my consciousness. Apparently, I had fallen asleep for a few hours because the portable lunch tray was on the side of my bed, and the soup bowl was cold. Before I could even get both eyes open, a shadow appeared. The other eye opened. It wasn't a shadow. It was a man dressed in black.

I shook my head and blinked twice, trying to recognize the human standing in front of me. He was wearing a white collar around his neck, and he was holding a Bible. His name tag showed the UC medical logo, which stood out, but I couldn't read his name.

That wasn't the name tag I had been looking for. I didn't request to speak to a priest. Maybe, he had the wrong room number.

"Lorrie?" he questioned.

"Yes," I answered.

I hadn't met the hospital chaplain, so I was curious as to why he was there to see me. The last time I remembered speaking with a Catholic priest was when I was eight years old in Sacramento, confessing that I wanted to kill someone when I got big (even though I didn't mention any names, I had one person in mind). I could see this man's furled-eyebrow expression that symbolized maybe something horrible had happened. He slowly moved his clenched fingers to his mouth as he tried to find the right words. He hesitated for a moment.

"Lorrie, how are you feeling this afternoon?" the chaplain asked.

"I'm dizzy," I responded. "I feel like I want to throw up. I'm not sure if it's nerves, the medication, or the disinfectant smell."

"It might be all of the above," the chaplain said. "Well, let me introduce myself. My name is Father Ryan, and I'm staff clergy here at the medical center. I was given a referral to visit you and see how you're feeling. I was wondering if there's anything we can do, or how I can personally be of help to you under these circumstances?"

I stared at him and bit my inner cheek, trying to comprehend the question he had just asked. I hysterically jolted up from the bed pillow like a jack-in-the-box.

"What circumstances?" I asked with a high-pitched tone. "Am I supposed to know something?"

He stepped back a few steps as if he was fearful that I was about to physically attack him. His mouth dropped open like he couldn't believe I didn't know. He stuttered for a moment, then compassionately stated, "Listen, your son is extremely ill. He's been transferred to the NIC unit, and he is in critical condition. The doctors are not sure about his diagnosis or anything else at this point."

My heart stopped beating for a few seconds as if time stopped. I couldn't speak…speechless. I dropped my head in between my knees and then squeezed with all my strength like a vise grip to muffle any more words of bad news. The tears of despair flowed down my cheeks. I could sense he was still standing there, so I looked up reluctantly. As our eyes met, I could tell that he had a nonjudgmental, nurturing spirit. He must have realized I was a heartbroken, confused twenty-six-year-old woman struggling to communicate anything. He probably presumed that it was a waste of time to probe or initiate any further conversation, so he quickly disengaged.

With a soft-spoken, gentle tone, he said, "Well, apparently, this is the wrong time to discuss this. I'll come back at a more convenient time for you."

I didn't refuse. On his way out, he looked back at me and stated, "I'll request that the physician come and give you more information regarding your son's condition."

I was dumbfounded. What was that all about? It didn't make any sense to me that the people in charge would send a priest instead of a doctor to discuss anything with me. Immediately, my defense mechanisms came raging forward, ready for battle, slinging verbal swords in my mind.

How dare they? What's wrong with these people? Doctors are trained for hospitals and priests for churches.

Wondering if that day was really a nightmare or reality, I reflected. If it was a nightmare, I'd wake up in a puddle of body sweat—relieved, grateful that it wasn't real. I pinched myself. My anxiety magnified. I could see both of my legs uncontrollably shaking underneath the blankets.

Can this be real?

I wanted to doze off and suddenly awaken with the nurse nudging my shoulder. I wanted to hear, "It's feeding time," with exuberant excitement in her voice. Then she'd place my healthy baby in my arms. I pinched myself again. Unfortunately, it's reality. *This is all my fault*, was resonating in the pit of my gut. But this time, those words lingered in my gut, then moved up into my heart. It hit me. I was no longer the victim; I was the perpetrator. That pinch of reality hurt deeply.

And what happened to the promise I had made to myself: "I'll never be like my mother?" I viewed my mother as a fragile, weak-willed, broken woman who put her traditional values of marriage above her children's safety. For years, I had been carrying the inability to forgive in my heart. I easily blamed my parents for all of my misfortunes, repeatedly refusing to take any personal responsibility whatsoever.

The irony of the confession (reflecting when I wanted to kill someone) I made when I was eight years old came true that day. But I didn't want to hurt my baby. Truth be told, I was a drug addict, not a monster. The thought of carrying on the heaping chain of dysfunction turned the pinch into a mental sting that had the potential to give me emotional damage forever. Guilt-ridden forever.

I wanted to die. Why didn't I just die? The only thing I could do for the moment was to focus on the unintentional portion that weaved a softer version of condemnation to my inner being. Somehow it made me feel less suicidal.

As I lay in the hospital bed drenched in body sweat, finally asking myself pertinent questions that made me perspire more, the phone rang.

"Hello."

There was silence on the other end of the receiver.

"Hello?" I said with pressured speech.

"Hi. It's me, Jason," he said with a sweetie-pie tone.

His voice had completely changed, sounding less irritable, like maybe he wasn't coming down from drugs anymore.

"How are you feeling?" he asked.

"Not good."

"What's the matter with you now?" he said with disgust in his voice.

"Well, if you were here, you would know."

"What are you talking about now, Lorrie? If you weren't so out of it, you would have noticed that I was there last night, but I just had gotten there a little late."

"Really? I guess I was under a lot of medication." I said.

"Yeah, I saw your family. Your sister was throwing dirty looks at me!"

"By the way, your wish almost came true last night," I exclaimed.

"Oh yeah, and what was that?" he questioned.

"Don't play dumb with me. That statement you made last night before I left, remember? You hoped that me and the baby would both die," I yelled.

"Oh, you know I didn't mean that. I was just upset about what Johnny said."

"And what was that, Jason?"

"That the baby wasn't mine."

"That's ridiculous!" I roared. "So…you just believe anything you hear, huh?" Before he was able to respond, I cut him off. "And for your information, the baby is in critical condition."

"Lorrie, that's not funny…stop messing around. I know you're just trying to get me back for making that stupid comment," he protested.

"Listen, I'm not messing around."

"You're serious, huh?"

"Yes. And they're not giving me any information about the baby's current condition. They act like they don't know. They did send a priest to come visit me. Can you believe that?"

"No way. Well, hang in there. I'm working on getting a ride to come and see you and the baby," he said with a little sincerity in his voice.

I was desperately pleading in my head that somehow he would pick up my vibes over the telephone. This is how I viewed the world and acted. Even though I sounded harsh on the outside, he'd be able sense that my voice was shaking on the inside. I wanted him to tell me he was sorry for not being supportive, how much he loved me, and he was on his way even if he had to hitchhike. I ignored the obvious fact that there were no obvious signs he was working on it. If only I could believe him, I could have been vulnerable. Maybe I could have told him I was really scared and lonely and to hurry up because I needed him by my side. I wanted to say, *Please, hurry up. I need you.* But my pride wouldn't let me.

"Don't bother, jerk!" I screamed and slammed the phone down.

I sat there and stared at the phone.

Now what did I just do? I thought.

At that moment, I wanted the nurse to come in and inject enough morphine into my veins that would cause me to go to sleep and never wake up.

While stewing on my pity pot for about fifteen minutes, a professional young-looking woman dressed in a blue suit with her hair in a tightly wrapped bun came up to my bedside with a thin file in her hands.

"Hello, my name is Ms. Wright, and I'm a social worker for the Children's Protective Services. We have received a complaint for child abuse because your baby's toxicology report came back positive for drugs. It's our protocol to notify you that we have put a hold on your infant, so he will not be going home with you upon discharge." She said all of this with an authoritative, stern voice.

"Well, I don't think the baby will be going home with me anyway, according to the old battle-ax in the nursery. She told me he's in the NIC unit," I said with tears falling from my eyes and gasping for air in between my words. Then I buried my chin into my chest.

"Well," she stuttered, changing her tune a bit, "I mean, once he is released from the hospital, he will be placed in protective custody until a thorough investigation is completed and we have more information about your circumstances and living arrangements."

She released a deep, heavy sigh and then boldly inquired, "How long have you been using methamphetamines?"

I wasn't expecting that question to be raised so soon during our introduction, so it had caught me completely off guard. It would have been helpful if she had taken the time to read my medical file a bit, then might have asked me some questions like, "What's going on in your life?"

I did realize that, indeed, my drug addiction was the primary reason for her much-needed intervention. I was petrified that anything I said might be used against me. Her approach displayed a stern demeanor coupled with a "got yah" attitude, like she was a prosecutor, and I could possibly go to jail. If she had taken a better approach, she may have noticed that there were many factors that also contributed to my situation.

After hearing her question, I looked shell-shocked.

"What?" I asked, stalling for time.

She repeated the question.

I got scared; then I immediately tensed up and raised my voice. "I don't know what you're talking about! Maybe the tests are wrong," I screeched as I shrugged my shoulders. I could feel the tension in my head and the frown line deepening between my eyebrows. It was obvious that I hated authority. How dare anyone ask me questions about my personal life?

The lippy smirk on her face told me that she took my statement too personally, as if I was deliberately lying to her. She couldn't see beyond her own ego, and I couldn't let down my wall of denial. Suddenly her pale complexion turned flustery red. It was evident that I struck a nerve at the annoyance level. I assumed that she was relatively new on the job, probably just finished school, probably brought up in a ritzy, high-class environment where her parents paid for her schooling. She was probably a spoiled-rotten brat who didn't know anything about my real world yet, at the same time, trying to save the world.

"You know, if you were living elsewhere in the country, you could be arrested right now, facing criminal charges," she warned as she spewed out statistics probably from a previous research assignment. Basically, this was her way of telling me she viewed me as such: a flat-out criminal.

Immediately I responded with a snap-back attitude as if horns just grew from my skull. "But guess what, lady, I don't live elsewhere, now do I?" I fired back with a sharp, snappy tone coupled with an intense snarky attitude. *Couldn't she sense I was in enough pain?*

It's too bad that we had started off on an ego-trip battle and failed to meet in the middle—somewhere that would have established a little common ground and understanding. Deep down, I would have appreciated her line of work. If only I had someone from Children's Protective Service to save my butt (literally) when I was little, maybe I wouldn't be in this situation, or maybe I would anyhow. Back in the early 1960s, there was no such department for children, at least to my knowledge. The only agency was the County Welfare Department, which required an annual home visit yet hiding another agenda: to inspect if the opposite sex was living there by the smell of men's cologne, grungy jeans with a belt buckle nearby, or cowboy boots lying around the house, etc. They acted as if she/he would have to use the bathroom, counting toothbrushes, gazing the basin for an electric shaver, snooping instead of checking for bruises and such. Mom was hip to their schemes.

Ms. Wright must had felt like she was getting nowhere with me at that point, so she handed me her card. "This case will be going to my supervisor for review and assigned to a caseworker," she snarled with her nose up in the air. Then she walked out.

What a witch! (That's the nice way of putting it.)

Within hours, my medical condition worsened dramatically. It became increasingly painful to go to the restroom due to the excruciating burning in *that* area. However, that was not as horrific as the torture I had endured when I was six years old. Nothing I had ever experienced could be comparable to that kind of burn.

I squeamishly hobbled back to my bed and pushed the Help button.

A new nurse came into my room and turned off the blinking red light but disregarded my complaint as if my symptoms were common after delivery and the burning sensation would eventually go away. Then she offered me a few suggestions.

"It's probably that the stitches are irritated. You can squeeze warm water from this bottle on the stitches the next time you go, okay?" the nurse said.

Suddenly, silence. I could no longer hear the ruckus going on next door. I had to admit, I was relieved when my roommate was discharged. I was miserably saddened and couldn't stand any joy around me. *You know, misery loves company.* I was especially annoyed that the hospital hadn't honored the specified visiting hours the night before. I felt like screaming, *Shut up!* On a good note, my roommate's visitors helped distract me from all the voices in my head.

After a few hours, I couldn't tolerate the burning sensation any longer. This had reactivated traumatic nerve damage in my childhood that was making me crazy. I started pushing the button more frequently throughout the night and quite obsessively. Word must have spread throughout the ward that I was a complainer, a nuisance, and rather than hand me a cup to diagnose a possible urinary tract infection, they conveniently handed me discharge papers. Shortly thereafter, the tubes were removed from my arms. I felt like I was on an assembly line of administrative processing that gave little regard as to where I was going.

I hate this hospital anyway. They're not getting rid of me. I'm leaving this place!

I sat up on the bed, stared down at my semipedicured pale feet dangling from the bed, gazed at my deformed-looking baby toe, and then chuckled loudly over my past stupidity. I couldn't help but laugh about why my baby toe was oddly crooked. A few months earlier, while vacuuming the living room, I noticed that the vacuum wasn't picking up debris, which possibly indicated the roller had broken. To test my theory, I prematurely stuck my foot into the bottom of the vacuum, and the roller sucked up my baby toe (I guess I was wrong about the roller). Not very smart.

I just shook my head, dumbfounded.

How my emotional roller-coaster state could fluctuate from weeping to laughing in a heartbeat was beyond my comprehension and was quite frankly bothersome. I was convinced that I was, indeed, "crazy." I started rocking back and forth just like an *insane* person would do, too lost for words, lost in spirit, lost in life—just a pitiful, confused human being.

Singing My Blues

I had to quickly snap out of my ocean of self-pity before I was confined in a straitjacket and thrown into a six-by-twelve padded cell like when Diana Ross played Billie Holiday in *Lady Sings the Blues*. To me, this was the lowest of lows of any addiction. The only upside was the fact that I wasn't a heroin addict. The perfect example to minimize my substance abuse.

My fear was that if the medical staff witnessed my fluctuating mental state, my discharge papers would turn into a commitment to the nut ward. I would no longer feel like county property, but I would be state property. I began to get rather paranoid—mainly because this had brought up my deepest fear that I'd one day be 5150'd, lose all my human rights, become a ward of the state, and permanently labeled a crazy lady. This fear-driven seed had been deeply planted in my brain early on. In fact, I would have recurring nightmares throughout my lifetime: I'm behind bars, balled-up in a fetal position in a corner with my back scrunched against the wall, staring at the nearby walkway of individuals who are pausing to look with their fingers pointed and whispering underneath their breath, "Such a pitiful waste of human life." Unfortunately, I had been in a similar situation as a child, and that continued to haunt me. The most hurtful experience is that most of those individuals mocking me were my so-called friends, laughing at me, "Look at that poor lost soul," and shaking their heads. Not one of them reached out a hand to me. Oh, how I wanted someone to reach a hand out to me. No one ever did.

Those graphic images were enough for me to collect my thoughts and rationally pull my mental state together so I could check on Dustin's condition myself. It seemed like I had been given the silent treatment regarding any information about the baby's health. I retrieved my personal belongings from a nearby closet and began getting dressed. I slowly moved my way through the hallway, still in enormous pain, and took the elevator to the desolate third floor. Then I followed the sign that read "Intensive Care Unit" on the tan steel door. I picked up the phone next to the door.

"Yes?" an older man's voice said.

"Hi. I'm here to see Dustin Baby Boy."

"And may I ask how you are related to the patient?" he asked.

"I'm his mother," I responded.

"One moment, please."

I stood there patiently waiting to hear the buzz sound to let me through the locked steel door before I hung up the phone.

The same male's voice returned to the phone. "Madam, I am sorry, but your infant is in an isolated unit until all test results come back. We cannot allow any family members in until we rule out contagious, infectious-disease factors. This is just public-safety precaution and hospital policy, so we appreciate your patience."

I stood there stunned and felt like I was going to faint. I couldn't believe my ears.

What the heck! Infectious disease? What is that?

Immediately, I felt this was a conspiracy to keep me away from my child because they were hiding information and just wanted to get rid of me. I sat down in the waiting area placing my hand on my forehead until my dizzy spells subsided. It was like my neurotransmitters were firing continually without any drugs.

I went back downstairs like a walking dead person; my face was as pale as my feet. I headed straight back to the room and sat on the bed. Immediately I felt stranded and abandoned. I stared at the TV and watched the actors' lips move, unable to register any cognitive function in my brain.

About thirty minutes later, I heard Jason's voice at the nurses' station.

"Excuse me, can you tell me what room Lorrie [so and so] is in?" he asked.

"Yes, sir. Room 206, a couple doors down on the right."

He walked into the room and stood there quietly. "Hi." He tilted his head slightly to the right. "What are you watching?"

"I've been looking at the TV screen for half an hour now, but I couldn't even tell you what it's about."

"What…it looks like you're ready to go home. Have they discharged you already?" he asked.

"Yes. I cannot believe that," I responded

"Well, what about the baby? Any information?"

"I guess he's in some sort of quarantine, and nobody's allowed in until some tests come back."

"What did they say is wrong with him?"

"Apparently, they don't know anything around here. Please, get me away from here before I snap and end up in a place that I will regret."

Mid-November 1988, Jason and I returned to the countryside, heading to the sixteen acres of land owned by Jason's grandmother who was currently residing in a rest home. I didn't say a word for that entire forty-minute drive. It felt oddly unnatural leaving the hospital without my newborn baby. However, I was eager to see Nicole and give her a big hug. I could feel like a loving mother instead of a heartless monster.

I wasn't a heartless monster. I was helplessly sick and shackled in my addiction.

Driving up to the property, we noticed the rain clouds were hovering over the traditional ranch-style house (probably built sometime in the 1920s), and Mother Nature's voice was howling just a few yards away. The trees that surrounded the house were dancing with the wind in different directions, which indicated that the next storm was probably closer than we had anticipated. As we pulled up around the backside of the graveled roadway, the house looked haunted, somewhat tilted from the earth-cracking movements over time that left its foundation unbalanced. Its spookiness had an unwritten story of its own.

It had been shamefully whispered that Jason's grandfather committed suicide. Shortly after his death, his grandmother married his brother, who also committed suicide—both suicides occurred on the property. Maybe that was why I had always sensed that the house was haunted, and we were invading the territory of ancestors' past. It wasn't like I was making something out of nothing. Seriously, I heard banging down in the basement, creaking doors as if a ghost had opened the door. I even observed the animals acting strangely and witnessed their fur stiffly sprout up like elderly porcupines. I knew that cats instinctively have a keen awareness of what the naked eye cannot see. When I approached Jason about my suspicions, he always had a logical explanation for all my concerns. He flatly refused to acknowledge that the house of his future inheritance (possibly) was haunted.

"The banging noise is from the old pipes underneath the house and the trees hitting the siding. The creaking noise is because the house's foundation had shifted over time, so the doors sway back and forth, and the cats act strangely because they're startled as a result of all of the above," he'd firmly insist. Even though we were both on drugs, he was an extremely bright individual. He had served several years in the armed forces and had communication skills that intimidated me. Truth be known, he could outwit me with little effort on his part. His logic outweighed my strong inner suspicions every time. I mean, how was I going to argue with no proof, just an extra dose of paranoia, coupled with extreme fear? Impossible!

The next couple of days were almost unbearable both emotionally and physically. The burning sensation was worsening every time I used the restroom. On the second day home from the hospital, I ran to the bathroom because I felt my pelvic bones literally expand to discharge whatever remained in my body—either afterbirth that was mistakenly left behind or massive buildup of blood clots from the hemorrhage. The process was almost like I gave birth to a preemie in the toilet (no kidding), but without all the ghastly labor pains. I considered bringing a lawsuit against the nurses for incompetence, but I had inadvertently flushed evidence against them down the toilet. What I was facing at the time, no one would believe me anyway.

The more and more I thought about this, the more and more furious I became. It was so evident to me that I had been released prematurely, and their actions exhibited gross negligence. I looked out of the bathroom door and glanced over to what could have been. I could see directly into Dustin's room, full of gifts from the baby shower and the paper plate decorated in multicolor ribbons streaming from the dresser to serve as a memento for his baby book. It hit me again. He may not ever come home. I may never get to put clippings from his first haircut, handprint drawings from kindergarten, dates of his first steps, or even pictures of his upcoming birthdays. It was too overwhelming. I fell on the floor and slammed my fists on the faded peach-colored bathroom tile, asking myself, *How could I have let his happen?* Truth smacked me directly in the face.

I wanted to deaden the pain by calling the dope dealer to come over and give me enough drugs to keep me spun for a week. I could then go into a sedated state (drug-induced-comedown coma, I called it) and wouldn't have to think about anything.

The least I can do is honor my son by not using anymore, I thought to myself.

Boy, that inner thought struck a retaliatory nerve. Whenever anyone called me a chicken, it sparked an upheaval of rebellion. It reminded me of my stepfather's favorite words: "poop-butt, sissy, ———," directed at us children. I would go to any lengths to avoid those name-calling insinuations about my character. Early on, my core belief was that if these statements came from my supposed role model, they must be true. Rather than swallowing his view, I was always on a risk-taking mission to prove him wrong. However, always at a cost.

The next day, my sister Lisa brought my eight-year-old daughter, Nicole, home to me. Her presence brought a ray of sunshine back into my life; the sight of her innocence put an exuberant smile on my face. Nicole had a meek, easygoing spirit and was considered my immediate family's pride and joy, having been the firstborn of the next generation. She had an olive-color skin tone with exotic distinguished facial features, as well as almond-shaped dark-brown eyes resembling her auntie Lisa. Even though she was still in the growing stage and carried excess baby fat, her high cheekbones remained noticeable—complements of a strong Cherokee Indian trait on her father's side. I hugged her so tightly, never wanting to let go. By her stiff body language, I could tell she was uncomfortable and didn't understand why I was so over-the-top affectionate that day. Normally, I wasn't a touchy-feely parent—by no means. Awkward for her, I'm sure.

She was disappointed that she couldn't meet her brother. Thank God, Lisa had already explained that the baby was still in the hospital for a couple more days, so I didn't have to go into detail with Nicole. Lisa realized I was still in extreme pain, so she took me to the ER. The staff concluded that I did have a severe urinary tract infection, prescribed antibiotics, and I was released. This only reinforced my suspicion of a cover-up conspiracy and the hospital's lack of concern for my medical condition during my hospital stay. On another note, we all know that methamphetamine use heightens paranoia, but I was absolutely unwilling to consider this negative aftereffect from the drugs and was convinced I was right. I wasn't aware of any hospital resources that would have allowed me to stay at the hospital until Dustin's health improved and was too ignorant to ask while I was in the ER—perhaps the medical social worker was unavailable? Lisa and her husband at the time were gracious enough to loan us their spare truck, which would allow us to visit the baby when he transferred out of NIC.

November 21, at 11:00 a.m., I heard a knock on the door. A short, petite middle-aged woman maybe of Latin decent sporting a friendly smile on her face stood at the doorway.

"Hi. I'm Maria from Social Services," she said with a polite, soft-spoken voice, then lifted up a badge around her neck that showed the county emblem. She held her hand out in an attempt to shake my hand as the icebreaker and nonchalantly lifted her eyebrows.

I complied.

I noticed that the heavy cluster of rain patches had passed, and the sun was attempting to show its face through the somewhat dissipated clouds, presenting a hazy overcast, kind of like my mood.

"Are you Lorrie?" she asked as her hair fluffed up from the chilly breeze that floated by.

"Yes."

"May I come in?" she asked.

"Well, of course. I already knew someone would be out to see me," I responded.

We walked through the living room straight into the dining area toward the country-style table parallel to the window. I pulled out a chair for her to show a little hospitality.

"First of all," she said, "I would like to apologize for the unexpected home visit, but I was unable to reach you by phone."

"I understand," I said, nodding.

Her demeanor was welcoming. It appeared she was a well-polished, seasoned individual unlike those I had met during my initial encounter at the hospital. She had excellent interpersonal skills that lowered my defensive mechanism right off the bat; she seemed to have been in the field for some time and related well to people.

"In case your baby's health improves to return home, I need to do a home inspection and make sure you can provide for your baby's needs or find out if we have any safety concerns before the court hearing. Now that I am officially your assigned caseworker, it's my job to make a recommendation to the court about my findings. Then, of course, it will be up to the judge."

I didn't have to ask about the details of upcoming hearings; I was fully aware of the court process.

Her tone of sincerity had taken the edge off the surprise visit, and she won points by referring to Dustin as "your baby" in her sentences. It seemed as if she was willing to keep the family together or at least willing to give me an opportunity to change.

I excitedly jumped out of my chair, having extreme difficulty controlling my emotions, ecstatic to have someone in my corner.

I then showed her around the kitchen, which I had newly decorated with the trendy *duck decor*, and eagerly pointed out the time-consuming, hand-painted job I had done refurbishing the cupboards white with baby-blue trim. I then escorted her into Dustin's room, crafted with all his new accessories, and turned on the mobile above his bassinet that chimed "It's a Small World After All." Then we went into Nicole's room to reassure her that my children actually had beds to sleep in. Since the rain had subsided, I took her outside and walked around a small portion of the property. I proudly showed off where my summer vegetable garden had been. I was trying desperately to make a good impression and prove that I was a functioning person and not the stereotypical homeless drug addict who sells her body for drugs. I conveniently left out the fact that Jason's crop had been stolen that particular summer as I gazed over to the muddy vacant lot and shrugged it off as slow-growing potatoes for good reason.

I chuckled underneath my breath and briefly flashbacked to when Jason was in the Bay Area for an appointment a few weeks prior, and I was alone in the haunted house pregnant and petrified. I suddenly heard our dog barking loudly and rapidly as if someone was prowling around the property. I panicked. I grabbed the heavy weapon from the wall rack above our bed, opened the window, and blasted three gunshots out of the window out of extreme fear. I didn't realize the powerful force of that hunting rifle: my right shoulder was severely bruised for days afterward. The blast set off a chain reaction. Not only were our dogs barking uncontrollably, but I could hear howling screeches from local animals from a distance. Whoever was scouring around that night wasn't after me. Apparently, they were after the herbs growing in Jason's lot—and I don't mean basil or oregano. I guess I must have spooked those trespassers, but not enough to keep them away from the property permanently. The potholes tell the rest of the story. No pun intended.

What was encouraging during our visit was that Maria nodded her head with approval of my efforts and continually offered verbal confirmation of mild satisfaction. Her nonabrasive attitude kept me somewhat hopeful for possible reunification.

We walked into the house and sat down at the table. Suddenly, she gently touched my arm with sincerity in her eyes.

"Lorrie, I've been working with ladies like yourself, and I've come to realize that most women have a story that molded self-destructive behavior before they ever start using drugs. Would you like to tell me about your background to give an overall picture of how we can assist you?" she asked.

Somehow I sensed she understood the vulnerability in my soulful eyes that opened a glimpse into my scar-filled heart from decades of relentless abuse. Momentarily, a sliver of that shame melted. *Maybe, just maybe—could I be honest and trust?*

Reflections from My Past

Looking back in an attempt to understand the generational norms in which I was born, I searched out the following as if I was on a mission researching a history project. My history—a mini-genealogy, you could say.

In the early 1950s, America's eye toward marriage was held in the highest esteem; so naturally, tying the knot during adolescence was considered the cultural norm in many respects. In fact, if youngsters weren't married fresh out of high school or shortly thereafter, there was a stigma attached for some of those individuals, as if something was seriously wrong. Given the attitudes prior to the feminist movement, it's no wonder my mother married my birth father when she was a year out of high school.

Having children was another priority for some during this postwar time period. Naturally, my parents followed the American tradition, and that's how I became a birth statistic in the latter part of the baby-boomer era the summer of 1962. The marriage between my biological parents worked semiwell for a couple years until the announcement of another baby on the way. The added pressure of more responsibility was too much for my birth father to handle, so he up and bailed shortly before my sister's arrival. I guess he wasn't looking forward to dealing with extra diaper duty since he was already working for a diaper delivery company, lugging cloth diapers day in and day out. I don't know that really—just sayin'.

My mother was deeply shamed by his abandonment. She was a brokenhearted single mother with one infant in diapers and one on the way. Mom was concerned about how others would judge her, the financial devastation and ultimately the loss of her marital vows that their union should last a lifetime. She was the first ever in her family to be labeled a "divorcée," and she felt like a disgraceful outcast. Back in those days, it was just flat-out absurd that a husband would abandon his/her spouse and children for any reason. Typically, even alcoholism wasn't a cause for separation, let alone messy housekeeping. Even worse, she felt as if she was ostracized within the Catholic faith, which deeply frowned upon divorce regardless if the decision for dissolution wasn't her choice. My mother eventually left the Catholic Church and would remarry without the church's blessing, which would come to pass far too quickly. Unfortunately.

In the few months that preceded this second marriage, I had met Rob only briefly a couple of times. Supposedly, my mother had met him during a night out with her girlfriends at the Pablo Club, a popular nightclub on 23rd Street in Richmond, California. Following their introduction, he had immediately impressed her by building himself up as a San Pablo police officer. Just the fact that he was employed was a plus, but a police officer was over the top in her eyes. His manipulative charm and smooth talk swept her off her feet and spontaneously captured her heart. Before she knew it, she had fallen for his trumped-up story without warning. Later on, it was revealed that he was fitted for a uniform indeed—as a security guard. Classic example of stretching the truth. Needless to say, by the time everything was revealed, it was too late. She was hooked.

Rob was in his midtwenties: tall, handsome, with long dark hair and a medium build. Beyond that, he resembled Clint Eastwood in a lot of ways. He was a perfect replica of society's renegade: tattoos (one with a lady's name) displayed on his forearm, a pack of cigarettes tightly tucked under the right arm sleeve of a worn-out T-shirt, and dingy jeans. He was most definitely hotheaded, demanding, and had a rigid personality. One word to describe his personality: *controlling*. What a contrast from my four-foot-eight Mom's meek, submissive, spiritually-based character. Oddball couple, you could say. According to my mother, he had two children from a previous marriage, the one area they had mutually shared. That discovery should have been a red flag to initiate a little investigation before plunging forward. By not digging further into his background, her decision to start anew changed the course of our lives forever.

Monday, January 2, 1967, started out like any typical weekday morning. I was finishing up watching the popular cartoon *Speed Racer* that early morning, singing, "Go, Speed Racer, Go." I dumped the leftover soggy cornflakes in the sink, then attempted to rush to my kindergarten class before the bell rang. That was pretty much my daily routine—procrastinating to capture that heroic ending to start my day on an upswing. Before I had a chance to dash out of the door, my mother suddenly rushed down the stairs wearing her tattered robe, and she held up her hand at me. She totally caught me by surprise because it was unusual for her to be up that early.

When she woke up, she didn't resemble the Hollywood actress Sally Fields as much as when she had been all dolled up with the trendy dippity-do hairdo and sleek orange lipstick on her lips, her favorite color by far. She would comment that orange complements her olive-color skin tone, and she stood by her selection with confidence even though those around weren't too fond of it, unless it was autumn, of course. I hadn't seen any other color on her lips other than different shades of orange, period.

"Wait, Lorrie, wait! I have good news," she excitedly expressed.

I stood in the doorway and waited for her news.

We weren't accustomed to good news except when my mother's high school friend dropped by occasionally and took us cruising up and down 23rd Street for a sightseeing excursion outside the projects. Richmond's 23rd Street was a popular main drag back in the day when bebop music, doggie diner, and oldie but goodie classic cars were the favorite pastimes.

"Over the weekend, me and Rob got married, so we're a family now," my mother said, proudly displaying an exuberant smile I hadn't seen in the years after my biological parents' divorce.

I wanted her to hear me—not what I was saying but what I wasn't saying. Dead silence.

I don't want a new daddy. I want my real daddy back.

I really wanted her to say that my parents had worked things out and we were all a family again (typical unspoken wish: to be daddy's little girl).

"You see, we're all a new family now," she affirmed, aiming for "family united" in her own way.

My shoulders rose to my ears; my body stiffly stood at the front door. I shook my head in disbelief, completely forgetting about the valiant ending of *Speed Racer*. This was not what I had in mind to start my day on the right foot, but I put on a fake smile anyway.

"Look," she said, waving the ring in front of her face as she moved her fingers back and forth, excitedly modeling the wedding ring that looked cheap.

It was obvious it wasn't the ring but the commitment she was excited about—and that she's found *the one*.

Daddy? I don't have to call anyone daddy if I don't want to.

"We're going to start this New Year on the right track," she said before I shut the door behind me.

After the news broke from my mother's mouth and I proceeded down the front-door steps, I strikingly noticed the god-awful smell outside that morning, which was basically usual.

Something must have happened at the refinery last night, I thought as I plugged my nose.

I trotted to my kindergarten class just up the street to the Hillcrest Elementary School, which by the way was located near one of the many oil refineries in the Bay Area. Frequently, during recess, we would hear the sounds of sirens going off from a distance, which was our cue to run inside the classroom and duck for cover to avoid any respiratory danger from the toxic chemicals seeping into the air. When this happened, I sprinted without hesitation to escape the rotten-egg smell whenever an explosion went off. I was a lightning-fast runner. Too bad I started smoking cigarettes a few years later; it ruined any future athletic ability for sure.

During the school year, I expected several drills at any given moment: fire-alarm drills, earthquake drills (as a result of the Bay Area centered on the San Andreas fault line), nuclear-bomb drills in case of retaliation from the Soviet Union, and chemical-spill drills due to oil refinery explosions. It seemed like I had my nose buried into the dingy beige tile floor underneath my desk rather than in textbooks. Sad reality. In kindergarten, I learned that this world is a dangerous place even before I memorized my ABCs. Yes, I'm being sarcastic, with a twist of truth here.

A couple blocks away from the school were low-income government housing units, which the small-community locals refer to as the Bay Vista Projects in Rodeo (pronounced *ro-day-o*). This was where I lived. It has been said (according to Google) that this small old-fashioned waterfront town used to be a hub for the annual cattle roundup back in the early twentieth century. That's how the town got its name. Makes perfect sense.

During playtime hours (jumping on the bed), Lisa and I gazed out of the upstairs window as we looked out over the mammoth steel oil containers located next to large cement tubes with charcoal smoke that barreled into the air. On a clear day, it looked like a giant imaginary checkerboard with multicolor circles throughout the area. With our youthful imaginations, we played our silly game. We pretended that the metal containers were the checkers on the board.

"I pick white," I'd say.

"I pick yellow," she responded.

And we'd go back and forth. We were happy campers as we played visual checkers in the sky. The awesome power of the imagination. Astounding.

Looking back, this scenery played a significant role in my survival later on.

Within a few months' time, things quickly started to change. My mother's belly grew like a watermelon, and we were expecting yet another addition to our family.

Mid-November 1967 became our first "on the road" experience. This had taken me by surprise initially, but soon it became a familiar theme for our family. Rob was always in trouble with the law, and he had difficulty facing the consequences. His solution was to pack up the family in the middle of the night and head to Ohio where he had relatives who stood up for harboring fugitives, or maybe they just didn't know. Not sure. My mother was an expert at keeping secrets, so naturally, I was in the dark regarding their decision until we carried our blankets, suitcases (which Mom prepared beforehand), and four-month-old baby sister, Shelly, out the front door—mind you, in the late midnight hours. We couldn't say a word. Besides, this was an era that normalized the "children are to be seen and not heard and do what you're told, no questions asked" parenting style. So, the fact that I didn't want to move away from my grandparents didn't matter to them. *No voice.* I was devastated that I didn't even get a chance to say goodbye to anyone. At that point, I didn't really know how far we were moving, but deep down, I sensed that this "road trip" was taking us far, far away. Those fearful, fleeting thoughts were parading around the unknown, but at least we were together, which eased the anxiety.

Our car was an unreliable older model, and it was only a matter of time that rather than on the road, we'd be on the side of the road all too often. Back then, I didn't realize that the occupation "mechanic" even existed. Car maintenance—are you kidding? We'd jump in the car, cross our fingers, and hope that the ole bucket would pull through. At least seven times out of ten, someone was underneath the hood as cars flew by on the freeway. If we had been a little more prepared, we could have made a variety of signs before leaving the house. When worse came to worst—and it always did—we could stand on the side of the road holding up the sign of desperation: "Water? Jumper cables? Gas can? Mechanic—anyone?"

Lo and behold, we had car problems in just about every state: breaking down, running out of gas, getting lost, and struggling with unexpected weather changes without snow chains. The only good that came out of breaking down was that we'd finally get to use the bathroom. Otherwise, "shut up and hold it" was the rule. When we finally arrived in Colorado, I remember Shelly was sandwiched between Lisa and me as we all began to doze off. Unexpectedly, we started rocking violently back and forth. We held on to each other tightly and braced Shelly securely between us as a car seat while the rear end fishtailed out of control. The tires skidded across black ice near Boulder, Colorado, which forced the front end of the car to the edge of a cliff after Rob lost complete control of the car. The car suddenly died. At that point, we were afraid to move or even breathe, expecting the worst. My mother instantly started saying the Our Father prayer, and Rob blurted out, "Little flower of the hour, we need you."

He lifted his head off the steering wheel, took a deep breath, then turned on the ignition. Amazingly, it started. The engine running sounded better than it ever had. My mother believed that we survived this only because all three of her children were in the car. That's the story anyway.

In the end, what should have been an eight-day road trip turned out to be a monthlong nightmare, or close to it.

It was the middle of December when we finally arrived at our destination in Springfield, Ohio. We pulled up in front of Rob's aunt's house. From the outside, it looked like just an ordinary house in the suburbs; it didn't take long to figure out I was highly mistaken. With a coat over my head to escape the rain and walking a little bow-legged to prevent an accident, I was looking for the bathroom with no luck. I politely waited for all the excitement and introductions to die down, and then finally asked, "Can I use the bathroom?" I directed my question to a potbellied, frumpy-looking woman dressed in a "moo-moo" gown with raggedy-looking slippers on her feet. Her disarrayed hairdo poked up in different directions like she had just rolled out of bed.

"Sure, but you'll have to go out yonder to use the commode," she said with a Southern twang, pointing to the backyard. Apparently, she was Rob's aunt Beatrice.

I stepped out back through the screeching patio door with Lisa right behind me. On the right-hand side of the yard sat a wooden weather-torn structured box that looked like it had gone through a few gusty windstorms.

How weird to have the toilet and the sink outside, I thought and quickly figured out we had arrived in nowhere land with an outhouse for a bathroom and a pump with a rod-iron handle for fetching water.

A few days later, I was petrified to start a new school in a different state, especially without Lisa by my side since she wasn't old enough to go to school yet. However, the rain clouds had disappeared, which I had taken as a good sign to start my first day of school. When we pulled up to the school, I noticed it looked like a historic college building covered with red bricks on the outer structure with several steps leading to the entrance doors. That school was three times larger than my other school. I took a deep breath, dreading the moment that I would be introduced as the new kid and have everybody stare at me.

My mother grabbed my face and squeezed my cheeks together.

"Oh, don't worry, Lorrie. This is our new start, new school. Besides, a lot of kids have to go through this, especially military families," she said then smiled, with a spot of orange lipstick smeared on her top denture. I laughed, forgetting my fear for a moment.

She then looked in the mirror and rolled her tongue over her teeth to remove the smudge before leaving the car. We walked down the dim hallway corridors to enroll me, heading for the sign that displayed "Front Office" above the doorframe. It looked as if the lightbulbs had blown out or the janitor was late. If I had yelled, like I felt on the inside, my voice would have bounced off the shiny buffed floor and ricocheted back to me—that was how vacant it was around there (which seemed pretty strange for such a huge school). Apparently, classes had already started, and by the looks of things, tardiness just wasn't an option, except for the janitor, of course.

After all the routine paperwork had been filled out, I was directed to room 2. I opened the classroom door and noticed three layers of windows up to the ceiling with steel bars covering the inner window while the morning sunrise glared through the cobwebbed corner and brought natural sunlight to the room.

"Class, meet Lorrie. She came here all the way from California," the teacher said as she cleared her throat and brought her glasses to the tip of her nose.

After the somewhat formal introduction, I immediately heard unwarranted snickering and phony chuckling toward the back of the room. I stood there paralyzed. Paying little attention to what the teacher was saying, my mind was focused on my future classmates, trying to mind-read. Maybe it was my name, or maybe the California part, or maybe it was just me, the way I looked? Feeling extremely insecure, I quickly dashed to the nearest chair to quiet my inner voice and get out of the limelight. Later on in the day, the girls were eager to let me know where they really stood by voicing their snide remarks.

During recess, I heard my classmates taunting me. "Look how she's dressed," they said and would laugh behind my back. I revengefully responded, "You *done-dare* brats (really the *B* word) talk funny. So there," trying to mock their Ohioan accent. I had learned this new vocabulary (profanity) when Rob was angry at me or anyone else. Since I was fuming mad, I felt it was a good time to repeat it. They were skipping so fast across the pavement that I didn't think they actually heard me, which was a relief, come to think of it. I would have hated getting into a fight on my first day of school and getting called into the principal's office. Not to mention, if I just so happened to lose the fight, I would have taken another beating if Rob found out. He would have demanded that I go back and fight until I won or else face his harsh discipline, which would hurt more than any kid fight could possibly do. Either way, I lose. I took a deep breath and wiped my forehead in relief. It didn't go that far. Suddenly I felt homesick for the familiar, like our small project apartment in Rodeo, even though it stunk like a sewage plant some of the time. If many of us were considered poor in the California ghetto, we didn't know it because we all looked the same. I quickly discovered I didn't like Ohio, and I desperately wanted to go home.

At least we had a bathroom and running water.

I didn't really consider myself poor until I had moved to Ohio. The kids there told me I was poor. I was not always fond of the clothing Mom picked for me, but at least my clothes matched, a fashion statement that my mother had instilled in me fairly early on. I wanted them to see me as I saw myself: prepared with matching clothes on my first day of school. I know I was in an early awkward growing stage: big blue eyes and sporting the Dumbo flyaway ears with my adult-looking nose outgrowing my baby face—not a good combination on an extremely skinny child. It hurt to think no one wanted to be my friend when I had no problem making friends in Rodeo, but I'd never admit to that hurt. Instead, lashing out in anger was safer for me. Rob bullying me and labeling me a "sissy" prepared me for no vulnerability or, at least, showing it. I'd be admitting that I was a weak-willed, scared, *sissy* girl, and that label brought heavy consequences on the home front. Even gender differences didn't matter as far as he was concerned.

When I saw my classmates eating a variety of foods rather than the same ol', same-ol' peanut butter and jelly day after day, their accusations about me being poor started to make sense. In retaliation, I was tempted to steal food from their backpacks, but I never got the opportunity. The teacher released class for recess then locked the classroom. The kids continued to see my poverty as ammunition for their humor.

"Look what I have—it's soooo good, and you can't have any. Ha-ha!" Sometimes it didn't bother me—except when they'd wave my favorite, a snowball cupcake (white and pink sprinkled with coconut on top and cream in the middle) in front of my face. I'd think to myself, *Yeah, you're lucky the teacher makes me go out for recess because none of you brats would have anything to eat.* I'd never have enough nerve to say it out loud because then they'd think I was a thief. When feelings were too negative, I reflected on going home to my sis. She was always happy to see me and made me feel like I was special.

So, welcome to Ohio.

With the fluctuating weather patterns and the chilling cold front moving across the south, my body was adapting to the climate change. Then something took me completely by surprise. Mom demanded Lisa and I go live with Rob's uncle John and aunt Linda until they found a permanent place for us to live. John was an awful, homely-looking man. The few teeth he had left looked decayed and had a greenish-brownish tint from decades of smoking cigarettes. In fact, he looked scary—not the kind of man I wanted to embrace during my first introduction.

In addition, his wife, Linda, was (let's just say) a large woman, at least by my standards, being a scrawny child. She looked like she struggled to keep air in her lungs and had a hard time getting around.

It seemed we had arrived on a scene from *The Beverly Hillbillies* before they struck oil (Lisa said that—funny).

Lisa and I kicked and screamed while they held us down as we watched our mother head for the front door. She tried to reassure us that this was only temporary as she looked back and said, "I'll be back to get you." I knew that despite her promises, it would be a long time before we saw her orange lipstick and those big brown eyes.

Our household duties consisted of the typical day-to-day chores, but also included rubbing Linda's crusty feet with lotion when she returned home from work. We knew what was about to happen when she started whining about "being on her feet all day." My first thought was, *Maybe they wouldn't hurt so bad if she'd lose some weight.* I know, I was being *mean*. When she came out of the bathroom holding a bottle of lotion in her hands, she'd say, "Girls, guess what time it is?" She looked at us as if this was the highlight of her life with her wide-eyed expression and that certain facial grin. Lisa and I looked at each other and cringed with disgust.

"It's your turn, Lorrie," Lisa said then looked at me with her tongue hanging out, like, *Yucky.*

"No way, it's your turn," I demanded.

"No, remember last night? I did it. Remember?"

"No, I did. Remember?"

We continued to argue back and forth until finally Linda, frustrated about our bickering, chose one of us to fulfill the dirty deed. The most dreadful part was when she moaned when my hands touched her hardened cracked feet—gross! The lotion squished through my fingers and turned brown from the wedged-in dirt stains. Her toenails were cracked down the middle, discolored, and had warty bumps growing on the edges of her toes. That disgusting visual magnified my already-upset stomach. Finally, I'd close my eyes because I didn't want to look at her hideous elephant feet any longer.

A couple weeks later, early Christmas Eve, Lisa and I overheard some drunken chatter between a few of Uncle John's drinking buddies at the kitchen table about their intent to "shoot Santa Claus" if he dared to enter the house without permission. Later that evening, we heard the pleasant sound of jingle bells and a masculine deep voice shouting, "Ho, ho, ho!" Lisa and I held each other's hands and squeezed with fierce anxiety, wondering what was going to happen to Santa. Immediately, the impossible happened—two explosive gunshots went off, one right after the other. We heard Uncle John's voice shouting at the top of his lungs, "Well, I shot the son of a ——. Taught his —— a lesson not to trespass on my property." He cursed God's name in vain constantly.

We couldn't believe our ears and remained stunned, speechless.

Lisa and I were taught early on not to exit the bedroom for any reason on Christmas Eve, so we closely tuned in with our ears glued to the door to listen for more information.

"Let's bury him out yonder," shouted some other unfamiliar voice.

As the commotion continued, we quickly jumped into the bed and placed the covers over our heads just in case they came barreling through the bedroom door and caught us eavesdropping and shot us too. The steam intensified with Lisa's every panting breath while I was holding my breath, feeling suffocated under those itchy, prickly wool blankets.

"Breathe, Lorrie," she told me.

"Can you believe this, Lisa? I think they shot Santa." My voice quivered with fear in a whispery tone.

"If we weren't here, Santa wouldn't have come to this stupid place," Lisa responded in between her sobs.

"It's all our fault. We can't tell anyone," I said.

"Well, I don't care what you think. I'm telling Mom," she angrily declared.

We had a particularly hard time falling asleep that night, but we eventually curled up next to each other in a spoon like position and cried ourselves to sleep.

Early the next morning, surprisingly, there were presents underneath their Christmas tree.

"Look, Lisa, they took the presents and put them under the tree before they buried Santa."

"Well, I don't want those presents," she whispered in my ear, then stomped her foot on the floor.

Shortly afterward, Uncle John's bedroom door flew open as Linda exited the bedroom wearing her gosh-awful country around-the-house moo-moo gown, smiling and saying, "Merry Christmas, girls." She was standing in the hallway holding her hands out in a welcoming position with an ear-to-ear-smile on her face.

We stood there in silence, thinking, *There is nothing merry about this morning.*

"Is Santa dead?" we asked in unison.

"Of course not. Your uncle John was playing a joke on you girls last night so y'all be really surprised this morning. He knew y'all be listening."

Then Uncle John showed his ugly face, shuffling his wrinkly cotton robe, laughing hilariously. "Gotcha, didn't I?" were the first words that came out of his mouth.

Lisa and I didn't think that was very funny but reassured him that he "got" us.

"Wow, you sure did," we said, shaking our heads up and down, affirming our body language.

That was a bittersweet Christmas. We celebrated the fact that Santa was alive, but we missed our mother terribly. Our anxieties grew daily as we wondered if she had forgotten about us and if she'd ever return to get us out of there.

Lisa and I stayed a few more months, which felt like an eternity. We jumped up and down hysterically, overwhelmed, that early-spring midday when our mother rescued us. Lisa hung on to my mother's leg and wrapped her little legs as tightly around her right calf to make a statement that she was not leaving without us this time. By the way, this was how Lisa got her nickname, *Monk*. Monkeys have the same clingy behavior. It fit perfectly. Lisa and I knew, whenever her nickname came up, it hit an internal cord that only we could really understand the true meaning of "Monk" through our experiences. Everybody else thought it was just her cute nickname. When Lisa mentioned what happened to us at the weirdo's house, our mother just shook her head and reassured us that we'd never have to go back there again. What a relief.

We arrived at our new house across town, and Lisa and I looked at each other with that twinkle in our eyes and the anticipation of exploring new territory. This house was located right across the street from the overflow, swamp-like marshland considered a runoff for Crystal Lake in Springfield. We started fantasizing about all the great possibilities for fun—swimming, skating, and playing together in our new backyard, like normal kids' play. There was a garage-like shed in the backyard, so we could play house.

Wow, this is finally our new beginning, just like our mother had promised. For starters, Lisa and I looked forward to dusk because we were awestruck with the fireflies' abilities to flash their booties, as we called it, off and on. Since we had been cooped up with the Beverly Hillbillies (as we considered them) and we didn't get to play outside, this amazing insect was our first-time experience. Like on an automatic timer, when dusk hit, we rushed out of the house just to watch their bottoms flash off and on. One night we decided to invent a night-light since our little imaginations were at their peak. We located a jar and poked holes at the top then dashed into the night on a mission to catch the flies. Once we had captured the fireflies, we dropped some grass into the bottom of the jar, and onto the nightstand they were placed. Our mother probably wondered why we didn't argue about bedtime, but we were anxious to actually see our invention in action. We quickly learned that fireflies are not made for night-lights.

Now and then, Lisa and I daydreamed about the lake across the street. We imagined all the possibilities throughout the four seasons, especially springtime. Due to the climate in Ohio, a thick ice formed on the lake that made it possible for us to develop yet another adventure. We put slipper-like shoes on and performed a slide-and-glide show on the ice. We held each other's hand and swung around and around like "ring around the rosy" until unexpectedly I heard unusual sounds beneath us. Suddenly I saw cracks forming on the ice in certain spots and realized that it was too risky. We had to get off the ice and quickly because the cracks were starting to surround us like a spiderweb. No, we did not fall in, but it was a very close call for both of us. However, it was fun while it lasted. Darn. But we were always on the lookout for the next possible venture to explore, not letting the restrictions get the best of us. Well…

We were bound to the house until we figured out our next "kids being kids" adventure (which was beginning to become more wishful thinking than anything else), and things became bleak. During that transition, my role changed. I had to take off my childish play, so to speak, and put on mother-like duties. It was apparent that Rob was irritated being unemployed, over-the-top stressed, or just darn-right mean by nature. The latter is a more accurate description of the man's spirit. However, with the other strenuous issues at hand, his explosive temperament worsened. So, Lisa and I learned how to walk on eggshells with precision when he was around.

I overheard Rob's demanding request to my mother, "The baby cannot sleep in our room. I won't be woken up in the middle of the night. Put her in Lorrie and Lisa's room and let them deal with her."

Later on that day, the bassinet was rolled in right next to our bed. I knew this was coming, so I was mentally prepared for "graveyard" baby duty with no say in the matter. Almost nightly, I woke up to change her and feed her even though I had to go to school the next day. I'd pretend to play house, just like what Lisa and I had talked about in the backyard shed, but this time, I had a real baby of my own. Baby Shelly was a beautiful little girl who had a light-brown skin tone, very large black eyes, and tons of curly coal-black hair, making her resemble an Indian papoose. Actually, she had the potential to be in baby commercials, but I don't think they had baby commercials back then. In fact, that time period was before the invention of disposable diapers and the baby swings, just good old-fashioned cloth diapers and arm swinging.

Shelly was a well-behaved baby who only needed care for her basic needs—not colicky, in constant need of rocking. Taking care of her was somewhat natural. However, there were many times after school that Rob looked at me and said, "Find the belt." He wouldn't say why. I just knew I didn't react quickly enough to Shelly's crying.

I was a comatose sleeper, and that probably explained why I had a problem of having frequent accidents (bed-wetter) at night.

A few months later, my mother was pregnant with her fourth child. I couldn't help but think about the additional pressure and responsibility I'd have. Let's face it. It was hard for me to imagine taking care of another baby. With my mother's pregnancy came additional duties. Lisa and I became responsible for nightly kitchen duty. Now this probably wouldn't have been so difficult if my mother had a routine, planned-out meal in which dinner was ready at a specific time. However, for whatever reason, the likelihood of having mealtime at the traditional 6:00 or 7:00 p.m. so that dishes could be done by bedtime was virtually impossible. If we even had a mealtime, it was usually 9:00 or 10:00 p.m. You get the picture. Since we were too short to reach the faucet, Rob conveniently supplied the two chairs, side by side, to complete the job. It started out fun until…

Rule 1: If one speck of food is left on a dish, every dish, silverware, pot, and pan is removed from the cupboards and placed on the counter to be rewashed.

With this routine came deep exhaustion, and severe fatigue quickly set in. The boiling tension between us was starting to put an undeniable wedge in our sisterhood.

During bedtime, I'd hear Lisa mumbling half-asleep to God, "Please, give Rob a job." I knew what she really meant: *Please get him away from us.*

Lo and behold, her prayers were answered. We were ecstatic. Not only was he away from us, but he paid less attention to the dishes, so we all went to bed earlier. When he got laid off, I'd tell Lisa to pray that "he'll die."

I can't help but mention Lisa's sharp-minded, quick-witted reaction to a situation that spared us. Unbeknownst to me, in Rob's mind, we deserved a beating for some reason or another. These "whoopings" occurred frequently and became almost the everyday norm.

"Lorrie and Lisa, find the belt. You're getting your butts [actually cussing] whooped," he yelled furiously at the top of his lungs. We were silent for a moment, and my body froze. Then Lisa brilliantly busted out with, "Daddy, you're wearing it." He was stumped. He then had an odd-looking grin, looked down at his waist, and hesitated for a bit. Then he went for it. He immediately pulled up his shirt, unbuckled his belt, and quickly slung it off his waist. This time, after it was all over, I squeezed Lisa's arm happily. Not only did she save us from the "hunt torture" but from considerable physical pain. Surprisingly, he was wearing just a regular leather belt, not the other two with the metal holes or the snap strap that caused intense pain for days to come. Lisa was brilliant at times. Now I can see that was God giving her words at the right time.

To stay away from Rob as much as possible, Lisa and I focused on our imaginations in the toolshed outback. We used it as our make-believe house to escape the madman who lived inside our real home. Sadly, due to the lack of garbage service, we watched the shed-like garage rapidly accumulate trash. It quickly became a dumping ground for rotting food and other perishable items that turned into maggots. It smelled like Rodeo. Oh, how I wanted to go back home to Rodeo. Instead of becoming our temporary place of refuge, it became a place of refuse—a home for rats and other crawlers like spiders, crickets, and pincher bugs.

Summertime also brought its share of challenges for us in our attempts to escape. We redirected our focus once again to the lake across the street. It was easy to focus on this area because sometime during the day, the sun made the water look like a sparkling lightshow. We couldn't wait to swim and play in the water and look for pollywogs and tiny frogs until our encounter with swarms of mosquitoes. As we'd scratch to get some relief from the irritation, our fingernails broke the skin, and bacteria grew and caused terrible infections, which my mother diagnosed as impetigo. Since she was working the night shift as a nursing assistant and had experience with medicating her own skin problems, she was incredibly skillful at treating our wounds. Bless her heart.

We lived there in Ohio for approximately eighteen months. Similar to how we had arrived in Ohio was how we left—uprooted in the same fashion in the middle of the night. This time, there were three girls and our newborn baby sister, Sarah, in the back seat. We were over-the-top excited to leave but had no idea where we were headed.

Chapter Reflection

This chapter brings up a variety of incidents that highlight the root of my blame toward not only my caretakers and peers but also society as a whole.

Back in Rodeo, I was too young to internally comprehend the potential health risks for all the individuals living in the impoverished neighborhoods due to the close proximity of the oil refineries. However, in adulthood, those experiences reinforced my self-fulfilling prophecy that the poverty-stricken individuals don't matter. No money—no voice. I carried this core belief into my personal experience on many different levels growing up. One can argue that this perception appears to be true in the worldly sense; however, in God's eyes, the opposite is true according to His Word. Bottom line—we do matter to God.

> *Give justice to the poor and the orphan; uphold the rights of the oppressed and the destitute. Rescue the poor and helpless, deliver them from the grasp of evil people. (Psalm 82:3–4 NLT)*

The idea of the Santa prank is unfathomable. The detailed activation, well-thought-out plans, the so-real props (jingle bells, gunshots, etc.)—it is insanely cruel and downright deranged to crush a fantasy as important as Santa, even just for childish kicks. It would have been nice if Rob warned us about his uncle's practical-joke character; in that, we would have been a little more prepared and not taken his hoax so seriously. On the other hand, Rob probably loved the idea as he slapped his uncle a high-five for delivering his so-called brilliant fright fest. I still have a hard time wrapping my head around this: immaturity, boredom, alcohol abuse, or all the above—who knows?

In addition, in my view, developmentally, for elementary-age children, it's almost impossible to separate fact from fiction, or separate ownership of adult-like problems like financial strain, family conflict, divorce, and other pressing issues. Therefore, I just assumed everything revolved around me. It was my fault my father left. It was my fault Santa died. It was my fault I wet the bed and, consequently, my fault we were dumped off with those strange people. This is something I didn't say; it was just how I felt deep down. Unfortunately, without healthy interventions to combat these falsehoods, the "my fault" syndrome became subconsciously automatic.

On a separate note, one of the most emotionally damaging repercussions of the beatings was hearing Lisa's torment when she went into the bedroom before me, more so than the actual physical violence itself—well, depending on which belt was used. I'm sure she felt the same way when the shoe was on the other foot. If I had a choice, I would have preferred being physically beaten more than to have looked for that so-called missing-belt agony. Just the thought of knowing a beating was coming brought an intense anxiety-producing mental strain, as well as the powerlessness we felt trying to hurry up and get it over with—impossible. So with that, it was like our mental state was being heavily pressed for hours before the physical beating had actually taken place.

It was almost as if he had hidden the belts from us purposely because when we finally found it, we'd find it in the most unusual, unlikely places, like buried underneath a pile of dirty clothes or underneath the couch. Looking back, I am convinced this was indeed his intention: to purposefully watch us suffer. There's a dictionary word for this: *sadism* (pleasure from inflicting pain, suffering, or humiliation on others), an excellent description at its core. This was our norm—slavery in our own home. The peer-to-peer conflicts also played a significant role in my silence. I felt like I was the only one with this experience and felt alone. In reality, countless individuals have encountered bullying, rejection, and humiliation at one point or another in their lifetimes but remained silent, creating the isolation. Makes sense. Just remember, you are not alone.

> *Don't be afraid, for I am with you. Don't be discouraged, for I am your God. I will strengthen you and help you. I will hold you up with my victorious right hand. (Isaiah 41:10 NLT)*

Today, during my spiritual journey, I thank God that I've realized—it's not my fault. Children are not responsible for an adult's decisions that cause them guilt, shame, or rejection early on. It was a pivotal moment when I finally learned how to separate the two. I also realized that we were not alone, even though Lisa already knew that. This type of abuse has been prevalent throughout history. In fact, God saw the agony of His own people being grossly mistreated, beaten, slave-driven, and he eventually provided a way out for them. This is exactly what He will do for all of His abused children if we trust in Him. I trust Him.

> *Therefore, say to the people of Israel; "I am the Lord. I will free you from your oppression and will rescue you from your slavery in Egypt. I will redeem you with a powerful arm and great acts of judgment. I will claim you as my own people, and I will be your God. Then you will know that I am the Lord your God who has freed you from your oppression in Egypt." (Exodus 6:6–7 NLT)*

*****

I had been sharing my story with Maria for a couple hours. I could tell she was intrigued with the introduction to my history lesson, but on the other hand, she had heard countless women's stories with similar backgrounds. The one thread that wove us all together like a tapestry was that we were unified in pain. Maybe she was doing a research paper, writing a book, or just knew I was suicidal. Maybe she was just interested in me? Go figure. I could tell she was getting a bit tired as her eyelids were getting droopy. It was almost 5:00 p.m., and she had to get back to the office and wrap a few things up before Monday. She pulled out her Day-Timer handbook, and asked if we could have another appointment early next week.

"I know that was only the beginning, and I am looking forward to hearing more," she said.

"Good, because what Nana did was unimaginable," I responded.

"Yes, I can only imagine, Lorrie. Next session, I guess I find out who Nana is. Hopefully we'll have more information about the baby's condition by then."

"I sure hope so," I responded and nodded in agreement.

Before walking her to the door, she said with a matter-of-fact tone, "Lorrie, thank you for trusting enough by opening up your life to me. You are brave and courageous." She then shook my hand.

Wow! Having gone from a drug-addicted monster to a brave and courageous woman is for sure a contrast. I think I like this woman.

Over the weekend, nothing changed, except that I was sleeping more and more—either depressed or making up for all the sleep I had lost over the years. Probably both. Dustin was still in the NIC unit in quarantine while specialists were teaming up to figure out what was going on. I drove to the phone booth and spoke to the nurses on staff about his condition—same news. I tried to remain hopeful that everything would eventually turn out okay, but this wishful thinking would fluctuate all too often. It was better for me to sleep than to think of the what-ifs continuously running through my head.

The following Tuesday, Maria showed up bright-eyed and bushy-tailed with a smile on her face as usual. I could tell that she was well-rested, considering it was the early workweek. Her high-volume caseload drama hadn't hit her like a ton of bricks; her makeup was evenly toned and brought a colorful glow to her Latina face, with her hair dipping down around her jawbone. She confirmed that there were no new changes in the baby's condition as the medical professionals were still running multiple tests trying to determine a diagnosis.

"Well, last week you shared the beginning of your life story. Do you feel up to continuing on? I believe you were about to tell me about Nana?" Maria said.

"Yeah, how did you remember that?"

"It's probably how we ended our last conversation. Besides, I jotted a note in my Day-Timer. So…who is Nana?" she asked.

"You'll find out soon enough," I responded. I wasn't ready to jump ahead and interrupt the chronological sequence.

"Okay, fair enough," she said, then nodded.

This tickled me that someone of her stature was interested in my life and brought a nonjudgmental, nonthreatening attitude that I burst into tears. Coming down from the drugs, topped off with the uncertainty of Dustin's health, I was emotionally wide open, unstable, and terrified. Usually, I had a hard exterior, rarely showed any vulnerability, and appeared unapproachable to keep people at a distance. This had been my safety net for protection, but this situation changed me—maybe I was sick of the façade (which was a lot of hard work) and obviously kept me wedged on a self-destructive path. After I calmed down with a few deep breaths, I continued where I had left off.

Bull Duke

On the road again. Our destination was with Rob's parents back in California. I'm not sure why we had to leave or if it was by Rob's choice; nevertheless, we were ecstatic about their decision. Lisa and I had felt miserable in Ohio. Therefore, we felt more hopeful going back to our place of origin near our grandparents, so this trip was much more enjoyable—almost an anticipation of excitement.

Moving across Interstate 80 on our way back to California, ironically, "I'm Goin' to Jackson" was playing on the radio by Johnny Cash and June Carter. My mother and Rob were singing the song together as if it had some kind of special meaning between them. Then my mother turned to us and shouted excitedly, "Girls, that's where we're going—right next door to Jackson."

Suddenly we're all singing, "We're going to Jackson, look out Jackson town," bouncing in the back seat to the music.

We fixed our eyes on one another in the back seat of the car and said, "I can't wait to see Balloon Grandma and Grandma Dorothy." Then we giggled with overflowing joy. We called our mother's mother Balloon Grandma because with each visit, she'd bring a bag of balloons, candy, and a variety of colorful stickers as our special treat. Grandma Dorothy is our biological father's mother, who was a very nurturing, delightful human being. They both loved their grandchildren dearly, and we knew it.

Lisa looked so cute with her stringy hair hanging over her brown almond-shaped eyes and a round rosy-cheeked face while the wind softly blew through the back-seat window. We were not born with any Asian decent; this facial feature was a biological trait that Lisa inherited from our father. That's it. I could always tell when Lisa was happy because her eyes closed as if she were sleeping; this meant she was smiling with her eyes. Honestly, I guess we both had that genetic trait.

Rob's parents' property was located outside of Sacramento in a small town in Amador County. There was a graveled path about a mile and a half off the main road in the middle of a run-down, "red-necked," pastoral ranch that looked similar to a setting from an old Western movie. As we drove down the path, I could hear cows mooing from the distance. This was a good indication that we were headed deep into the countryside that was surrounded by ancient overgrown oak trees. An additional half-mile dirt road covered with small rocky pebbles looped around green hillsides and led to the ranch-style home. As we made a left turn, I saw the rocky pebbles flying up from the tires, creating a dust cloud behind us. No paved roads in those neck of the woods. No doubt about it, we had arrived in the country because several bulls and cows were grazing along the green hillside. I could sense that not many people came to this area because the cattle stopped eating and stared intensely at us as we drove by—like they weren't used to the company.

To the left of the house were bushels of wood that were laid near a huge tree trunk, and I spotted an antique-looking ax lodged dead center in a stump. The property was secluded as if we were in a sinking pit surrounded by minimountains. The only neighbor was a half mile down the rocky path whom I concluded must have been in the wrecking-yard business because the house was fenced in with several beat-up rusty vehicles, scattered car parts, tractors, and old farming equipment that apparently hadn't been used in years. There were tumbleweeds and dead grass all along their property.

As we approached our destination, it looked like a typical old white ranch-style house. It had peeled paint hanging off in some areas as if the house had gotten beat up from previous winter storms (kind of like the outhouse in Ohio), and it was bordered by a wire fence with a gate leading to the entrance. A gust of wind filled our faces, followed by the smell of dry hay mixed with the fresh aroma of cow patties. When Lisa and I got a strong whiff, we called it "bull duke," then cracked ourselves up. We had our own silly language that only she and I understood.

The layout of the house unveiled a three-bedroom structure with a massive living room decorated with antiques on every wall. I could sense that Rob's daddy wasn't handy with a broom and would much rather be outside than clean house since the furniture was covered in dust, and thick cobwebs looped around the ceiling like dingy gray baseboards. I continued to gaze around our new environment. By the looks of the ceiling, I could tell other creatures lived there too.

"Mommy, there are too many spiders in this house," was the first thing I was worried about.

"Oh, they're just daddy long-legs. They look scary, but they're harmless. They won't bite you because their legs are too long for their bite to reach the skin," she told me.

An entry door was located in the hallway that had a drop-down stairway leading to the attic that looked spookier than the spiders. During the tour of the house, Rob's father, nicknamed Gramps, pointed at the stairs and threatened us. "If you kids dare act up, I'll put you up in that there attic and hang you by the hook," pointing upwardly to the ceiling.

I guess the spiders were going to be the least of my worries after hearing that comment. I then looked at Lisa and whispered, "I hope he was just kidding." It was hard to tell because he wasn't smiling and had a poker face. We then walked into the kitchen. The pantry closet door was open, and I noticed plenty of canned nonperishable food, which was pleasant to the eye, considering we had gone to bed without anything to eat in Ohio many nights. To be quite frank, it was much better to go to bed hungry than to deal with the nightly dishes' saga with a full belly—well, maybe not. Hunger pains are no joke either. Let's just say, we were delighted about plentiful food at our disposal. However, we had no idea that too much food would be used against us. Mind twisted—from one extreme to another.

It didn't take too long to figure out that Gramps was definitely rough around the edges, lacked etiquette, was rowdy to say the least, similar to a mountain man with a raspy, hoarse voice. He had no problem spewing vulgar language topped off with the *F* bomb after every other word, as if he had had limited contact with human beings and was cursing at the cattle all day long. It seemed like he was always dirty from hard work: hands grained with grease stains from working on broken-down cars, fingernails caked with dirt, and overalls coated with slivers of wood chips from chopping wood for the iron stove. Meanwhile, Rob's mother worked in the meat department at a grocery store, so she believed in having enough food on hand in case of an emergency. Rob's mother was a big-boned, heavyset woman in her early fifties with fluffy curly gray hair who wore thick bifocals. She appeared to be a sweet-natured, grandmotherly figure whose nickname reflected that of a nurturing caregiver: she was known as *Nana* to the family.

Along with Gramps and Nana, we were introduced to their family pets: a pit bull with one blue eye and one blind eye (named Joey One-Eye) and a black Doberman pinscher named Blackie (nicknamed Heffa), which appeared to be temperamental. Based on Blackie's growl, my intuition told me that this was not a people-friendly dog—trained not to like strangers, to attack on a whim, and to protect the surroundings at all costs. We'd hear stories about Joey One-Eye's prey and imagined his jaws locking onto our body parts. Gramps said Joey had previously devoured a bird and left all the feathers lying throughout the yard. Their feeding bowls were located in the entryway of the kitchen, and the only way to get to the bathroom was to cross over into the kitchen if the back-patio door was dead-bolted. There was absolutely no way Rob's parents would consider changing the position of the bowls for us because the dogs were family members; obviously, we were just visitors.

Lisa and I developed a preventive plan that if the dogs were feeding, we'd just potty outside. Feeding or not, Blackie constantly nipped at us, sometimes even drawing blood. Whenever we'd run to get help, Gramps unmercifully responded, "If you don't want to get your —— bit, stay the —— away from the dog. You know how she is. And stop being a sissy." I could see his jaw muscles pulsating during his response like he absolutely despised sissies (weak-willed, cowardly individuals).

Humm, like father, like son? Makes sense—learned behavior.

Gramps undoubtedly preached that dogs can smell fear, and that was a for-sure way to get our —— bit unless we "listened up." Even though we were petrified, we tried hard not to show our emotions. We then got sick and tired of the intimidation, so we put on an extra pair of pants. Now we thought we've outsmarted everyone, even the dogs. Ha!

Can anything be more frightful than Rob, spiders, the attic, and unpredictable dogs?

We started a new school that was several miles away in a nearby town and had to catch the yellow bus near the main highway. Because there was only one school bus going to Jackson, Lisa and I had to wake up at the butt crack of dawn and leave early enough to walk that one-and-a-half mile dirt path to catch the bus on time, or else. On our way, several bovine observers openly stood along the path and gave us a direct eye-contact glare and intense stare with their coal-black eyes and thick flared nostrils. We tried carefully not to make much noise by bringing attention to ourselves. But unfortunately, with the mixture of our heels hitting the tiny rock pebbles and the crunching sound throughout the graveled dirt road, it was virtually impossible to be left unnoticed. With every step we took, we witnessed their determined look, cautiously watching our every move, their heads slowly turned in our direction, as if they were thinking what to do next. Trust me, we dittoed their every move. As I looked back to see where the bulls were, Lisa straightforwardly said, "Don't look at them, Lorrie. Maybe they can smell that we're scared just like Blackie and attack us."

"All I know is, if they are going to attack, we need to know when to haul butt," I fired back. "And, Lisa, hide that red lunch pail under your arm. That's probably making it worse."

"Oh, yeah? Then keep on lookin'."

The cows were less intimidating than the bulls, of course. Luckily for us, there were far more cows than bulls most of the time. Although the cows vocally communicated their disapproval of our presence loud and clear, we weren't sure if this was their distress moo call to their mates for protection or a call for a group attack. Nevertheless, after they had dropped their heads like bulls do, we were unmistakably shivering with fear. There was no faking this one. Ten pairs of pants wouldn't have saved our behinds, only our own two feet. My eyes were heavily concentrating on their feet (something I had previously observed on some sort of cartoon) to see if the hooves were digging into the grass like, *Charge!* with their eyes ablaze. The only fencing was on the outer perimeter without any barriers separating us from the cattle. Our goal was to get across the fenceless gate as fast as we could; only then were we safe. For some reason, the cattle would not cross over that metal grid pounded into the ground with gaps in it. It looked like a tic-tac-toe board with big holes in it. I guess they were afraid they would fall in. Our lifesaver. When our adrenaline stabilized, we looked at each other and shouted, "Bull duke!" We slapped each other a high five, then heaved a deep sigh of relief because we had surprisingly survived another day.

Many school days, Lisa and I walked side by side, arm in arm, with steady eye contact, focused on high alert, dreading the day that the bulls would finally attack. Lisa usually prayed for protection, silently mumbling underneath her breath or humming a comforting melody to distract our fears prior to bull contact. I'd admire how a five-year-old girl could be so brave when I was the older one, yet she was stronger than me. She had a unique way of making hard times easier—that validation of reassurance that we'd be okay someday. Later was my chance to return the favor when my favorite song "Downtown" by Petula Clark periodically hit music airways after being released in 1964. It was such a popular song that even four years later, radio DJs still chose to play the song. I sang that song on the way to the bus stop and daydreamed that "someday" we'd be out of the country and somewhere downtown around a lot of people. Every day, I told myself:

> We will be safe downtown...
> We will be safe downtown...

When winter came, it brought an intense strain to our eyes due to the time change. It was dark when we left the house, making it difficult to watch the cattle's eye movements or body language, but we were grateful that we had excellent eyesight. Sometimes we were just flat-out lucky. The bulls were elsewhere on the property or, better yet, nowhere in sight. Even though we had our challenges getting to school, there was an instant relief when my feet stepped off the school bus and hit the school grounds. For some reason, I had a special relationship with my first-grade teacher, Mrs. Ball. Maybe it was because she believed in me, even though I was struggling academically. I would perk up when I'd hear her say, "That-a-girl!" I adored her spirit, her inner beauty, her soft-spoken voice, and I regularly shared Mrs. Ball with Lisa on our way home. Mrs. Ball reminded me of our biological grandmothers, and she provided an emotional safety net, an "I feel secure when I am around her" kind of feeling, even though I couldn't label it as such. It just was.

"I hope you get Mrs. Ball for your teacher next year, Lisa. You will love her."

"Are you kidding? I don't want to be here next year," she exclaimed. She did have an excellent point.

Back on the home front, it was virtually impossible for outsiders to sense any abuse because Nana was a master manipulator, an expert deceiver. She made unannounced school visits and pretended to be a concerned grandparent by checking on our academic progress. She then used the information as ammunition against us later by letting us know how stupid we were. Nana got a thrill picking out our frilly, lacy dresses that we dreaded in the wintertime and wrapped our hair in pink rubber curlers (which looked like clothespins with tiny holes) so tightly to present the Shirley Temple look with spiraling ringlets. This was more for her "look-good" persona than for our good-look benefit. Like clockwork, when the antique cuckoo clock chimed six times, it was time. She sat in her faded blue rocking chair with the comb and brush resting on the crochet arm cover with several rollers close by her feet. This routine was Lisa's worst nightmare, more so than the bulls: having her hair yanked, pulled, rolled up smack-dab to the scalp. Probably because our hair was so baby-fine thin, we were worried our hair was going to all fall out. Our only relief was when she stopped for a moment, then strangely caressed our earlobes several times like she had a fetish with rubbing ears. After the hair-pulling routine, it felt like my temples had been stretched to their limit.

"What is she trying to do, make us go bald? Can't she see we barely have hair as it is?" I complained to Lisa. I dare not whine or complain to Nana about the pain—just take it and shut up.

"Sis, my head hurts," Lisa would whine, obviously going through the same pain as me.

"Yes, I know. It's giving me a terrible headache too. Just wait. It will go numb in a little while. At least in the morning, the rollers will be out, so try not to think about it and go to sleep," I'd respond, trying to take my own advice.

Nana made it very clear to us that she was perceived by others as a long-standing, respectable community participant and was noted as a well-established, churchgoing, charity-giving, so-called productive citizen around the countryside. She used this technique to brainwash our minds not to share our "family business" and threatened us that things would only get worse if we failed to listen, planting the seed of doubt that maybe she was right. This was a preplanned setup, no doubt. More accurately, psychological head games.

"Besides, no one would ever believe you anyway," she'd say as she looked directly at me purposely, like, *Don't even try it*. Then she would go on to say, "Lorrie and Lisa, you know I've been living here for a long, long time, and people here know and respect me, so always keep that in mind." Then she smiled at us with her grayish teeth and those wicked eyes that magnified threefold from her thick bifocals. Scary.

"Do you both understand what I'm saying?" she'd ask while she tapped her foot on the floor, flung her hand on her hip, and glared those demonic eyes that penetrated more than those words.

"Yes, ma'am, we understand," we'd say, nodding in agreement.

Her demeanor was undoubtedly convincing. Even though I wanted to tell someone what Lisa and I had been going through, that seed of doubt grew out of control, and the possibility of the latter didn't even register anymore—different kind of horns in my future.

Chapter Reflection

Writing about this experience brings back the intense feelings of intimidation and fear that permeated our bodies at that time. It reminds me of the movie *Forrest Gump*. "Run, Forrest, run!" Jenny would scream so that Forrest could escape the neighborhood bullies. Same scenario, but *bulls*, not bullies, were our adversaries—both scary for little kids. Back then, it was said that the color red irritates bulls. While that is not the case to my knowledge today, my instinct tells me that Nana deliberately bought red for that purpose.

Nonetheless, we felt frightened and helpless. It became a normalized mindset for us to remain silent. The unspoken message here was that what I said did not matter, I didn't matter, and that no one would have believed me anyway. My belief system told me, "Every little person goes through this and how much different it will be when I get big." In the meantime, that self-talk worked enough to protect my mind or, rather, it was God protecting it. I just didn't know it at the time. I see now how God gave us something to hold on to in order to keep our hope alive. In my case, it was the song "Downtown" that helped redirect my focus and cope with homelife. The lyrics reflect to forget all my troubles, escape my worries, and finding someone just like me who would understand. For heaven's sake, I was only six years old and felt this song was written for me at the time. I wrapped my arms around my shoulders and gave myself a big hug. I reminded my inner child, *You're all right now. God is in control. God sees everything.*

> *Nothing in all creation is hidden from God's sight. Everything is uncovered laid bare before the eyes of him to whom we must give account. (Hebrews 4:13 NIV)*

HEET

During that time, little did I know that having experienced the bulls' horns around the outdoor perimeter, I was about to experience Nana's *devilish* horns firsthand behind her closed bedroom door. In the mid-1960s, there was a medicine that was used to soothe agonizing arthritis pain and reduce the swelling for patients suffering from the disease. It was a dark, deep-red liquid substance; it looked like blood in a bottle. It had a wire applicator with a cotton, cloth-like swab connected at the end of the wire that was stored in its container. The outside of the bottle said *HEET*, surrounded by flames around the word.

"Lorrie, come with me. You peed in the bed last night, didn't you?" Nana screeched as she walked ahead of me, then grabbed my arm forcefully behind her.

I remained silent and followed her into her bedroom, not sure what was about to happen. I watched her pick up the bottle as described above from her dresser, all prepared for her demonic act.

Nana stared me down with her large magnified eyes bulging behind those ugly thick bifocals like a demon-possessed monster ready to devour me. It was terrifying.

"Lie down," she said, then nudged me onto her bed and pushed my shoulders back. She violently ripped down my underwear, held my legs down with her knees, and placed the swab saturated with the red liquid on unthinkable places.

The burning sensation was so out-of-this-world excruciating that my organs wanted to jump out of my body to save themselves from the torment. I screamed for help because it felt like my private and bottom area were literally on fire, just like the visual emblem on the bottle. No one came to my rescue.

She threatened, "Shut up, or you'll get more."

It took all my strength within me to stop my natural reaction to scream, but somehow I managed the pain by gritting my teeth together as hard as I could. I felt my jaws locking up due to the intense strain. Then it happened.

I feel like I'm floating now. I can see this room from the ceiling. Looking downwardly, the dresser drawers are open with clothes loosely hanging out in disarray. The top of the dresser is cluttered with empty perfume bottles coated with thick dust particles, costume jewelry, antique trinkets, knickknacks, *and miscellaneous papers.*

I see Nana's backside, a middle-aged woman, heavyset with broad shoulders, bushy, wiry hair, hovering over me at the end of the bed. Her stance is that of a wannabe wrestler eagerly prepared to pounce on the helpless, fragile little girl.

Forward motion, I see a scrawny, boney-looking six-year-old little girl with baby-fine sandy-blonde hair shaking violently from side to side, her jaws tightly clenched, distinguishably outlining her tiny jawbone muscles protruding from both sides, as if her teeth were glued shut in an anguished state. Her eyes are tightly squeezed shut. I can see the lines on her forehead like the wrinkles of old people. She is rapidly shaking her head back and forth with her arms folded across her chest like she's going crazy. The bedcovers are all over the place, like she has been tossed from one side to the other. I can see the tears gushing from the corner of her squinty eyelids.

Why doesn't somebody save her?

That part is over now. I'm back.

I held my breath and put my fists to my lips to prevent my mouth from opening. Still burning, I wanted to run around the house like a crazy girl, but I was plastered to the bed with Nana straddled over me like a vulture, underpants pulled up. Nana demanded that I go sit on the living room floor in front of whoever was there. I was unable to discern who was there or who wasn't due to the distraction of the intolerable, insufferable pain. Maybe I didn't want to know. I had to move quickly in an attempt to cool down the intense burning throb of chemical burn. As the heat sensation continued to intensify, my bottom effortlessly bounced across the oriental rug—rather a natural reaction to the torment. My goal was to get as much air as possible for any kind of relief. A half hour had gone by when my bounciness somewhat slowed down, then eventually stopped. I buried my head in between my legs and pressed my knees into my temples as hard as I could, took a couple deep breaths, and then waited for the final departed words.

"Now go to bed," she hollered.

I had red stains from the HEET on my underpants. I didn't know if it was blood. I was petrified that I was bleeding to death. It felt that way.

When Lisa was excused to bed, she came in, lay right by my side in secret, hugged me, and said, "I'm sorry, sis."

"Don't you think that people that go to church are supposed to be nice?"

"Yeah," she responded.

"Then why is Nana so mean?"

"She is the devil."

We embraced and cried ourselves to sleep that night, although many, many similar nights were to follow—countless, to be exact.

Two days later, the same routine: I followed Nana to her bedroom. She then picked up the bottle, so I knew what was about to happen. It was too painful to watch my little girl in utter agony, so this time I went back to Rodeo when I used to play checkers in the sky with Lisa. My happy place. Here I go…

I'm now a giant overlooking the refineries. I'm so strong I can pick up the oil containers and play checkers with Lisa in our minds. She's a giant too. I pick white; she picks yellow. I'm good at this game and usually beat Lisa, but sometimes I let her win. These are happy times. I want to stay here forever.

I wet the bed again and again…why?

Many nights, I tried my hardest not to wet the bed by not drinking any fluids before bedtime; I even considered Lisa's suggestion to pray and told myself, *I'm not going to wet the bed tonight*. But no matter how hard I tried not to, I did anyway. Throughout the entire day, I knew I was going to come face-to-face with that evil tyrant.

Unbeknownst to me, Nana checked my bed area after I left for school, and she remembered like clockwork every evening before my bedtime. This presented a challenge for me to concentrate on schoolwork with those dark and heavy thoughts reoccurring in my mind. It was so odd that she'd have a pleasant attitude, not dropping a hint of punishment when I returned home from school. I sighed with relief and thought that maybe she had forgotten when she arrived home from work, as if I had nothing to worry about. I cringed later that evening when I heard my name called, but I was a step ahead.

I prepared to play imaginary checkers with Lisa, making the process more tolerable—not that it was ever tolerable. I remembered asking the question, *Where is Mommy?* I then told myself, *She's not here*, lying to lessen the ultimate betrayal.

Within a week's time, my mother did attempt to protect me. Early one morning, she had woken me up and shook me, put her hands over my mouth with one hand, put her other finger to her mouth, and whispered, "Shh, shh." She directed me out of bed. She quickly picked up the mattress like "Superwoman." She flipped it over and put a clean set of sheets on the bed. Her actions proved in my heart that maybe she did love me; she was just as scared as we were. That was a good day for me. However, it was a onetime deal that came and went. The HEET had taken a toll on my mucus membranes. Instead of becoming a way of correcting my bedwetting, it was actually causing more damage and making it virtually impossible to hold my urine. The ruthless stinging spasms throughout the day due to the nerve damage were rapidly increasing. To cope with the pain, I held myself tightly, crisscrossed my legs, hopped around, and held my breath until the stinging sensation stopped. The spasms were unreasonably unpredictable with no notice as to when they would strike.

One particular day, Lisa and I were roughhousing in the living room when things got a little out of hand. I don't remember exactly how, but Lisa accidentally broke Nana's vase that was of sentimental value, supposedly passed down from generations. Lisa was told by

Nana that when she got off work, Lisa was going to get the HEET as punishment.

I thought, *Yeah, now Lisa will really understand the HEET.* I wanted someone to understand.

Later that evening, Lisa entered the bedroom, and I heard Lisa screaming. My heart dropped. How could I ever want anyone to feel that kind of pain? I was guilt-ridden at just the thought.

The next morning, I said, "Lisa, I'm so sorry. It hurt really bad to hear that."

"Guess what? I'm going to share a secret with you, but you have to promise not to say a word to anyone, okay?"

"Okay, I promise. Lips sealed."

"Pinky swear?" she asked.

"Pinky swear," I responded; then we locked fingers.

"Nana really didn't give me the HEET. She had me pretend that I was getting in trouble, so I had to fake scream so everybody would think I got punished."

Lisa confirmed what I had already known: Nana hated my guts, and there was nothing I could do to change that. I couldn't help but feel sorry for myself. However, at the same time, I was relieved that Lisa was spared from unbearable agony.

But I always wondered, was she really telling the truth or not? It was true.

Being that Nana had worked in the food industry as a meat wrapper, she was overly compulsive regarding excess leftovers and food waste, or she played her game question of, whose belly will burst first? For whatever reason, we were the recipients of her habitual obsession with neurotic, mind-twisted behavior. With that in mind, she heaped piles of food on our plates like our bellies were that of obese hungry mountain men. She seriously expected us to eat all of it, reminding us about the starving kids in Africa. She could have easily prepared less food in the first place, but no. There had to be another purpose.

I was ready for the challenge because I flatly refused to lose this game, defending my title. See, I received a new nickname, Garbage Can, because considering my scrawny size, I could pack down the food. I often survived first round; however, when the monstrous serving spoon circled into round two, I was in mega trouble. It literally felt like my tummy was about to burst open. Obviously, I lost. Garbage can or not, it was too difficult without throwing up on my plate. Lisa usually lost at round one, actually throwing up, especially if it was oatmeal (my favorite, though). I would have helped Lisa out if we didn't have eyes staring at us.

Consequences for losers: Throw up, I lose. Leftovers on my plate, I lose. Feed the dogs, I lose. Complain, I lose. Majority of the time, I lost. Nana then made her entry into the dining room, shaking a bag of Japanese red-hot chili peppers in the air above our heads. I heard the crackling sound of the bag intensify as she got closer and closer to the kitchen table.

"Girls, guess what time it is?" She snickered with her wicked smile on her face, enjoying every second.

Yes, we knew what her clock signified: *Burn, baby, burn.*

The plastic bag contained small dried-up semiwrinkled deep-red chili peppers. The first bite was unbearable. Any bite after that was more torture. I instantly felt like the green dragon I had seen on cartoons but had invisible hot smoke barreling from my mouth, saliva dripping with spicy heat burning both sides of my mouth, eyes burning from the spicy flames, nose dripping clear fluids, and my tongue hanging out while gasping for air—nothing but hellacious hot air. I began panting like the dog when she was hot—no help. I ran into the kitchen sink for water and quickly discovered that water made the burning ten times worse. Then I figured that Nana already knew that; that's why she didn't stop us. I'm sure if water would have helped relieve our circumstances, she would have intervened in a flat second. I wouldn't make that mistake again. Only time was the answer: sitting it out and waiting for the spicy fire to slowly simmer, then eventually disappear.

Newsflash: unbeknownst to me at the time, spicy foods to that degree, once digested and discharged from the body, made you feel the burn—hot, hot, hot—from one end of the body out the other. Shocking reality.

Chapter Reflection

As I reflect on these acts of "punishment" in adulthood, it pains me to think that Nana intentionally chemically fried me. It's no wonder I could not stop wetting the bed. It's also saddening to be proud of the nickname "Garbage Can" and identify with myself as a piece of trash—even going so far as to defend that title. The psychological impact this created in my life was profound and led to a degrading sense of self-worth. When I originally wrote this section years ago, I obviously had some healing to do. I found myself name-calling (with great intensity) this ferocious, mean-spirited woman. In fact, I identified with the movie *Sybil*, holding strongly on to the victim role. Rightfully so. However, revisiting this, it has been easier for me to generalize her behavior rather than her deliberate attack on an innocent child. It may have been mental illness, her own childhood abuse, or demonic forces that caused this type of malicious act. Somehow it makes it easier to comprehend, eases the heartache somewhat, and is a confirming reflection of my healing today.

This timeframe in my childhood also marked the beginning of the rejection I felt from my mother, which only intensified as I got older and manifested itself into a deteriorated relationship. Although I was too young to comprehend, it was far better for me to pretend she was absent rather than accept the truth that she witnessed what happened to me and failed to intervene. When the reality finally hit me, I hated her. I wanted her to stand up for me and protect me, but I guess she was petrified too. This perception of her fear was much easier to accept than the idea that she just flat-out didn't love me. I see that now. She was a victim as well—no power, no voice, unable to protect me or herself, for that matter. It has taken me a long, long time to get to this understanding, see past my own wounds, and develop any sort of compassion for her.

In my spiritual journey today, I've come to realize that God did not commit the despicable acts; the evil forces did. However, He did allow it so someday it would somehow be used for good. In fact, He went through the fire with me. I now see that's the only way I could have possibly withstood such intense pain without literally losing my mind to a point of no return and still be the woman I am today—a living miracle. I survived because He was with me. My constant reminder: there was a purpose for my pain.

> *I know the Lord is always with me, I will not be shaken, for he is right beside me. (Psalm 16:8 NLT)*

> *For we know that God causes everything to work for the good of those who love God and are called according to his purpose for them. (Romans 8:28 NLT)*

We may never know what brings out the worst in people, but what I do know is, God knows, and it's by His grace that I can feel compassion today. I have comfort knowing that I am a child of God, called for a valuable purpose, precious in His sight and His masterpiece. I hold tightly on to these Scriptures that have been imprinted in my heart.

*****

During my sharing, I noticed Maria's eyes turning bloodshot as if she worked all week with no break, but it was only Monday. This was completely the opposite from her earlier bright-eyed and bushy-tailed appearance. Her mouth dropped open in shock as if she couldn't believe her ears, but she maintained eye contact with a nod of validation throughout bits and pieces of my horrific ordeal. She was listening with intensity and began to get teary-eyed at times, which brought an "I'm being heard" feeling—finally.

Telling the HEET part of my story to Maria was the most stressful. Toward the end, I began to get hot flashes, flushed like I had a fever, and I began getting light-headed with an overwhelming confusion, almost like another out-of-body experience was about to surface.

Obviously, I had PTSD. I just didn't know the word for it.

I had tapped into the symptoms with the utmost familiarity that used to be so natural for me: I'd forgotten. Oh shoot. I knew parts of my body wanted to leave as if I was literally reliving this experience. I started to panic. I knew that no matter how compassionate Maria was, there was no way she would understand if I started acting out. She would label me crazy. My fear was not only that this would prevent Dustin's homecoming but that I would lose Nicole to foster care. I immediately shook my head and reassured myself that I was just sharing and excused myself to the restroom. I nonchalantly walked into the bathroom, closed the door, waited a few seconds, breathing heavily, splashed water on my face, and sat on the toilet seat. "I'll be okay. I'll be okay," I convinced myself. Instantly, Lisa popped into my head and flooded my mind with her music, which reminded me, *I am okay*.

When I walked back into the dining area, Maria looked just as overwhelmed as me. She was sitting at the table with her fingernail perched on her front tooth and elbow on the table, like she was in heavy thought. She sighed and shook her head.

"Wow, Lorrie that was a lot to take in. You should have warned me. I think we both need a break." Then she sipped on the, by then, cold coffee. "You know, I'm going to go out and get myself some lunch, and I'll be back around two-ish) Is that okay with you? Maybe you can share a little more before Nicole gets home from school. As a matter of fact, when does Nicole return home from school?"

"Being that we're in the country, she usually doesn't get home until about three thirty," I responded.

"Good. See you in a bit. Also, I'll stop at a phone booth and check in on Dustin's condition while I'm out."

A couple hours came and went, and she returned promptly at 2:00 p.m. On one hand, she looked rested a bit, as if she enjoyed her lunch; but on the other hand, she had an uncertain look on her face.

"According to the nursing staff, the only changes are that more specialists are involved with his treatment, so we should know something soon, hopefully sooner than later," she passed the information on to me since I didn't have access to a telephone.

After hearing her feedback, I tried to comfort myself, reassuring myself that Dustin was in safe hands with the medical professionals. I lied to myself. Deep down, I didn't trust that hospital, considering my own treatment there, and I desperately wanted him transferred to Children's Hospital in Oakland where, in my opinion, the *real* kiddy doctors were. The hurry-up-and-wait was frustrating, similar to the powerless moments I felt as a child.

"Okay, ready to continue?"

"Ready."

Fiery Darts

Back then, my mother's skin condition, which was somewhat left unnoticed in the past, had worsened over time and became obvious. She had an allergic reaction to fragrant dish soaps, harsh laundry detergents, and cheap perfumery lotions, which irritated her sensitive skin and caused frequent breakouts in a horrible rash. But not just any rash. Watery blisters would emerge. When the rash progressed, her skin started to crack and create open wounds. Quite frankly, it made my stomach turn seeing the liquid ooze from her skin cells. It was painful for her to keep gauze wrapped over her skin due to its stickiness during bandage changes.

At that time, the best medical treatment was air-drying the wounds. I knew she felt shameful and embarrassed during those breakouts by the way she tried to hide her hands. The only help that Lisa and I could provide was to complete those ongoing household tasks, especially washing dishes and cleaning dirty laundry by hand—not to mention the crap-load of diapers for two infants. No washing machines back in "them there" days. Well, maybe for rich people. The closest appliance to a washing machine was a wood-framed washboard with a heavy plastic material in the middle that had bumpy see-through grooves used for scrubbing. You old-timers know what I am talking about. This item was generally sitting in the big bucket with two wooden rollers attached by brackets for wringing out the clothes. Lisa and I felt this was the least we could do to help our mother since she absolutely could not put her hands into the soapy water. We turned it into a game and sometimes would throw suds at each other and laugh like kids do. We actually enjoyed the task of wringing out the items, but we had to be cautious not to lose our fingers in the threading process.

Well, it was pretty clear that Nana hated my guts and would rather see me dead, but she also hated our mother. Even though Nana was aware of my mother's skin condition, she made derogatory, demeaning statements to us about her character, but never to mother's face—only to her children. It would usually go something like this: "You know, Lorrie and Lisa, you have a no-good mother who is lazy and a-good-for-nothing so-called wife." The part that made me snicker was when she'd say, "I don't know why my son would choose to marry a woman like that."

We felt the opposite. We didn't know why our mother would choose to marry a worthless pig like her son. Then she'd go on and on: "She doesn't know how to keep the house up nor take care of her own children. In fact, she doesn't deserve to have any children in the first place." Her choice of words pierced through my heart because I knew our mother had a condition that prevented her from doing certain things, and Nana took advantage of the situation and turned it against her. I swallowed the shame that came with the inability to defend our mother. I always wished I could look her straight in the eye and say, "—— you!" But I knew she could see it in my eyes. Sometimes my body language was stronger than my words—unfortunately, to my own detriment.

Besides getting past the bulls, attending school was a temporary relief. Excitement built when school pictures arrived, and like many other children, I desperately wanted to hand out photos to my teacher and fellow classmates. You know, write a little something on the back to make it memorable. Considering Nana had purchased the pictures (the "look good in the eyes of the teacher" act), I approached her and asked permission to give some away. When I did so, she gave me the direct eye contact, with the stern and evil glare through her thick bifocals, her eyebrows squishing together and her forehead wrinkled, deepening with every facial expression as if to say, *How dare you even ask that?* I got the picture!

She threatened, "Don't you dare give any pictures to your friends. I'm warning you."

I thought that was kind of ridiculous, considering the duplicates, but I didn't even think about going against her demands. Within the next couple of days, the entire photo packet was missing, and the accusations flew at me.

"Lorrie!" She cursed God's name in vain over and over. "You deliberately disobeyed me, didn't you? I know you took those pictures to school," she said as her voice got louder with every word.

"No, I didn't, I swear. I'll find them and prove it," I pled.

"Well, you better start searching," she demanded, shaking her finger at me.

Oh my gosh, not the dang hunt again, I thought. Now, I knew where Rob got the idea; must have happened to him as a child. Regardless how I was feeling, the search began with Lisa backing my efforts, like we were a tag team once again. We frantically searched the entire house, leaving no item unturned. I was bound and determined to prove my innocence, although I fretted and sweated every moment. I could see Lisa's frustration building as time went; and all the while, it brought back the stress of the "hunt" in Ohio. Those tireless, endless efforts went on for several days with the frequent question asked with raised eyebrows, "Did you find the pictures yet?"

Homework? Are you kidding? Who in the heck could concentrate on school knowing what was in store for me? It was useless. I had to just take the heat, so to speak. I gave up the search. Oh boy. Then it happened. Nana arrived home one evening. She slung the front door open, holding something in her hands, shook her fists at me, and angrily shouted, "Look what I found in your desk at school."

I couldn't believe my eyes. The blood instantly rushed to my feet, and I was about to faint. She then snarled at me and called me a liar and insisted that I 'fess up. "Do you know what happens to liars?" she shouted. I watched her bushy eyebrows furrow more deeply.

"I'm not a liar. I'm not going to admit to something I didn't do!" I could feel my face flushed with anger. I looked at my mother, pleading with my eyes for her intervention, protection, and belief in me. "Mom, I didn't do it. Please, please, you have to believe me!" I shouted.

My mom put her hands up, like all the evidence was stacked against me. She then shook her head with disgust. I freaked out. I then began running around the living room, begging anyone to stick up for me. Hatred of injustice started to fester within. Even though I couldn't put a label on it, I could feel it. As I looked at everyone in the room, there was frumpy ole' Nana with her hand on her hip, Mother two feet away from her with a smirk on her face, and Lisa with almond-shaped eyes that were not so squinty as they were widening by the minute. I knew she knew something but couldn't say it. I then exhaled from all the screaming that literally felt like all the air left my body as I shrank like a shriveled balloon, exhausted. There was no way out—but to *admit* to something I did *not* do.

How in the world can I be guilty just because someone bigger says I am?

I was having a hard time accepting this reality.

My mother left the room for a moment and returned with a belt in her hands.

"Pull down your pants, and I mean now!" she demanded.

I looked at her like, *How could you?* and shook my head with disappointment.

The first thing that came to my mind was that Nana had now turned my mother against me. To my recollection, she had never been violent toward Lisa and me up until now.

"Now turn around and bend over."

I began belly-flopping on my stomach, squirming over the armrest of the blue chair. I held my breath and waited for the blow. Suddenly the impossible happened. I heard my mother screaming and the sound of the belt buckle clanging as it hit the floor. I looked up to see what had happened, and my mother was running around the living room holding her rear end. "The dog bit me!" she shouted.

I was stunned. Moreover, Lisa was dumbfounded. The animal that once was our enemy was *now* our protector. Astonishing!

My mother was torn up both emotionally and physically that she had completely forgotten about my butt whooping.

But Nana—would Nana forget too?

At our usual torture evening time, the setting had changed. "This is more for lying than actually disobeying," Nana calmly stated while directing me behind her into the kitchen area. She snapped her fingers as she directed me to sit on the white-painted high chair similar to a barstool that was placed in the middle of the kitchen. There was a tall heating lamp overlapping the high chair. I sat under the florescent heating lamp that was supposed to be used for indoor sunbathing and was instructed to stay put. After several minutes had passed, I could feel the heat rays begin to pulsate through my hair follicles and into my pores. Within an hour's time, my scalp started to burn as the sweat dripped down my brows. My scalp was burning. It's like she had it all timed—long enough for me to feel the heat, but not long enough to cause blisters and lose my hair.

"Time's up," she said, then directed me to bed for the night.

The best escapism was "downtown" as I lay there in my bed.

I am twirling on the sidewalk with my hands up in the air, distracted by all the busyness. Tons of people were coming and going with packages in their hands, as if it's the holiday season—billboard shows lit up, whistles blowing, bells ringing, the sound of traffic congestion, engines running and horns honking. Chaos. But I love it. I am safe with all the people watching.

Someday, I thought and sighed.

Although most of my days were nightmares in that environment, I'd visualize the upcoming holiday season, the most enjoyable time with this family. They'd present a certain kind of softness when it came to the holiday cheer, family gatherings and such. Rob had a sister with five children, two of whom were close in age to Lisa and me, which made it more enjoyable during family events. During the Easter holiday, the family's annual traditional campout at Lake Camanche and massive Easter egg hunt was a thrill, complemented with Shirley Temple curls, girly lacy dresses, bonnets, leggings, and white patent leather shoes. The holiday attire didn't stop us from exploring the huge open-range park surrounded by water and popular for hiding spots, no matter how dirty we got. Sometimes the family rented log cabins near the forest pine trees—great for the upcoming egg hunt.

In addition, the Christmas holiday was usually a special event and a time when my outlook on life was brighter, like any other six-year-old, which was my age at Christmas 1968 at Nana's. More than anything on my Christmas list, I wanted Santa to bring me the new baby doll that had been repeatedly advertised on the TV commercials. This was a First Baby Doll, the next best thing to the real deal. She had a hole in her mouth for feeding, then the water disappeared, and then she'd go potty. It was kinda silly of me to want a fake baby since I had been taking care of two real, live babies at home. Yet I had put this doll on Santa's list numerous times.

Early Christmas morning, we'd travel a couple towns over for the celebration, feast out on a humongous breakfast, and wait for the clock to strike 10:00 a.m. before we opened presents. That family had a time schedule for everything, probably because the man of the house had worked as a prison guard, and structure was the key. Nana's granddaughter was a few months older than me, and she was obviously the favorite by far. The tradition was that each person would open one gift at a time while the others waited until it was their turn. I was stunned when Mandy's turn came around, and I watched her facial expression of excitement as she held up the Baby Alive box after eagerly ripping off the reindeer wrapping paper. I could see the little girl holding the baby in her arms, just like the commercial, and the little bottle sticking out of its mouth on the front of the box. I could barely hold on until it was my turn.

Oh, I bet I got one too, I thought as my Indian-style legs bounced up and down, my knees heavily knocking the carpet with utter excitement. When I opened my gift, it wasn't the Baby Alive box. It was a cheap plastic baby, similar to the ones at the Dollar Tree, whose lips were sealed shut. Immediately I wanted to take this so-called present and throw it right at Nana's face. Hatred was growing deeper, deeper toward her daily into the depths of my soul. I had to think again. There would be steep consequences. I had to shove all that rage down, smile with gratitude, and say "thank you," plus give her a hug as if I was pleased with the gift. Man, I hated being robotic and phony just as much as I hated her.

As the holiday vacation ended, I continued to have difficulty academically with frequent negative progress report showing checkmarks of "unsatisfactory—needs improvement" inserted in my red folder attached to homework assignments. Although Gramps had a rough side with his harsh voice and foul mouth, he did display a vigorous, righteous spirit when it came to my education. He'd say to me, "—— Californian schools are more advanced than —— Ohioan schools, so we have to get you —— caught up, so you don't —— flunk first grade," with a serious, deep tone. "You hear?" He'd point his finger at me and declared, "It's time to pay —— attention."

Every evening, he sat with me hour after hour, tutoring me in math and English, quizzing me after each sectional lesson, frequently dropping the *F* bomb in between every other word.

"Stop being a stupid —— and listen to what I'm —— teaching you," he'd say when I'd fail a quiz. He took great pride when the progress reports returned, showing "Satisfactory Improvement" since he obviously didn't have much confidence in the school system's ability to teach. One thing is for sure: he really taught us how to use foul language. I felt bad for Lisa because I knew she was also struggling greatly with academics and received no extra help at home. She sat there and just watched with puppy-dog eyes, waiting patiently for Gramps to ask her questions, but he never did. Speaking with my sister recently about this, she said even though he didn't deliberately teach her academics, he taught her how to count because she counted his curse words when he was teaching me. I thought this was hilarious because she did learn something from him after all. Awesome.

During that time, an upcoming early spring weekend day, we made a somewhat random visit to Gramps's father's house due to his deteriorating health condition. He was extremely frail, a poorly nourished ninety-year-old who was confined to a wheelchair. During our visit, I noticed he had taken a turn for the worse. He lethargically sat slumped over, sort of hunchbacked, His head tilted sideways in the wheelchair and shockingly exposed all body parts. He sadly looked like a skeleton: his rib cage was visible, and wrinkly skin with age spots and zero elasticity hung off his bones, lacking muscle tone. A plastic bag was filled with dark urine hanging on a metal pole attached to the wheelchair that hung above his head. It was disgusting to see that dark-yellow, almost-brown fluid openly visible, but I suppose it was unpreventable back then.

Within the next couple weeks, during a routine checkup at Gramps's father's house, someone threw a banana peel on the living-room floor, and the finger was pointed at me one too many times. I was getting sick and tired of being the guinea pig for accusations. *Oh, heck no, not this again!* I thought. My heart began to race with panic, and the fear-based adrenaline started to build instantly.

Without questioning everybody in the house, Nana immediately looked at me and yelled, "Lorrie, did you throw that banana peel on the floor?"

"No." I shuddered.

"Yes, you did," Gramps screamed. "I saw you."

"I didn't even eat a banana today," I said, trying to defend myself.

"Well, Gramps says he saw you. Are you calling him a liar?" Nana sarcastically questioned with her hand on her hip, the way she did when she wanted to demonstrate her beastly power, and pounded her foot on the floor like an elephant.

"No. Maybe he saw someone else. It wasn't me," I fired back.

Nana looked at Gramps with a meaningful smirk on her lip and an indentation in her forehead.

"Well, I think Lorrie is calling you a liar, honey. What do you think?"

"Humm," Gramps said, tight-lipped. "I think she is."

"Lorrie"—cursing me and God's name in vain as usual—"you need to admit that you threw that banana peel and then tried to get out of it or else," Gramps demanded.

"But I didn't do it, honest," I said, shaking my head.

"I saw you," he said, refusing to back down.

You're lying, I thought and glared at him intensely with my eyes budged. *How can you do this to me?* I wanted him to read my mind, but he was so preoccupied with Nana escalating the situation. At that moment, I looked at the doorknob like it was calling my name, *Run—run as fast as you can.*

Okay, this is it. I'm out of here. I thought. My head turned toward the door, and without hesitation, I bravely darted out the door as fast as a six-year-old could run, fearful for my life, as if I was on the school grounds in Rodeo. My bravery shocked myself. About a couple blocks down, I could hear feet hitting the pavement; Gramps was in fast pursuit and gaining ground. I managed to get a few more blocks down the road before his hand nabbed a handful of my hair, which felt like my neck had been jerked out of socket; then he tackled me to the pavement. He literally kicked me in the butt all the way back to the house. Thank God, he was barefoot. I think he kicked off his shoes so that he could run faster. When we walked in the door, Nana was standing there with a razor strap swinging it round and round, ready for me. I received an unremitting beating that day right next to the banana peel with my belly on the hardwood floor.

"Did you throw that banana peel on the floor then lie about it?" he explosively screamed.

"No, I didn't do it." My face then flushed with anger.

With every swing, I could feel my legs bobble up from the automatic reflex due to the impact of the blow. He repeated the question, time after time as the force was getting stronger and moving down to my thigh area, then to my legs. Finally, when he questioned me after the seventh time, I had had enough; then I screamed, "Okay, yes."

He demanded, "Then say it."

"I threw the banana peel on the floor and lied about it."

"That's what I thought. Here's one more for lying, and here's another for running away, and here's another for making me run after you barefoot."

Then it stopped with the final departing words, "Pick up that —— banana peel and throw it in the garbage where it belongs."

I couldn't get off the floor, so I lay there momentarily until the stinging let up and I mustered enough strength. I stared at the banana peel, telling myself, *I guess I did it. I just don't remember.*

Then they went into the kitchen and went about their business like nothing even happened.

Chapter Reflection

The beating was awful, but the reshaping of my character was much worse in the long run. Bruises disappear; psychological damage sometimes never does. I have to admit that a piece of my dignity was stripped that month—from the school-picture incident to the banana-peel ordeal. The brewing anger that I had no rights and having to admit to something I didn't do created my "get them before they get you" attitude in early adulthood. Justice failed me in childhood; there was no such thing as justice, as far as I was concerned. I ultimately developed a "no respect for authority" attitude. Luckily, today the irony of this experience has brought a shift of gratitude for my criminal defense employer, which put things into perspective. I used to ask myself, how can I work for an employer that defends the people I used to despise? Like with my past situation, not everyone is guilty just because an authority figure says so. They fight tirelessly for the oppressed each and every day, and I witness their dedication to represent their clients wholeheartedly. Today, a piece of bitterness melts.

In my adult life, I had to let go of these strongholds and perceptions that were causing more damage than good by omitting my belief system and start clinging to God's Word (rather than the unjust experiences of my past) for hope and healing. I realize that Jesus is my personal *Defender*, for I stand firmly on His promises in His Word.

> *He made heaven and earth, the sea, and everything in them. He keeps every promise forever; He gives justice to the oppressed and food to the hungry. The Lord frees the prisoners. (Psalm 146:6–7 NLT)*

*****

I hesitated to continue any further with my story as I could tell that Maria was heading toward exhaustion, or I had overloaded her listening-skill capacity. It was hard to differentiate if she was overwhelmed, bored, or burnt out as I'd catch her gazing up to the ceiling a few times within the last hour. This was my cue to stop, considering we'd been at it all day.

"I'm wiped out," I told her. "I think I need a nap now."

"I think I need to go home and go to bed," Maria responded.

Then we both chuckled a bit.

"You know, Lorrie, I just don't know what to say, given that you just have shared your heart and soul to me, and I'm completely overwhelmed and speechless. I'm going to need a couple days to process what I just heard," she said, then took a deep breath, like she regularly practiced yoga.

She had just answered my question without realizing it. The fact that it wasn't boredom was a relief. She was an initial catalyst for a healing journey. I doubt if she even knew.

I had to trust her. She wouldn't take all this information and turn it against me in a court report, would she? Could that be possible? I looked into her eyes, searching for an affirmative answer. I found sincerity behind those dark-brown eyes and an angelic glow. Standing at my front door on her way out, she validated my newly trusted instinct. We smiled at each other.

"Maria, I should have a phone within a couple days. I'll call you when I get my new telephone number."

"That would be great, so you can have better communication with the hospital staff." She then presented a hopeful smile and quick nod. "Listen, if I don't hear from you, I'd like to continue in a couple days, if you feel up to it."

I nodded in agreement.

"But I am going to need a couple days, and you do too."

I stood at the door and watched her walk down the steps.

She looked back at me and stated, "You are a survivor." Then she waved goodbye. I had never heard that term before. Yet on the other hand, I've never shared my story with anyone in such detail and intensity.

Even though I felt a little lighter letting go of some of my burden from childhood, the stress of the baby's condition carried a heavy weight in my heart and an overwhelming sadness throughout the household. I was barely fighting off drug cravings without the support of Jason doing the same. It was as if he was keeping himself numb medicated on pot to relax and spun on meth for energy. He was a yoyo, up and down so he didn't have to think about the terrible mess we made from our choices. All the while, I had to struggle to stay clean (abstain from drugs), feel all those dreadful feelings I didn't want to feel, and live with it. My resentment toward him was building, and the idea that he chose to "check out" was making me bitter, not better.

Getting out of bed was pointless and strenuous. Most of the time, I wished I'd never wake up. But I did have a daughter who was hurting too that I needed to consider. So I did.

The next morning, my friend Kathy surprisingly showed up at my door and offered to connect telephone service in her name since the telephone company turned me down based on my past credit history—you know, pills before bills in an addict's mind. She knew it was a struggle without unreliable transportation and walking to the phone booth was exhausting. The next day, we had telephone service, which reduced some of the household tension. However, it spiked up when we received the same old news from hospital staff. Dustin had now been in NIC for five days with little to no improvement. According to the doctor, it was difficult to treat his medical condition without a proper diagnosis, so they were trying a multitude of medication options in hopes of tackling the problem.

I called Maria and left her a message with my new phone number. When she called back, she scheduled another meeting on Wednesday.

The story resumes…

Lucky Booth

Mother's labor pains hit on January 4, 1969. She was rushed to the hospital, preparing to deliver baby number five. We waited anxiously, crossing our fingers that she would finally deliver our new brother, that much desired baby boy she'd always wanted, and then she'd stop having children. A couple days later, she arrived home with our baby wrapped in a pink blanket. We shrugged our shoulders and asked, "So what'd you name her?"

"Mary Jo," my mother said. "Well, that's it. No more."

We all knew what she meant. There was an acceptance tone in her voice. Maybe "Jo" was chosen as a middle name because this name was the closest she'll ever get to a boy's name after considering a new surgical procedure to prevent pregnancy. Nevertheless, we were excited to meet our new baby sister.

It didn't take long for another offensive nickname to be added to our sibling circle. Besides "Garbage Can" and "Blanket ———," "Dead Eye" landed into the trio of Gramps's gibberish because Mary had one eye that seemed to wander off at times (a lot actually).

"Look at the funny-looking eye [his description more demeaning]. You can't tell what she's looking at, you or the wall," Gramps would say, then laugh. I have to say, he had a unique way of pointing out our deficiencies as a way to humor himself, then broadcast it to those around him.

Considering that our family was outgrowing the number of bedrooms that were available at Nana's, my mother decided it was time to move on into our own place (that decision couldn't come soon enough for me). I'm sure that was her excuse to Nana, but we knew otherwise. Her choice to move us was one of the most ecstatic, indescribable moments in my lifetime. We happily carried our boxes into a two-story house in Plymouth, California, which was located in a nearby town approximately five miles east (it wasn't far enough away, but it was still a cause for an elated celebration).

The second story had a loft-like structure that eventually became our bedroom. It was quite different from what we had been used to. We were elated to be out of that country hole of fire and bullcrap (literally) and grateful that my mother didn't leave us behind. The frequent reminder that "I would rather starve than continue to live there" would shortly become a reality, just like in Ohio.

Considering our new addition, the hassle for my mother to pack up the infants for a quick in-and-out trip to the local am/pm grocery store would have been overwhelming. Our highlight of the week was when my mother handed us a note to purchase her cigarettes, as well as other items on the list; then she sent us on our way to the closest market that was near the main highway into town. There was a telephone booth on the corner that we named *Lucky Booth* because Lisa and I were lucky just about every time we entered the booth. Instead of turning into a superhero like the *Underdog* cartoon after entering the phone booth, we turned into instant moneymakers. We took turns pushing down the lever on the upper right-hand corner and listened carefully as the coins fell to the bottom—our very own slot machine. Our faces lit up with an ear-to-ear smile, and our eyebrows rose when we heard the coins hitting the metal.

"Clang, clang!" we yelled with excitement. We'd jump up and down because we knew we were about to be the "two little kids in the candy shop." Tootsie Rolls, Smarties, Banana Taffy, Pixy Stix, and cigarette gum were the childhood favorites. It was exciting to count the change and calculate how much candy that amounted to. Lisa had tapped into some spiritual power—God, she called it. She was good at finding hidden treasures, especially when we were in need. I didn't believe in all that nonsense, so I called it luck. The timing couldn't have been more perfect.

Not too long after our move in, Lisa hit a gold mine in an old shed containing about a year's supply of canned goods. She came up to me and screamed, "Hey, Lorrie, come here, follow me. Look what I found." I followed her to an old shed, and I saw the plywoods rotting, which was obviously a breeding ground for termites, in some spots and broken fence boards in other parts (which made for easy entry access). The property was barren and unoccupied, so onward we went.

"I looked to see what was inside that hole, and all I saw was food. Mommy will be so happy when we bring this food home," she said. "I'm going in after it." She then got her body in motion.

She fearlessly bolted through the hole, not worried about the cobwebs, spiders, or the darkness. Not more than a few minutes later, I could see her dirty hands coming through the hole, slinging out dented cans of fruit cocktail with rust clinging to the bottom edges, some weathered cans with unreadable labels, and other mystery cans with no labels at all.

"Just maybe God hears our tummies growling," Lisa said, aggressively throwing the cans out like a football player.

"Are you crazy? What God? If there was a God, guess what? He hates us. You just got lucky, that's all."

"Just be quiet. You're ruining it," Lisa fired back at my negativity.

She shut me up with that stern remark. I remained silent as Lisa crawled out of the shed, having made a grocery basket out of her T-shirt, and shoved as many cans as she could in her homemade basket and told me to do the same.

I could tell she was problem-solving by the look on her face. "Hey, we'll save some of this stuff for the weekends since we get free lunch. That way, it will last.

We didn't even care that some of the food was outdated, dried-up pork and beans without sauce, and the syrup from the fruit cocktail had showed signs of fermentation. I guess hunger drives out any potential food-poisoning risks. Eat it and then deal with the consequences later. My favorite was the creamy peanut butter in the gigantic can topped with all the saturated peanut oil. There were no consequences after eating my peanut butter on a spoon.

Lisa and I would go to any length to satisfy our sweet tooth. One day, while we were visiting Rob's sister-in-law's house, we saw two silver dollars sitting on her daughter's dresser. We couldn't help but notice how different and shiny the coins were, like they dropped off the coin press. The appreciation for that piece of metal was obvious, but even more so, we looked at each other and knew what those coins were equivalent to. We didn't hesitate to dash immediately to the local neighborhood market shouting out different names of candy we could buy on the way. We thought we'd have an extra supply just in case Lucky Booth stopped producing. When we were finally confronted about the missing money, there was no way we were going to admit to stealing. Apparently, the coins were of sentimental value, which, in my mind, meant more severe consequences and only reinforced my denial. My mother gave us a piercing glare with her big brown eyes, along with her stern tone, and demanded admission. It would have been better to just tell the truth.

Undoubtedly, I had underestimated the neighborhood connection with the market owner. When asked if he'd come across two silver dollars recently, he blurted out, "Two little girls about five and six years old came in and bought two hundred pieces of penny candy with new silver dollars." At least that's what my mother said that he said.

Ouch. We were flat-out busted.

Before then, it was already overwhelming for family and friends to have open arms when "Jenny and all her kids" came to visit, but then it became "Jenny and her two thieves." We had dampened the welcoming spirit, for sure. Luckily, to take a little pressure off our mother, the store manager exchanged the silver dollars for a two-dollar bill (due to the sentimental value); however, we still had a price to pay. My mother didn't believe in spanking too much after the dog had bitten her behind. However, she had promoted her new parenting philosophy we referred to as "restriction queen" more often than I'd like to admit. She believed in matching the punishment to fit the crime, so she put us on a one year's restriction from sweets of any kind. Lisa and I glanced at each other with little smirks because our mother didn't know about Lucky Booth. We shrugged our shoulders behind her back like, *Ha!*

Rob wasn't around much during our stay in Plymouth. He was probably in and out of jail most of the time; or as my mother referred to it, he had out-of-town business. However, one day when he was present, a situation arose that flipped my mother out when she caught us playing doctor with her friend's children who came over to visit. We were all under the covers in our loft-like bedroom when the door suddenly opened.

"What are you kids doing?" she asked. "It's just too quiet all of a sudden."

I cautiously raised the blanket a sliver, just enough for my eyeball to peek out, then poked my head out from the bedcovers. I noticed by the look on her face that she was extremely upset. While the others started stuttering, eagerly searching for a valid explanation, I explosively burst out from the top of my head, "We are making a bed tent." I surprised myself with that sudden answer. That idea might have flown with her, but considering that we were partially dressed, she just shook her head in disgust.

"I'm going to let your father handle this crap," she said.

Suddenly my hairs felt like they were popping out of my head pores. My eyes bulged as Lisa and I looked at each other, and without saying a word, we knew what we were in for. When the children left, Rob entered the room and told us, "Listen up. I'm not going to beat either of your butts. I want you to pretend like you're getting an ——-whipping by yelling and screaming when the belt hits the bed. Is that understood?"

"Yes, sir," we responded. Lisa and I couldn't believe that was happening. He enjoyed beating us; why would he pass that up? Without a doubt, we complied without questioning, just in case he was about to change his mind. After we faked our whipping and he left the room, we stared at each other dazed and confused about the whole situation but at the same time grateful we had been spared a beating.

"Wow. Can you believe that?" I asked in utter shock.

"I guess he's more concerned about dirty dishes and snitches than playing doctor," Lisa said.

We didn't stay in Plymouth for any significant length of time to call it home, maybe six months. When Rob was on the run, we followed. I was initially excited about our past moves (other than the trip to Ohio), but this upcoming move was extremely disturbing to me. For some reason, our mother thought it was necessary for Nana and Gramps to be temporary caretakers of Shelly while we got settled back in Rodeo. When I heard this news, hatred toward my mother began to fester. A huge knot developed in the pit of my stomach, consumed by an unsettling nausea. My thoughts started playing like a horror movie with diabolical images about harming Shelly—the lies, the hot peppers, and the HEET all flooded my brain as if it was yesterday. I was still experiencing stinging spasms (in my private area) that reoccurred frequently, making it impossible to forget my experiences. They only reinforced the detestable possibilities that could go wrong for Shelly. As I continued to ponder, obsessing about the little one I had taken care of, protected, and treated as my own now being ripped away from me, I became resentful and crazy. It felt as if a giant hand reached in my chest and yanked my heart out. I nervously slapped my hand on my chest and gasped for air as if I was trying to keep my heart intact—ultimate betrayal in my eyes.

I angrily began pleading with my mother. "You have to go back and get her. I'll take care of her. Please, please, you just can't let her stay with those people."

"Lorrie, you have to remember. This is only temporary until we get settled. That's it," she rattled on, trying her best to reassure me by defending her position.

There was a familiarity to those words. My only hope was to reflect back to the last time I had heard them. She actually did follow through and rescued Lisa and me from the Beverly Hillbillies. I tried to believe her, even though, deep down, I really didn't.

*****

I had been sharing my story with Maria for some time now and could feel my body getting tense. I glanced over the mounted china cabinet to see what time it was; then I shook my head with disgust over the tweaked paint job I had attempted several weeks ago. It looked ridiculous. It was now 11:00 a.m., and as far as I was concerned, it was time to take a break and get a little whiff of the winter breeze since it was beginning to get a bit hot and stuffy in the dining area. The house had its original antique heating system mantled on the floor, which, to me, presented carbon-monoxide dangers seeping up into the house (too hard to prove). Jason would roll his eyes and call it nonsense whenever I complained since he worked in the heating/air conditioning field. Isn't it ironic? The painter's house needs paint, the mechanic's car needs fixing, the housekeeper's house needs cleaning, and my heater man blows out hot air. I didn't go into detail with Maria about my many household suspicions, fearful it might set off a chain reaction into even deeper depression, and then I'd really look like a paranoid schizophrenic. I shut my mouth and headed toward the door for some fresh air.

I could sense that Maria was not emotionally wiped out as she was a few days ago. She appeared alert, like the caffeine had kicked in, and the possibility of me sharing another chapter was good before we called it a day.

"Well, I have to say, this part of your story was much more tolerable than I had anticipated." Then she sighed. "I enjoyed hearing bits and pieces of good times in your childhood, which I'm sure gave you some much-needed hope at the time, huh? But I can tell by your reaction, you're about to bring up more painful experiences that pertain to your sister Shelly," she said, and then she put her hand on my shoulder for comfort. "Excuse me. May I please use the telephone to check in with the office? It will only take a minute."

"Sure can," I graciously said, *thanks to Kathy's generosity.*

I opened the front door to let a breeze flow through the house for a few minutes. Maria finished her telephone conversation and sat back down at the table.

"According to my clerk, I have about one more hour left before a scheduled office visit that I failed to pencil in. Is that enough time for you?" she asked.

"Maybe time for a couple more chapters," I responded.

"Very well then, let's continue. By the way, please remind me, how old where you then?"

"Seven and a half years old."

Pissy Pot

So we were on the road again. This time, our destination was Rodeo, where I had shared my glorious pre-Rob memories and before we had left for Ohio. We pulled up to a tan apartment complex, possibly twelve units with similar-looking units across the front patio facing parallel to one another. During our return to Rodeo, it seemed that my mother was unusually tired most of the time because she slept a lot. I think she was depressed about leaving Shelly behind, and that was how she had dealt with it—by checking out. When she was unavailable, Lisa and I climbed on the countertop, frantically searching for anything to eat. There was one item we could pretty much count on: peanut butter. We had peanut butter on a spoon, sometimes for breakfast, lunch, and dinner. My mother said it "sticks to the rib cage and satisfies the hunger pangs longer." She was right.

One day while I was playing outside on the front patio, I couldn't help but notice the neighbor's curtains wide open. There was a kitchen table below the window with a beautifully decorated fruit bowl. However, instead of fruit, there were many assorted colorful coconut-covered candies heaping to the top. They reminded me of mini snowball cupcakes, only mini-size portions. Instantly, those flashbacks from the kids in Ohio antagonizing me, licking their lips, munching on snowball cupcakes, and tauntingly voicing the fact that I couldn't have any haunted me. I wasn't about to be put through that again, if I could help it.

I knew I had a few months left to complete the "no sweets" restriction, and there was the fact that Lucky Booth was now history since the recent move, so I decided to enter the apartment through the sliding glass door and nabbed two handfuls of the candy. I left a few pieces in the bowl; then I bagged up the majority and placed it under my bed for future enjoyment—just in case the neighborhood kids attempted to tease me about how poor I was. *I'll show them*, I thought. Even though the candy was a bonus, any kind of food sitting on the table that day would have been history.

Although I didn't get caught in the act, Mrs. Beals, the neighbor, definitely knew someone came into her house. She probably had a good idea it was me or Lisa because we were always begging and borrowing food around the complex. Without saying a word to anyone, she prevented it from ever happening again. Thereafter, her curtains remained closed rather than an aggressive knock on our door. Due to the lack of repercussions, I thought I was pretty darn slick and ahead of the game. I was starting to become a manipulative rookie mastermind, topped off with a nibble of candy to award my ego, or so I thought.

However, I was mentally unprepared to deal with what was about to happen next: Rob's idea for bed-wetting prevention. Obviously, I was still having problems wetting the bed. After being torched at Nana's, I couldn't believe I was still having that problem. Anyone in their right mind would have stopped wetting the bed immediately, right? Looking back, I think it created more damage and made the problem worse, as you can imagine. Night after night, I woke up in a soggy mattress. I felt ashamed and embarrassed in my silence, but that would soon change.

About ten o'clock midmorning, Rob came into our room holding some items in his hands.

"Put this on right now," he demanded, holding up a bib and the cloth diaper. "No shirt or pants. You're going to sit outside near our front door on the walkway, stick the bottle in your mouth, and suck on it." Then he rattled off what my lines were going to be. I could not believe my ears.

My body froze up in an instant, and I was heading for panic mode.

"No, Daddy, No! I promise that I won't wet the bed anymore." *I hated the fact that I had to call him Daddy.*

"Shut up! You're going to learn this lesson once and for all," he screamed at the top of his lungs. He then looked at Lisa and said, "Go 'round up all the neighborhood troops. Make sure to get all the kids from school, whoever you can find outside. Is that understood?"

"Yes, sir," she responded.

As I sat there on the dirty walkway half naked with my legs crossed, trying hard to hide the fact I was wearing a despicable diaper, I could hear the footsteps from a distance getting closer and closer. I began to sweat profusely from nervousness. I could feel the warm sweat dripping down my eyebrow as if someone just sprayed me with a hose. The gallivanting sound reminded me of a crowd of upcoming spectators, running and laughing as if they were on their way to a circus sideshow around the corner of the apartment complex. As they all approached me, Rob looked at me with his glassy piercing eyes, and then he nodded for action. This was the cue to start my lines.

He glared at me intensely. Chills ran up my spine into my head as if ants were crawling all over my head.

I had to get it over with.

I put the bottle in my mouth. My hands shook violently. I felt terrified of the children's reaction; this increased my trembling tenfold.

Rob then gave me another nod. It was showtime.

With every "goo-goo, gaa-gaa," the neighborhood kids burst out and laughed hysterically so hard, nearly bent over in a hyena position with their arms wrapped against their stomachs, and shouted, "Ooh, look, she's a big baby."

They continued pointing their fingers at me and repeating it over and over again like a popular chant. I couldn't look at them. All I could do was bury my head in between my legs to hide the instant blood flush to my face, consumed with shame. I was undeniably so humiliated that I began to drift in a deep trancelike stare. My urinary muscles slightly lost control, and I literally peed in the diaper, making their statements true. *I was an overgrown baby. It's true.*

Rob stood upright, laughed with them, and nodded in agreement while his arms folded across his chest, which signified an attitude like, *I've got the power.*

Then he gave me that final nod. Showtime was over. As I got up and looked back, I saw a wet spot on the concrete of my butt print. From that point onward, my nickname changed from Garbage Can to *Pissy Pot*. I tried to erase that disgraceful experience, but it was impossible. The neighbor kids continuously reminded me, pointing their fingers at me, whispering in one another's ears, and giggling underneath their breath.

Sadly, this place is no different than Ohio.

Even though Rob started the fiasco, he was completely unaware of the aftermath he had created during school hours. In my mind, being labeled "Pissy Pot" was bad enough, but "Poop-Butt-Sissy-——" would have been worse, so I kept it to myself since most of the verbal abuse occurred on school grounds.

"Wah, wah, big baby," was like a broken record day in and day out. Finally, I became fed up and decided to roll with it and fired back.

"You —— —— want me to pee on you? Keep it up."

They'd say, "Ooh, ooh," then run off.

Yah, you'd rather be p——d off than p——d on, I'd say to myself, then giggle. Indeed, I did get satisfaction from their wimpy reaction. I guess you could say I was a bit fed up and spiteful.

Morning after morning, I'd wake up frozen and ask myself, *Did I, or didn't I?* I frantically patted the area around my bottom and held my breath. Surprisingly, I never wet the bed again. I didn't know if I should hate him or love him.

One thing is for certain, my confusion—I became internally relieved to finally put those actual bedwetting days to sleep forever—but unfortunately the memories never fall asleep.

We stayed in Rodeo for a very short period of time, more like a pit stop. Basically, I felt the same way leaving Rodeo as Ohio, which I didn't think was possible. Next destination was Sacramento, the capital of California, which to me sounded like an important place to live. My mother had two girlfriends in particular who persuaded her to move closer to them. Actually, she didn't need much persuasion. Starting anew seemed to be the family motto from the beginning—rather than running from the law. However, her optimistic philosophy had rubbed off on me. This was my chance for a new start without the label of "Pissy Pot."

We moved from an apartment to a house on Woodland Street, which environmentally was a slight step-up from the Rodeo ghetto. I think Rob chose this isolated house due to its semiseclusion from other neighbors; it was the only house that sat farther back from the street (this was ideal for Rob just in case the "pigs" were after him). Visually, we could see whoever was pulling up in the driveway from a distance, given that a long dirt path would ultimately lead up to the garage. This provided a getaway plan for Rob to climb out the back window, if need be.

The language around our house seemed to change. Whenever Rob mentioned "the pigs coming after him," Lisa and I looked bewildered. We shrugged our shoulders at each other because we were confused.

"How can pigs be after someone? They're too fat to run," Lisa said.

Later, we found out from the neighborhood kids that he was referring to policemen. We guessed that policemen smelled bad. We were incredibility bright in some areas and completely naive in others. You'd think we'd have this one embedded into our brains by then.

My mother carried that optimistic spirit about getting a new start and leaving the past behind with one exception: the absence of baby Shelly. This continued to weigh heavily on my heart as I waited anxiously for her return (since we had supposedly gotten settled into our new place on Woodland Street). On our first day at school, my mother tried to be a good example by volunteering for room mother duties. This responsibility included supplying cupcakes, cookies, and juice to our classmates on special holiday parties, especially Valentine's Day, Halloween, and the annual Christmas party. Our best parties were when the holiday fell on "Mother's Day," the 1st or 15th of each month. In our family, "Mother's Day" was twice a month—the beginning and the middle of each month when all the needy welfare mothers got paid by the government. This was the time when we all waited impatiently for the mailman to arrive. In all honesty, we were starving by then. We listened carefully for that particular motor tick of the mailman van, then looked out the window for the American flag emblem for confirmation and shouted, "Hey, the mailman's here!" We dashed out of the house to greet the mailman. Most of the time, we didn't even give him a chance to put the mail in our box before we ran up with our hands wide open. We had one thing in mind: hurry up and get to the post office before it closed.

The post office was the place where we received multiple food-stamp booklets, the bills that looked like multicolored play money. My mother would stop by the Wonder Bread store around the corner from the post office. Pastries and other bakery goods just seemed fresher due to their advertisements painted on the window rather than the local grocery store.

Our mother made sure our classroom parties were successful, no matter what. Another attempt to normalize our new beginning was when she responded to a sign-up sheet we had brought home for Girl Scout participation. Lisa and I were excited that she contemplated enrolling us in the troops, considering our tight budget and difficulty making ends meet. She made it happen. We attended our first meeting in the elementary school auditorium along with several other parents. It was obvious that some of these girls had been participating for several years. Some came fully suited up with their red Miss America bands across their chests and pranced around showing off several patches throughout their uniforms. Some of them were huddled into groups chanting songs that they had learned from previous years. Lisa and I looked at each other nervously and wondered how on earth we were going to fit in with these cliques.

"Hey," whispered Lisa in my ear, "what do you think about this?"

"Looks like fun, but I feel weird," I responded. "How about you?"

"Yeah, me too, but at least we have each other." Then she smiled. That was always our unspoken truth, but this time, she voiced it.

During the orientation process, our mother filled out more paperwork. We didn't know it at that time, but we later found out that we were accepted for a sponsorship that included our initiation fee, and uniforms would be provided by our unknown sponsors. However, our mother would be responsible for the monthly dues. Lisa and I wondered how she would be able to follow through with our limited welfare income. Undoubtedly, the thought of my mother getting a job was unlikely with two infants at home. Moreover, Rob was too preoccupied running from the law, and that disabled him from maintaining any type of stable employment. Mother called him a "freeloader" behind his back. In addition, she didn't receive any child support from our biological father. At some point, he was found in contempt for failure to pay and was remanded into custody for three months. He still didn't pay.

Of course, after a few months into Girl Scouts, the monthly dues accumulated without payment, and we were banned from the meetings. Lisa and I retaliated. Instead of letting those uniforms hang in the closet and collect dust, we decided to put them to good use. We developed a plan to use those outfits and collect donations from all the "rich houses" to give to the needy. On weekends, we fitted up and solicited anyone who was willing to support a good cause. We chose a nearby community across the railroad tracks in another school zone, mostly the elderly, and crossed our fingers that we didn't knock on a door where an active Girl Scout lived. Lisa and I skipped down the street fully suited up, chanting, "Who said we can't be Girl Scouts?"

We did consider our family as a part of the needy clause, so our actions were fully justified. Lisa and I placed money in places where our mother thought she had dropped it or pulled money out of the couch cushions and said, "Look what we found in the couch. It must have fallen out of your purse."

We got addicted watching our mother's face light up, completely surprised, especially if she needed cigarette money. We would get a kick out of knowing that we had contributed to her happiness in some way, and that was enough to keep the behavior going. Of course, we had our own stash for "nickel candy"—inflation. We could never let our mother know what we were doing because she would have marched us right to the Girl Scout Association, admit our wrongdoing, and apologize—not to mention give the money back. We knew she held firm to her "good girl" Catholic roots: stealing was a sin and not justified no matter how needy we were. However, one exception: the "goodie box" (I'll explain later). Besides, the possibility of being labeled "scavengers" getting back to our classmates was another deterrent to keep our mouths shut. I was not about to claim a new negative nickname in our new neighborhood. Our enthusiasm continued to feed off the benefits enough to keep the scam going within a six-month period, but eventually we were forced to stop. Why? We outgrew our uniforms (we were *hustlers* before we knew there was a word for it).

Although we continued our month-to-month struggle financially, our mother had difficulty setting boundaries when it came to rescuing stray animals in the area. She was an absolute animal lover and easily persuaded to open our household doors for these unwanted pets. Lisa's favorite, Harry, an overgrown sheepdog, was almost rideable like a horse for our younger siblings. Harley Davidson, a miniature white poodle, was obviously the alpha dog for his breed. His hyperactivity and feisty behavior were on my list of favorites. He reminded me of myself. I thought it was rather silly to name a poodle after a motorcycle, but this was obviously the beginning of Rob's obsession with the so-called boys' toys. Then the cats multiplied. I'd hear my mother sternly reprimand the animals when they'd start whining for food.

"Go catch a mouse, you darn freeloader. And that goes for you too, Harry and Harley. Go outside and catch a bird." She'd point to the door as her voice escalated.

Not too long after the Girl Scouts' ban, I asked my mother, "Why do we have so many animals when we can't feed them?" I mean, shoot, there was no such thing as dog-food stamps.

Her response was, "I can talk to them, and they don't talk back."

We laughed when she said that. She'd go on to say, "Besides, they have survival instincts to fend for themselves if they have to," with a matter-of-fact tone. Being what it was, the chances of getting our cats spayed and neutered didn't even register. So you can imagine.

I remember one time in particular when Lisa ran into the house, her face pale white as if she had seen a ghost. She admitted to me that she observed Rob catching the kitties in the backyard and crushing their heads with bricks. This was his ruthless answer for pet control. We contemplated telling our mother but chickened out due the "snitch" label and the possibilities that could bring for us. We thought he might take us in the backyard and smash our heads with a brick since he had always made it clear that snitches die. We were too scared to tell.

Then the unthinkable happened. Baby Sarah's belongings had been boxed up and carried out of the front door. I was bowled over with shock. Instead of Shelly returning home, right in front of me was another sibling headed out of our household, and I felt overwhelmed with grief. In my view, I saw animals coming in and my sisters going out. In my attempts to get my foolish mother to come to her senses and reassess her logic, I began pleading like the last time, only this time, accusatory to some degree.

"Why did you give Sarah up too?" I yelled at her. That was exactly how I saw it.

"I didn't give her up!" she yelled back at me, her face flushed with anger. "Me and her father have decided that it was best for Shelly to have one of her sisters with her for a while."

Oh yeah, always what Rob wants, Rob gets, I thought. *How can I possibly go up against him?*

For some reason, I just knew this had little to do with Shelly. I was smart enough to know that if Shelly needed a sister, she could come home and have all her sisters with her. From that point on, I thought my mother was a weak-willed liar and should have demanded Shelly's return home.

No matter how hard it was to put the past behind and start anew, there was conniving Rob ready to make his next move like a chessboard mastermind. *Who's next?*

My mother did have something up her sleeve in hopes to make up for sending the girls away—in attempt to slap on an emotional Band-Aid to stop our tears. She planned to give us, Lisa and me, a seven and eight-year-old, surprise party since our birthdays were so close together. That event came as a total shock to me because parties were meant for other families who had money; we had accepted that throughout the years. However, my mother had always celebrated our birthdays in other special ways. She enjoyed sharing our birth experiences and how we had arrived in the world, and she underlined phrases in the birthday cards that had special meaning from her to us. She obviously planned out this particular party in detail, including several neighborhood children, the traditional pin the tail on the donkey, sock-hop races, and other customary activities for the celebratory event. However, while my mother was busy monitoring the schedule, Rob had a different plan to spike things up that didn't include the typical children's beverages to suit the occasion. He handed me a glass of red liquid that looked like cherry Kool-Aid, nodded with an acceptance gesture, and said, "Drink up."

I could smell a strange aroma coming up from the glass as I tipped the glass toward my lips. I stopped and looked at him strangely like, *What is this?*

He said, "Don't ask, just do it."

After the first sip, my tongue felt a stinging sensation that clarified that my senses were right on: this wasn't any fruit juice. I glanced at Rob again and witnessed his quick, firm nod. I didn't hesitate any further. As I continued to sip, its bitterness and strong alcoholic aftertaste made my tongue numb. The first gulp was the hardest to get down, so I held my breath, quickly swallowed, and shook my body so I didn't throw up.

"It's good, isn't it? Rob asked.

"Yeah, I guess so," I responded, fearful of what he might do if he thought I was being a sissy in front of all my friends.

"Good, then finish up," he said while he held another glass in the air, like, *This one is for you too.*

Since my tongue was already numb, the second round was easier to swallow, so I guzzled just to get it over with. Within the next hour, I blacked out. I woke up the next morning face-first in my own vomit. I was so confused, my head spinning, my hair saturated with puke, an excruciating pounding headache. I could barely remember what happened to me or how I even got into bed. I lay there disgusted with myself because I was a sissy for not wanting to be a sissy—then I shook my head. I remember thinking that if alcohol made people feel that sick, why on earth would anybody want to feel that way? While I muddled in turmoil, it suddenly dawned on me that my party was over, and I missed it.

Happy 8th birthday to me and the unforgettable gift from Rob. My first drunk experience will undoubtedly always be remembered (even if I didn't actually remember—I remember).

Long after the birthday hoopla died down and weeks had come and gone, the absence of the girls started weighing heavily on our hearts once again. The loss was overwhelming for Lisa and me. Most of the time, we tried not to think about it or simply change the subject to prevent a breakdown whenever anyone asked, "Where did Sarah go?" But for some reason, the popular KFRC radio station was making it difficult for us to push our emotions aside. A song with her name had hit the airways by storm, and the listeners' demands for replay was at its peak. Lisa and I burst into tears whenever we heard that song, no matter where we were. The teardrops fell like a waterfall of sorrow steaming from my eyes. It literally tasted like saltwater. The impact of Lisa's lamentation set off a chain reaction, almost as if we were in competition of who could weep the hardest. Lisa always won—slobber and snot, all mixed with tears. The strangest notion was when we thought about turning on the radio to escape the grief; our fingers couldn't reach the dial. We could not betray their memories. So indeed, we listened, sang, and sobbed together.

When our mother witnessed our distress, she tried to comfort us by reassuring us that we'd see the girls often with family visits, holiday vacations, and during the summer months until their homecoming. We had a hard time believing her. Despite her wishful words, the frequent visits were a joke in the beginning. It appeared Gramps and Nana didn't make the visits a top priority, or it surely seemed that way. However, Mother did make every effort on her part not to abandon the girls, at least to let them know she was still in the picture. When our vehicle was running properly, we made the trip just like she said we would. We'd all hop in the car in hot pursuit to visit, and we were overjoyed to make sure they were okay. I despised it when Nana put on her phony persona, acting as if she was so happy to see me when, in fact, I knew differently. I was awfully disgusted at myself when I was forced to act as phony as her by hugging her as if I missed her too. In my heart, I wanted to kill her.

I continued to tell myself, *One day when I get big…*

Chapter Reflection

Writing this piece brought back an overwhelming surge of emotion. On one hand, I hated this man for putting me through such gross humiliation and relentless shame; but at the same time, I felt grateful that I was cured from wetting the bed. The hatred was birthed in my heart at such a young age and grew uncontrollably rampant over the years. I first hated the world because I internalized that it hated me. I desperately needed God to intervene and penetrate my hardened, callous heart and give me a new one. (He did so, I'll explain later.) I am convinced I would either be in prison, a mental ward, or dead, but instead I am sharing my story behind my own household walls rather than the jail cell walls. Amazing. Something that I could have never achieved on my own. I am so grateful to God for giving me a new heart that has allowed me to replicate His love first. There was absolutely nothing that I did to earn His love. I was severely damaged, and He chose to pull me out of the pit.

We love because he first loved us. (1 John 4:19 (NIV)

In my spiritual walk today, I can identify with Jesus's humiliation—the mocking, the betrayal from so-called friends, and the rejection. I know that He knows my pain, shame, and seeks to heal me from all brokenness. In fact, He wants that for all of us. That is why He chose to give His life so all who believe can have hope and a future.

These scriptures touch deeply into my soul, which completely erase the hatred I used to carry for decades. Now the opposite is true today.

> *You keep track of all my sorrows. You have collected all my tears in your bottle. You have recorded each one in your book. (Psalm 56:8 NTV)*

This is what God has to say about our circumstances—past, present, and future. No tear wasted.

Our Safe Haven

Three years had passed. There were some summer months and vacation holidays when Lisa and I missed seeing the girls due to biannual visits to our grandparents on our biological father's side. Our mother's lecture prior to leaving to Grandma's house was not to blab our dirty laundry to anyone—period. She had handled it somewhat differently from Rob's demonizing "snitch theory," although reinforced secrecy on her own terms. She'd made it a point to sit us down, look us straight in the eye, and reiterate not to share our family business about "anyone, anywhere, anytime"; we knew she meant Rob's behavior. She targeted me especially because I had a tendency to speak my mind spontaneously without thinking twice. I called it my nature; mother called it "big mouth." She'd look at me, and suddenly her eyebrows met in the middle and created a deep crease in her forehead, so I knew she was serious.

"Lorrie, you're the one with the big mouth! You have to promise to keep your big mouth shut!" Mother sternly stated.

I remember thinking, *Oh great! Garbage Can, Pissy Pot, now Big Mouth. Boy, I can't wait to get to Grandma's house where "honey" sounds better—more positive.* (For the record, my mother eventually changed my nickname to Lambie, but I always knew she meant: Loud Lambie. So funny to me now.)

Between the both of them, what were two little girls to do? Without a doubt, our lips were sealed.

Being on our way to Grandma's house created that butterfly feeling of excitement in the pit of my stomach, especially as we approached the Orinda exit. Lisa and I bounced on the back seat, knees wiggling rapidly as we passed that distinguished local downtown theater that had ORINDA displayed vertically on the top of the building. Our grandparents lived in an upper-class suburban community located up a steep hill that overlooked Highway 24 from their fenced-in backyard. It always seemed a bit cooler as the ocean breeze swished through the Orinda hillside, which was a relief from the hundred plus temperatures that I was accustomed to in sweltering Sacramento. Without a doubt, Grandma's house was a safe haven for us.

As we pulled up in her driveway, there she was at her familiar spot, waving her hand with a contagious, exuberant smile on her face like she hit the lottery. Within seconds, she came outside with a floral tailor-made apron on, swooped us up in her arms, and began to verbalize how happy she was to see us. We already knew. Grandma's nature was similar to June Cleaver on the old-fashioned sitcom *Leave It to Beaver*. She had a gentle spirit, welcoming eyes; polite, soft-spoken tone; and always dressed up in high heels. She also loved to entertain her guests and was an immaculate housekeeper. There were many memorable experiences at Grandma's. For one, Lisa and I sat up on the bar tools around the countertop and pretended like we were at a fancy restaurant, stared at the crystal hummingbird that dangled from the kitchen window (Lisa has this in her window now since Grandma's passing), and watched the variety of rainbow colors when the early morning sunlight hit the glass-like object. Grandma had been up since six. The KGO talk radio played in the background while she stood in the kitchen with her apron on, ready to serve us.

"Now, girls, what would you enjoy for a bite to eat, *or* have you both decided what you're having this morning?" she asked.

We folded the newspaper and spontaneously rattled off whatever came to mind. Nine times out of ten, Grandma had the items on hand. Lisa and I looked at each other astounded that she had that much food handy. *And* there were always toiletries available.

"Wow, we didn't even have to go ask the neighbors to borrow anything," we'd say. We then whispered in each other's ear and said, "Grandma's rich."

Lisa and I enjoyed not only Grandma's cooking but the fact that time stood still as we had her full attention, and the whole world revolved around us when we were in her company. However, we did get upset about having to wait thirty minutes to go swimming out back in the pool. Grandma was adamant about letting our food settle first because she said cramps could affect our ability to swim and put us at risk for drowning.

We spent most of the day in the pool until our skin was wrinkled like a raisin. When lunchtime rolled around, instead of getting dried off and dressed to go into the house to eat, we'd enjoy catered lunch outside. Grandma would be holding a tray of sandwiches, cups of fresh fruit (cut-up pieces of watermelon, cantaloupe, honey dew melon, sliced apples), and those odd-shaped Bugles chips that we loved putting on all our fingers as if we had long, pointy fingernails. Then we bit them off. Most of the time, Lisa and I didn't leave the pool unless it was chow time.

When evening rolled around, and Grandfather arrived home from work, I could see the disappointment in Grandma's eyes that he wasn't as excited to see us as she was. I did make an effort to hug him, but he stood up tense and distant, sometimes stiff as a board. Grandma said, "Hug the girls!" He patted us on the back, which was sufficient enough to satisfy Grandma's wishes, at least for the moment. Even at our young ages, we realized it was difficult for him to show affection; his emotional vulnerability was completely opposite from Grandma's loving nature. At least he wasn't abusive. Just silently shutdown at times but harmless. He was more of the intellectual type: well-educated, a brilliant chemist who owned his own business. He enjoyed playing the organ, learning different languages, and playing bridge with their friends on the weekend-evening get-togethers. Although he wasn't the touchy-feely type, he had a wondering eye for other women. When they did entertain friends, he anxiously waited for the females to dive into the pool in their bathing suits, preferably bikinis. After a few martinis, he had no shame when placing the goggles over his eyes so he could watch their every movement underwater in slow motion. He didn't fool us.

At 6:00 p.m. sharp, dinner was served on the nicely decorated table with an ironed tablecloth, matching dishware, and polished silverware placed on napkins in its proper order. Grandma, with her soft-spoken voice, would say, "Girls, get washed up for supper." We loved hearing those words.

I looked forward to dinnertime because she cooked our favorites, including frozen peas for the veggie. Afterward, I had mint chocolate chip ice cream for dessert, and Lisa had French vanilla, our favorites. Lisa and I ate as fast as we could to finish dinner before Grandfather in order to beat him to the television set.

I could tell that Grandma knew she had some teaching to do regarding our despicable table manners.

Grandpa enjoyed the nightly routine of watching the news (featuring current events, especially the Vietnam War rhetoric that seemed to catch people's attention), so our game plan was to control the television set before he had the chance. I'm sure he knew about our scheme, but he never let us know. We always thought we had the upper hand.

Then there was bedtime. Even though Lisa and I weren't too excited about the grueling nightly routine of bedtime, I couldn't wait to dive into the guestroom bed, made military style, and make contact with those top-of-the-line smooth linens. When Grandma peeled back the bedspread and prepared to tuck us in, I'd do a back-flop, my full body weight onto the bed. I think this monkey behavior annoyed her, more so because I was making a mess out of the bed, but she didn't make a big fuss about it. I waved my arms and legs back and forth like I was creating an angelic figure in the snow. I loved when my skin touched the sheets. I used to think Grandma had some special secret about maintaining the softness and fresh smell. Then she'd place the covers underneath our chins, tuck us in, and handed me my fox fur I had inherited somehow. It was a white fox fur: one end was the face with a pointy nose and wire clampers underneath. I could squeeze the clampers together to open its mouth. On the other end was its tail, surrounded by hardened claws attached to the feet. For me, it was my security fox.

Grandma noticed Lisa's face drop with disappointment when I latched onto the fur. She whined, "Grandma, I want a fox fur too." One minute later, Grandma came into the room carrying a brown fox fur. She had taken off her fur collar from a suit she had worn on her wedding day so Lisa wouldn't feel neglected.

"Ha-ha, I got Grandma's wedding fur, so there," Lisa would remind me that I'm not so special after all. She had always felt that I was Grandma's favorite; now she was not so sure.

Although those were comforting moments, the constant uneasiness remained. That unsettling worry of, *What's going on at home?* was frequently on my mind. I'd look at Lisa and say, "Maybe Grandma would let us call home tomorrow," and then I felt more at ease falling asleep for the night. The next day, we'd hear Grandma on the telephone talking to our biological father. She said, "I have the girls over. You should come by to see them. They would like that," with her polite, soft-spoken voice.

Lisa and I waited impatiently. There were times he dropped in, too busy to hang out, or left abruptly and said he'd be back or didn't show at all. We got used to it and considered ourselves lucky when he did show his face. At times, it was noticeable that time had passed because his appearance changed significantly since our last visit. Either he had put on some weight or grew a full beard like Kenny Rogers. He did resemble the country singer, especially with facial hair. Still does, to this day.

However, his brother, Allen, pretty much made himself available. He had a way to distract us from our disappointment with a full schedule planned out for the day. Uncle Allen was a fun-loving, free-spirited, happy-go-lucky character who always ran around barefoot. He wore Hawaiian shirts and had a Volkswagen Beetle with stickers all over the car: peace signs, psychedelic love flowers, and messages that promoted "world peace" on the bumper. Apparently, our country was distraught and shaken up over the Vietnam War. Berkeley protesters proudly demonstrated their "freedom of speech" rights all over the newscast. When we were with Uncle Allen, we were compelled to promote world peace as well. While driving in the car, Lisa and I held up the peace sign using our *V*-shaped fingers and count how many people driving by would give us the *V* back or honked at us, giving an approval. "All You Need Is Love" by the Beatles played on the radio while two little girls jumping around in the back seat shouted, "Peace and love!" We were ecstatic when another Beetle bug drove alongside us, revved the engine, and exhibited the same enthusiasm, displaying their peace signs and honking down the Bay Area highway.

Lisa and I thought Uncle Allen was magical because he had knowledge to find all the fun places that kids love: water parks, summer community events, music festivals, cookouts, and the like. When we arrived back at Grandma's, we were too wiped out to think about our father's absence. Eventually, however, fun events became more and scarce when Allen met the love of his life. He did try to include us in the beginning. I remember when we arrived at his apartment. He rolled out the hide-a-bed in the living room, got us settled in, and proceeded to enter his bedroom with his girlfriend Cynthia.

"Hey, Lisa, I wonder if he's going to marry her," I said as we lay there with worrisome looks on our faces. Before another minute passed, I yelled, "Uncle Allen, I have a headache."

He went into the restroom to run water over a washcloth with medicine to take to relieve my headache; then he tried to get us settled down again. After a few minutes, Lisa yelled, "Uncle Allen, I have a bellyache."

He came in with another washcloth to put on her belly for comfort, then tried to get us settled again. After a few minutes, I yelled, "Uncle Allen, I'm hungry."

He came back in and explained, "You both can't possibly be hungry. We just ate." Then he tried to get us settled again. We were quiet for a moment then yelled, "Uncle Allen, we're afraid of the dark."

He came in and turned on a night-light. "Now, you girls, please try to get some rest. We have a busy day tomorrow." Now we could tell he was a bit frustrated to the point of irritation.

Finally, Lisa and I ran out of things to ask for. We eventually fell asleep.

I don't think he ever realized the penetrating fear Lisa and I had of losing him that night. In our own little-kid way, the chaos we had created was an attempt to disrupt any future plans that might interfere with our bond. In our minds, first comes love, then comes marriage, then comes baby in the baby carriage—and out with Lorrie and Lisa. And that's exactly what happened—in that order.

At least once during our visit, Grandma planned a shopping expedition which included clothes shopping for us, as well as picking up miscellaneous items she needed around the house. I was flabbergasted at Grandma's ability to keep her balance in ritzy high heels as she trotted down the one-mile steep hill toward downtown with Lisa and me right by her side. I assumed that she developed that skill from walking down the hill frequently since she had never driven a car in her lifetime. She was ecstatic when BART (Bay Area Rapid Transit) arrived on the scene, which made an easier access into Oakland's shopping district. She couldn't wait to give us our first train ride, which she had kept a secret until we approached the station. After a long day of shopping, we arrived back at the Orinda Station. Then she called Grandpa to pick us up so we didn't have to climb that dreadful steep hill. She must have known the combination of high heels and carrying packages would be too much of a struggle, no matter how skillful she was.

The hardest part about Grandma's house was leaving. Her tradition upon our arrival was a spitting image of our departure. She had all our nicely folded, fresh-smelling belongings neatly organized in different compartments, all ready to go, with one exception: the foxes had to stay behind. She insisted on carrying the luggage out to the car, refusing any help, while we stood there waiting for our goodbye hugs. As we drove away, Lisa and I crawled on the back seat with our knees bent, looking backward out the back window, and she'd be in the same position waving goodbye and blowing kisses. Teardrops fell like Niagara Falls as we proceeded down the hill; then Grandma disappeared from our eyesight.

Upon our arrival back to our house in Sacramento after our two-week vacation, there were more secrets lurking around the household, and the hush seemed to be the norm about what had happened to our mother. She was still in bed in the later afternoon, her body wrapped up in bandages as she rested while we tiptoed around the house, respecting her sleepy time. My natural response was to investigate what had happened, so I pried and asked questions to find out what all the hush-hush was about. According to the sources around the neighborhood, she and Rob went camping at Lake Berryessa with some friends, and apparently my mother got "plastered" drunk and passed out directly in the sweltering sun for several hours. She had gotten severe burns on her body and had to be rushed to the hospital. Then it got worse. After they administered penicillin, without realizing she was highly allergic to the medication, her body went into shock, and she almost died.

It was also mentioned that Harry (our sheep dog) had died while we were at Grandma's. Lisa was devastated since she was so attached to her overgrown pooch, and this added more salt to our wounds. Supposedly, our neighbor who lived right behind us shot Harry in a fit of rage for trespassing on his property. He alleged that Harry was killing his chickens, so he felt justified to shoot Harry dead. That was just too hard for us to believe. Lisa and I had it in the back of our minds that maybe Rob killed Harry as a means of pet control, especially with his history of animal cruelty. It was hard to know the truth since we were not there to witness what actually had happened. We did not let this go.

"Maybe we should get to the bottom of this ourselves and go ask Mr. Swartz what happened," Lisa suggested.

"Yeah, but if he really did shoot Harry for trespassing on his property, maybe he'll do the same to us," I responded with paranoia. It was just too risky to be pestering the neighbor about the killing, so we had to let it go. But we always wondered what really happened that summer.

We were glad to be on the road again after Harry's death. It was hard to look at Mr. Swartz's property every day and think about the possibility of Harry dying there, if it was true. Instead of moving across the state or any other long distance, our mother found a bigger house on the same Woodland Street a few blocks down the road. Not only were we excited about more living space, but there was a larger backyard with a miniature-looking cottage that Lisa and I decided would become our getaway house from all the unnecessary stress of dealing with Rob's mood swings (maybe a mental health crisis). The fact that we didn't have to change schools again and didn't have to make new friends was a huge bonus.

Not too long after our move, Rob started hanging around a group of individuals who were different from most of society. They had wacky nicknames of body parts and makes and models of automobiles preceding their first names, like "Cadillac Bill" and "Mustang Joe" who didn't believe in washing their Levis. To prove his loyalty and get "props" from his newly found peers, Rob gave his own personalized touch by urinating throughout the blue-jean fibers, marking his own putrid scent and "to break them in," just like an animal. The more grit, grease, and grime that produced a glossy shine and a leathery texture was the goal. In fact, the ultimate goal was to get the Levis filthy and heavily coated with dirt so that the pants could eventually stand up bodiless. The process was pretty disgusting to witness.

Rob made it perfectly clear that if my mother ever washed his Levis, he'd kill her, and "That goes for the both of you too," he told Lisa and me. I would often think, *Is he out of his mind? I wouldn't even think about touching those grungy, stinky pants if he paid me.* Then Lisa cracked me up when she pointed out, "Lorrie, don't you think if we touched his pants, he wouldn't have to kill us because we would die from his *icky*?" I died laughing. "And he has the nerve to say policemen stink." Then we both were practically rolling on the floor.

Most of his friends had long shabby, greasy hair (to match their pants) with hairlines parted in many directions that exposed their scalp even when pulled back in a ponytail. Some had bandanas displaying a skull in the middle of the forehead wrapped tightly around their heads, Fu Manchu mustaches hanging halfway to their necks, or beards resembling ZZ Top—all mixed with hoarse, raspy voices. They usually had smashed cigarette filters clenched between their nicotine-stained teeth.

One night, one of his friends, a well-known hit man (which we had interpreted to be that he hit people a lot), came over bragging about robbing a security-armored Brink's truck, and all the while he was picking human skin out of his teeth with a toothpick. Apparently, it was said he had gotten into a fight and bit his opponent's ear off. He was a burly man and someone who had the ability to intimidate just by his looks alone. Then there was a peculiar couple, Coo-Coo and Mirabelle, who moved in the cottage out back and were obsessed with snakes. Not only did they bring more chaos in terms of unnecessary commotion and weirdness, but they had stolen our getaway cottage that Lisa and I had our hearts set on just to get away from the constant madness. They owned a boa constrictor as their pet snake and took enormous pride wrapping the reptile around their bodies as a garment. They'd walk around the house flaunting their animalistic fashion mixed with "how do you like me now?" grins. It was all surreal. They housed the snake in our garage-converted family room (which by then was called Rob's playhouse), stored in a wooden chest when not wrapped around their bodies. It was hard to know at times if the snake was on the loose in the family room or if Coo-Coo and Mirabelle had the snake in their possession. It absolutely freaked us out at times when we'd find the shredded snakeskin throughout the house with the boa nowhere in sight. With every tiptoe I took, I was extremely alert about my surroundings, on the lookout for the ten-foot long reptile and apprehensive about entering any room in the house. I didn't consider complaining about being petrified because Rob hated "poop-butt, sissy ——," as he called it and would probably make me hold it, so I faked being "tough," although I wanted to shed my own skin and disappear entirely.

Our environment started looking like something I had previously watched from a horror episode, filled with the eerie, creepy energy accented with a touch of Rob's decor: several shapes and sizes of skulls throughout the house. His skull collection became an obsession for him and a constant nightmare for us, and he knew it. There was one skull in particular that was strikingly similar to a human skull that had a candle holder on the top of its head. Rob placed a lit red candle as the topper and waited for the red wax to drip down the skull's exterior, yielding the "dripping blood" affect. Then he waited for the wax to harden. The creative masterpiece served as a reminder of his golden rule: snitches die.

Every time we looked at the skull, which by the way was hard to miss since it was displayed right above the television set, it engraved his statements deeper into our brains. Then there were those smaller ceramic skulls with the big black hollow eyes and big rats that sat on top of the skulls' heads. Lisa would crack me up when she pointed out, "Well, at least, we don't have to buy Halloween stuff." I had to agree. We laughed to the point that our stomachs hurt.

Strangely enough, at times, an odd smell seeped in from the garage and circulated throughout the house, which meant Rob and his buddies were smoking the "peace vase" again. They'd all gather in the garage-converted family room, sitting Indian-style on the floor surrounding a colorful lime-green see-through vase-looking object that looked like a miniature octopus. It had eight metal posts with hoses attached to each individual post sticking out from the sides in the middle of the circle. As they sucked in the air, I could see the water bubbles popping up inside the vase as the grayish smoke cloud darkened with every puff, and then slowly it dissipated while they puckered their lips and held their tight-lipped breaths. Shortly afterward, their entire demeanor changed as they laughed loudly, told dirty jokes, curse, playfully made fun of each other, and bragged about whose motorcycle was better. I was relieved that the tension was gone.

During one of these groupie gatherings, I was enticed to join in since there was one empty hose lying there on the floor. Since I was fascinated watching the water bubbles in action, I decided to give it a try. Besides, it seemed to make people seem less edgy and more harmonious. During the initial stage, I was instructed to observe the proper way to smoke marijuana. As I took a deep breath in, my lungs began to expand from the smoke, and my throat felt like it was on fire. As I tried to fight the harshness, I started choking and coughing because I just couldn't hang on any longer. I immediately determined that the "peace vase" wasn't my cup of tea, even if the bubbles were interesting to watch. Of course, I was called a poop butt, sissy, —— for not being able to hang with the "big boys."

Although the clan got more and more playful throughout the daytime, come nightfall, Lisa and I became involuntary recipients of Rob's need for approval as we were used as yoyo puppets in his live comedy show for their nightly entertainment. While sound asleep in our bedrooms, we were awakened by his angry voice, shouting, "Lorrie and Lisa, get your —— up and get out here now." His voice penetrated through the bedroom door.

I'd nudge Lisa. "Oh no, Lisa, what did we do now?"

"Slave duty time, Lorrie," she said.

Half asleep, we jumped up like awakened from a nightmare. Instant sweat poured from my armpits as I firmly responded, "Yes, sir," military-style.

"Go get us all a beer and make it snappy," he said, army style.

We scurried to the kitchen on command and carried cold beers from the refrigerator.

He and his buddies were sitting lined up on the couch and throughout the living room. He then said to them, "Watch this." He snapped his fingers, pointed to the floor, and shouted, "Comprende." I don't even think he pronounced it right, trying to speak Spanish.

We dropped to the floor. He then snapped his fingers again, this time with one finger pointed up in the air. Lisa and I immediately jumped up on command, again and again. It felt like we were human yo-yos as he pulled our invisible strings, and we bounced to his command while his buddies laughed and admired how well-disciplined we were—like animals. One of his friends remarked, "——, you've got them trained." I could tell by his puffed-up demeanor and that "look-at-me-now" grin satisfied his giant ego hearing that comment: his bad—— persona portraying that he had the ability to "pull strings" might actually make him look like he was somebody. As the laughter died down, we headed back to our room.

"What was that all about?" I questioned Lisa as the nervous adrenaline continued to pump through my brain, my hands shaking like a leaf.

"He was showing off again like usual," she said.

"Wonder how long this is going to last?" I asked.

"Hopefully, not long. You know what? I'm praying for him to go to jail so we don't have to deal with him anymore," she said, her eyes looking much wiser than her years.

"You better pray long and hard," I responded.

As long as new buddies were introduced, the comedy show continued to emphasize total mastery over his little pawns, meaning us, to covet the crown of power; and the possibility of being appointed to a higher rank in the clan was at the forefront due to his show-off behavior. He didn't verbalize it, but we just knew it. We just couldn't put it into words yet.

Not too long after this repeated fiasco, the telephone rang. It was the call we had been waiting for. Excitement started to build as I nosily listened to Mother's affirming words: "Oh, you're in jail again. What for this time?" Then there was silence for a few seconds. She went on to say, "Well, you might have really done it this time. You might be gone for a while."

I nudged Lisa and said, "You must have prayed long and hard, didn't you?"

She smiled and didn't say a word. Instead of screaming *yes* so loudly that Mother could hear, Lisa and I went into the room, shut the door, and embraced each other while jumping up and down in sequence, arm in arm with each other. Our feet were jumping off the floor as if were on an invisible trampoline flying up in the air. I suddenly got the vision of Rob sitting in a cell with the steel bars slamming behind him like the episodes I had seen on *Dragnet*; at the same time, our steel bars had finally opened. We were free at last!

With Rob's absence, we had the opportunity to finally be kids as we played outside, grateful that we didn't have to be Rob's welfare slaves. Our mother had two girlfriends who lived on Woodland Street as well, Sherry and Joan. They both had daughters about Lisa's age, Theresa and Lucy. After a hard day's play, Lisa came in looking pathetically puzzled, shaking her head.

"What's the matter?" I asked.

"I just don't understand either one of them two. It's like we all can't play together. When I play with Theresa, she wants me to hate Lucy. When I play with Lucy, she wants me to hate Theresa. Why can't we all play together? They only want to be my friend when they're fighting with each other and want me to pick sides. That really bothers me."

"Well, don't play with either one of them," I suggested.

"Then I'll have no one to play with," she responded with frustration and threw her arms up in the air.

"I guess that's something you have to deal with," I said and shrugged my shoulders.

Elementary-school-age games kids play. Pretty typical for children to get territorial with friends.

Lisa's friendship dilemma had been circling around for some time until one day she pranced through the front door carrying an eccentric strut in her step. Something was different about her demeanor as she looked at me with a "smirk-eating" grin as if she had news to share.

"What's going on? Why the grumpy look?" I questioned.

"I'm sick and tired of playing with Theresa and Lucy and dealing with their silly crap, so I've found a new friend to play with. She's in my class, lives on the same street by Lucy's house. I really like her."

"That's good. What's her name?"

"Savannah. But everyone calls her Savannah-Banana," she said.

"Well, it sounds like you have finally solved that problem you've been dealing with," I affirmed.

"Yeah, now I don't have to feel caught up in the middle of those two anymore." She sighed, bringing a sense of relief to her voice as she was telling me. "Yay!"

It was the middle of summer with scorching-hot temperatures while I witnessed Lisa and Savannah-Banana playing in the sprinklers, venturing out to the neighborhood creek to catch tadpoles and pollywogs and then taking turns riding Savannah's bike down the two-mile poorly paved road with no sidewalks. Savannah obviously had strong height DNA because she towered over Lisa, which definitely gave her an advantage playing tag. As they ran around dodging each other, Savannah's lanky, thin body, along with her quick footwork, left Lisa in the dust. Savannah's ponytail stuck straight out like Pippy Longstocking's behind the colorful headscarf while Lisa's extra-baby-fine hair instantly flopped with moisture from body sweat. They both didn't seem to have a care in the world as their faces beamed with glee from their newly found friendship, and nothing else mattered for the time being. It was pleasant to witness Lisa's joyful spirit, which, unfortunately, was few and far between. I guess you could say things were looking up.

Days before the school's new year started, we went with our mother "goodie box" hunting in hopes to get school clothes to help us scrape by and save money. We called this particular location "goodie box" because sometimes when we saw toys, like games, dollhouses, and baby dolls, Lisa and I shouted "Goodie!" We didn't care about the clothes as much as Mother. First, we took a cruise by the Mayflower grocery store to scope out what belongings people had dropped off at the gigantic green metal box that looked like a giant mailbox. It had a handle that opened the box that was extremely heavy but was the point of entry to access the items. The problem was that Lisa and I were too small to reach the handle, so Mother dropped one of us in the box; then we'd throw out the items as fast as we could. Sometimes we were lucky because the box was stuffed full, so the donators dropped off stuff surrounding the box onto the driveway pavement; a much better view of what was available. For some oddball reason, I seemed to get more of a thrill from the sneaky act itself, doing something we're not supposed to be doing rather than receiving the material items.

Our mother said, "We're not stealing. People give this stuff away for the poor people who need it, and guess what? We're needy, not greedy." Made perfect sense to me.

However, the part that tickled me the most was going back on the mission at night in hopes that our earlier scope out was still there. I started bouncing on the back seat with excitement when I laid my eyes on the items still there and immediately pointed. "That's mine! I called it earlier."

We rotated duties. One of us decided what was valuable, the other slung items into our vehicle, while the other was on the lookout for the "cops." Of course, our mother's preference was household goods and clothes. Our priorities, hmmm? As we drove away, Lisa and I shouted, "Goodie!" feeling the excitement building as we'd be home soon, and it would feel like Christmas in the summertime. These were good times—Rob's long-awaited absence, new wholesome friendships, and anticipated goodie-box goodies. How long would these good times last?

Chapter Reflection

I shake my head with amazement regarding the resiliency of children. What an adjustment for any kid. Scrounging around looking for food at home, sneaking a fried chicken leg from the frying pan before our 10:00 p.m. dinner while Mom catches me in the act, screaming, "Lorrie, you're a vulture. Bring that piece of chicken back this very instant!" Survival of the fittest changed to survival of the quickest in my crafty mind. If I did not capitalize on the opportunity, there was a pretty good chance there would be nothing left.

On the flipside, there were prim and proper manners at Grandma's with plenty of food at every dinner table setting. Washed up for supper, sitting up straight, napkin tucked into my shirt, I'd say, "Please pass the butter," or "May I please be excused?" It must have been challenging for Grandma to watch us slip into heathen habits, such as reaching across the dinner table and snatching food with my fingers rather than patiently waiting my turn using the proper utensils. And the biggie—chewing food with my mouth wide open, chomping, and smacking probably annoyed her to pieces. She had received a degree in home economics and owned one of the first ever made handbook guides on etiquette. Naturally, she had a strong opinion about normalcy and the way family life should be. I can still hear Grandma's words: "Ooooh, my, girls," giving us a hint of her disapproval when we acted out rather than reprimanding or shaming us in any way. Sometimes we got it. Most of the time, we didn't. It was difficult to shift etiquette gears when we've developed *hoodlum* survival skills for years.

We also attributed Uncle Allen's departure from our lives due to our unruly, erratic behavior. We figured they did not want to expose their children to riftraff heathens and corrupt their children's good upbringing, being raised properly and all. Looking back, I don't blame them, and I may have done the same to protect my children from us too. However, it was double rejection for us. Even though we knew it was coming, it was awfully hurtful to accept the reality of his actions.

In my spiritual walk today, combating the negative self-talk, those relentless attempts to deplete my forward progress, self-esteem, worthiness that only comes from *the* enemy is a never-ending struggle. However, I try to catch those thoughts before they get out of control and rely on God's promises: who I am in Him, that I have a purpose to fulfill, and His unconditional love for me rather than all the despicable lies that I've held inside for so long. Instead, I refocus those thoughts with God's truth and affirm that He will never reject me. I hold on tightly to His promises.

> *Fix your thoughts on what is true, and honorable, and right, and pure, and lovely, and admirable. Think about things that are excellent and worthy of praise. (Philippians 4:8 NLT)*

> *Instead, let the Spirit renew your thoughts and attitudes. Put on your new nature, created to be like God—truly righteous and holy. (Ephesians 4:23–24 NLT)*

> *However, those the father has given me will come to me, and I will never reject them. (John 6:37 NTV)*

*****

I couldn't help it. I had an enormous smile on my face sharing this part of my childhood as I looked at Maria. She had a ditto ear-to-ear smile on her face that matched mine. She was feeling the sense of "good times" with me. Without saying it, we both knew this was perfect timing to call it a day—on a positive note. She looked up at the clock, and we both nodded.

"You know, I've been thinking," Maria said. She cleared her throat, hesitated for a second, as if she wanted to think about how to say it, and then delivered a question. "I want to suggest something for you to consider before I leave today, okay?"

"Okay," I responded.

"As you are aware, I have much-needed responsibilities with other clients that require my attention as well, and I need to distribute my time equally and fairly based on many contributing factors. And believe me, you are high on my priority list. So with that being said, I want to put it out there for you to consider writing parts of your story from here on out. Of course, we'll continue to meet, just not as frequently, and I definitely want you to share what you have written if you choose. I just don't want my lack of presence to interrupt your storytelling process as I can see you're on a roll. It's my belief that this progression is therapeutic and helpful for your healing journey. Also, I have a great therapist in mind for you to work with who can help you sort through any abandonment, anger, sadness, and/or other negative emotions that may come in between you and your recovery. You don't have to give me your answer today. Just think about it."

She paused for a moment, her eyebrows lifted, her mouth presented in a tight-lipped grin, like, *Okay?* Then she presented me with a genuine smile. How could I not smile back just to let her know my nonverbal response—okay.

"I'll think about it," I responded.

I then watched her as she gripped the winter coat from behind the chair, put it on, then proceeded to the front door.

"Let me know if you hear any news about Dustin before I do, and I'll do the same," she said on her way out.

Immediately following her departure, I started mentally tripping. Bothersome questions were flying in my head from one extreme to another. *Is this her nice way of abandoning me herself? Is she tired of hearing my story? Is she pawning me off to someone else? Does she want me to put it in writing to use against me in court, or is she actually telling the truth?* I had to remind myself that this was a good day and not to let this doubtful committee in my head ruin that. I began the positive self-talk to combat those annoying thoughts.

She hasn't betrayed my trust at this point, and she does have other duties to fulfill. I'm not the only one on her caseload. I should give her the benefit of the doubt. Besides, she did mention that she wants to hear what I have to write.

The next day, I thought about it; then I stared at a pen lying on the table. It was my sign to pick it up. Here goes…

Check

Yes, I knew it. Like they say, every good thing has an ending eventually. The terrible day finally arrived when our freedom was stripped away. The reality hit us when Mother announced, "Girls, your father is coming home."

Lisa and I became paralyzed, stunned by her words. "But we thought he was going to have to stay in jail until his time was up," I questioned. I knew this from eavesdropping in her initial telephone conversation a few months earlier.

"His time is up because he had been rewarded time off his original sentence for good behavior," she responded.

Lisa and I were flabbergasted. They have got to be kidding. How could he be rewarded "good time" for anything?

Our mother must have witnessed our overwhelming disappointment when our lips dropped and our chins scrunched that our facial frowns couldn't go unnoticed.

"Girls, your father is a changed man now. Having been in the clinker has taught him a big lesson."

Lisa and I looked at each other like, *Oh boy, she didn't fall for that line, did she?* Maybe she was just being optimistic. For me, I got the visual picture that the latch on our outer bedroom door was now locked and our freedom lost once again. I knew he'd eventually be back, but not so soon.

Upon his arrival, he did appear somewhat different, excited about the family reunion. As he walked through the front door, he held out his arms and anticipated for our bodies to burrow into his stomach, then gave us all a massive bear hug. The first words that came out of his mouth were, "How are my baby girls?"

To my surprise, his tone sounded warm and welcoming.

Did he really change? I thought.

It was way too early to tell. Even I knew that.

Within a day or two, he spoke about selling his motorcycle to have extra spending money so that we'd be able to have a good Christmas that year. He always did have a soft spot for the Christmas holiday season, so that didn't change. However, it became more noticeable that he decided to let go of his past and begin anew, which finally affirmed Mother's deepest wish for our family. Lisa and I were able to sleep all night without being called for slave duty. He hadn't reminded us repeatedly about "what happens to a snitch" and didn't go ballistic when the skulls were no longer present on the TV stand.

However, the most noticeable action that had me somewhat convinced that *maybe* Mother was right about his so-called change was when the motorcycle found its way to another owner. More shocking, he started taking a more interactive approach toward family time like game night—more spontaneous timing than the traditional scheduled nights. The spontaneity was upon us. He taught me how to play the game of chess and how to defeat my opponent by thinking ahead. "Get them before they get you," he'd say. "You have to be smarter by thinking at least three moves ahead to outsmart your enemy, and always beware of what your opponent's strategy is." He'd show me what I thought was his personal "slick" moves, like the "three-move checkmate" and, if that didn't work, the "seven-move checkmate." He also taught me how to corner your opponent's king, the versatility and advantages of the queen, and explained to me that sometimes the pawns are used as a sacrifice to trick your opponent when the time is right. He'd present that certain arrogant smirk after his move like he's the master at the game of chess and knew it. My competitiveness sprung into high gear when I'd hear him say, "Lorrie, ready to let me kick your —— in chess," just at the opportunity to outwit him.

Lisa and I would compete against each other to get extra practice hours, hoping that one day we would be able to repeat his all-too-often victorious word: *checkmate*. I so desperately wanted to return the jaw-dropping shock just like he defeated me when I didn't see it coming.

"Dang," I'd say. "One of these days, I'll do it."

One day out of the blue, Balloon Grandma and Grandpa, my mother's parents, came from the Bay Area to visit. We were without a doubt overjoyed to lay eyes on them due to their unannounced, spur-of-the-moment visit.

I would perk up when Grandma told me that I was her special "godchild." She made that statement often. It was music to my ears, but in my heart, I knew it wasn't true. I never had the courage to tell her I didn't believe in God, fearful of hurting her feelings, besides spoiling her positive image of me. I didn't want to ruin that for her or for me having such a special position in her eyes. That would be ignorant.

Actually, I thought she had me mixed up with Lisa.

How could I tell Grandma that I wasn't special at all? Besides, my personal view was, if there was a God, God must hate me. Therefore, it was less painful for me not to believe.

She grabbed my face, puckered her lips, and smacked twenty fast repetitive smooches in a row on my face. Sometimes her breath smelled like booze, cigarettes, and coffee all rolled into one breath, but I didn't care. Her smooches were better than mint chocolate chip ice cream in my book. I knew Balloon Grandma had a little too much to drink if her wig was cockeyed, tilted sideways, or slightly lopsided on her head. Lisa and I would crack up if Grandma had forgotten to comb the back of her wig, and the noticeable shiny knitting material would show. Then we'd gladly fix it for her. How we loved our grandma. I noticed that her smoking habit had taken a toll on her appearance as the wrinkles along her outer lip began to deepen with every puff, or perhaps it was from all the smooches she gave—maybe both. She was incredibility affectionate and not afraid to show it.

I overheard my mother stating that Grandma had a hard life growing up, which made me admire her even more. I could see why. Grandma was the eldest of twelve children. I was surprised to find out

Grandma's mother was still having babies when Grandma was having babies; that seemed odd to me. In fact, Great-Grandma died while giving birth to my mother's younger aunt. Amazingly, Grandpa was one of twelve children also. When his mother passed away, his father married a widow down the street with twelve children. I immediately envisioned a bus with twenty-four children smashing their lips against the fogged-up windows as the bus rolled down the street for an outing. A family field trip for real!

"No wonder why they got the heck out of Minnesota and moved here—to get away from all those kids," I told Lisa. We both laughed.

As always, Grandma came prepared: a car loaded full of groceries, sandwich bags filled with stickers, balloons, and candy for our special treats. Lisa and I thought we had mastered her nickname to match her giving nature. We were proud of that.

On this particular visit, Grandpa's and Rob's voices rapidly rose from the living room, which eventually turned into a screaming match. It was only a matter of time when tensions erupted since we all knew those two didn't see eye to eye. I heard Grandpa as he screamed at Rob for leaving a loaded pistol lying on the coffee table. This was weird because I didn't see any gun in the house.

"Are you crazy? One of these kids could get a hold of that and think it's a toy," screamed Grandpa.

I ran into the living room when I knew I shouldn't. I saw Rob's finger pointed in Grandpa's face, threatening, "You're not telling me what to do, old man. This is my house"—screaming foul, degrading obscenities—"and if you don't like it, get your —— —— out of my house. As a matter of fact, you're not welcome here anymore," he shouted and jerked his finger toward the front door. Grandpa wiped the sweat off his bushy eyebrow with his hands trembling. His face was beet red, like he was holding his breath and ready to explode. He bit his lip.

My eyes fluctuated back and forth from the gun to my mother's pleading voice, "Rob, please." I saw Grandpa's eyes shift to the gun as well. He was smart enough to put his hand to his mouth to stop the escalation before something terrible happened that he'd regret.

"Come on, Margie," he said to Grandma. "Apparently, we're not welcome here anymore. Get your things and let's go."

Grandpa looked down at my mother as he towered over her. "Changed man, huh?" (I guess she had pulled the same line on them too.) He rolled his eyes at Mother with distain that she fell for his brainwash once *again*. "Jenny, if you choose to stay married to that monster, I disown you." His eyes were blazing as he stared Mother down with contempt.

We all knew he meant business.

All the adrenaline I had just acquired from my body's fight-flight response instantly dropped to my feet. I stood there numb, speechless. I was dying inside for Mother to respond, "Wait, Dad, we're coming with you," but she never did.

That loss was a nightmare for us. Deep down, I knew if our grandparents disowned Mother, that meant they disowned us. Unless…

That night, Lisa and I held each other just like the time we thought Santa had died and cried ourselves to sleep with our goodie bags from Grandma tucked underneath our pillow.

Before I fell asleep, I whispered to Lisa, "Start praying."

Distraction had a way of putting painful memories on the back burner, although not completely forgotten.

As time went on without a word from our grandparents, I tried not to think about our loss and looked toward anything positive in the foreseeable future. Even though the temperatures dropped and brought a damp, chilly breeze in the forecast, we felt optimistic that Rob having sold his motorcycle had some making up to do. However, no Christmas present in the world could replace our grandparents.

The upcoming holiday season worked in our favor as usual, which seemed to penetrate a softness of heart in the atmosphere around the holiday season. My mother seemed to use her crafty imagination to put some realisms in Santa Claus and tried to make this particular Christmas extra special. She placed treats out for the traditional jolly fellow the night before. When we woke up that morning, we knew he had arrived because tiny leftover cookie crumbs were scattered on the plate, and there was hardened milk residue around the glass with a thank-you note left behind exclusively from Santa. We were elated believers.

As the holiday season wrapped up, so did the festive spirit among us. Truth be told, Rob's criminal behavior resurrected. I knew in my heart of hearts it was only a matter of time. It appeared that amnesia crept in regarding the previous dire consequences he got of jail time. In reality, the fact that he was an unemployable convict probably added to the "screw it" attitude. It didn't take long for him to resort to old habits, maybe a couple months in. Soon our front door reopened to the "buddy scene" again while the guys gathered around and devised plans on how to make quick money.

One night, they pulled off a drive-in robbery that turned our garage into a "fast-food" minimart in a matter of minutes. Packages and packages of frozen food—hamburgers, hot dogs, and frozen burritos—were at our disposal. Bags and bags of cigarettes—Lucky Strike, Benson & Hedges, Marlboro, and Pall Mall—filled the concrete floors in the garage.

At least they don't have to worry about cigarette money now, I thought. When I voiced this to Lisa, she exclaimed, "Heck with the cigarette money, Lorrie. Now we don't need to worry about food money." There again, she had a great point.

Mother had a "don't ask, don't tell" policy because their behavior didn't fall into her "needy" category. Robbery couldn't be justified, even if we were starving in January like most poor folks after Christmas. Things progressively got worse over time, although I managed to escape slave duty from time to time.

One dusky mid-August evening, I approached the house as I usually did after returning from my best friend Renee's house singing "Tears of a Clown" by Smokey Robinson & the Miracles. Naturally, whenever I heard the soulful beat, I began swinging my arms and hips, dancing down the middle of the beat-up pavement, singing the lyrics. I appeared happy-go-lucky and joyful. Dancing in the street was my outside demeanor, even though I was dying from sadness, loss, and shame on the inside. This song had special meaning to me: it *was* me.

Renee and I definitely had a pattern of wearing out new songs, playing it over and over when the 45-record hit the market. As we tried to memorize the lyrics and choreographed new dance routines, we pretended to be famous singers and used our fists as make-believe microphones. It was an absolute breath of fresh air to be in a peaceful environment and escape my problems through music and fantasy. I enjoyed hanging out at Renee's. Her mother was a dear heart who reminded me of my absent grandparents. Oh, how I missed them terribly.

Renee was the baby of the family and pretty much spoiled by my standards, although not by hers. Her parents were much older and might have given birth to Renee in their late forties (I'm assuming, but I really don't know). Her mother looked much older in comparison to my mother. The deep tanned creases along her forehead, center cheekbone, and outer mouth proved her passion for gardening, to say the least. Not to mention the sun exposure during the summer temperatures probably sped up her aging process—maybe.

Renee's parents owned a duplex that had been converted into one large house that sat on a corner lot with a beautifully landscaped yard (her mother's gift). A door was installed in the middle of the wall that connected the two duplexes together. Renee's room was located at the other end of the duplex as if she had owned her own apartment. This setup was heaven-sent for any preadolescent. I longed to have her living arrangement; I envied her.

As I began to climb the porch steps, it hit me. I despised my reality even more so now that I had something to compare mine to. Regardless, I took a couple of heavy sighs, and I twisted the doorknob. I felt sticky and icky from the blistering heat, which caused dirty sweat beads to roll off my forehead.

As I headed to the bathroom to get cleaned up, I heard Lisa sniveling in our bedroom. Her cry was muffled, and her hands were cupped over her nose. I opened the door. She was lying flat on her stomach, her head buried into the pillow to soundproof the scream as I witnessed her legs move up and down with every, "Ah, ah, ah."

"What's the matter?" I asked.

She continued to weep and didn't say a word.

I pried further. I had a feeling in the pit of my stomach that something really bad had just happened.

"I got beat," she caught her breath to answer my question.

"How long did it take you to find the belt this time?" I asked.

"That's not the problem, Lorrie. I don't care about that or the beating. Rob took Savannah-Banana away from me." Her cry escalated louder and louder as she put greater emphasis on *Savannah Banana*.

"What happened?" My eyes bulged out, expecting the worst.

She panted for a moment and then caught her breath. "Savannah and I rolled up on our bikes to spray each other with the hose. When we got there, Rob was standing on the porch and screamed at me, 'Why did you bring a —— n—— to my house? There are no n—— allowed at this house ever. Got it?'"

"What did you say?"

"But she's my friend. But he told me, 'Oh, —— no, you will *not* have a n—— as your friend. Get your —— in the house and find the belt.' But that wasn't the worst part."

"Oh no, what?" I asked.

"He stared at Savannah with that ugly demon look of his and said, 'You get your black n—— off my property before your parents find you hanging from a tree.'"

"Oh my gosh, he did?" My jaws instantly dropped to my neck. "What did Savannah do?" I asked.

"Her mouth flew open, and she took off running down the street scared to death."

"I hate him!" She then flopped her face back into the pillow and started wailing again. "She was my friend," she cried as she lifted her face up from the pillow then dropped down repeatedly.

"I hate him too, Sis."

She turned over and looked up to the ceiling. Her eyes were going back and forth as if her thoughts were racing a mile a minute. I could tell that Lisa was seriously searching for a resolution.

"I know. Maybe if Savannah doesn't tell her mom what happened, I can sneak over there and play without him knowing. That is, if she doesn't hate me now."

I was crushed as I witnessed Lisa in so much pain despite her beating. It was obvious that she was heartbroken to the core.

All of a sudden, I heard Rob screaming at me from the dining area, his voice echoing off the naked hallway walls that were covered with our family tree of dirty handprints. "Lorrie, get your —— out of that room. That n—— lover is in trouble."

"You better hurry before you're called a n—— lover too," Lisa whimpered.

Around the same time period, I was introduced to another one of my first lessons. My mother's friend Joan had a teenage daughter who babysat us when my mother was burdened with totting us around while she ran errands, paying bills, etc. Teri was judged by others as the unruly teenager who didn't respect authority. She was an attractive, nicely proportioned sixteen-year-old whom the neighborhood referred to as a "wild child." Her obvious infatuation with the clan and Harley Davidson motorcycles turned into flat-out obsession, and she voiced her idolization and the desire to become just like them someday. *Easy Rider* was her favorite movie of all time.

One day, she enticed me to smoke a cigarette while on duty.

"People who smoke are cool," she told me. "Don't you want to be cool, Lorrie?"

I desperately wanted to be cool, so I responded, "Yes."

"Then smoke this, like me," she said and held the cigarette up to my face.

Undoubtedly, she thought she was pretty darn cool.

"This is how you do it." She took a puff, inhaled, then blew smoke out from her mouth.

Hmm, that looks easy.

"Watch this," she told me. She took another puff. This time, she snapped her jaw, which created several grayish smoke rings in a row.

Wow, I thought, *that is supercool.*

"Now watch this." She illustrated another trick. She took another puff, but instead of smoke coming out of her mouth, it looked like smoky railroad tracks evenly lined up streaming from her nostrils. I had seen enough. Her demonstration of "coolness" was convincing: if I wanted to be cool, I had to smoke.

"Give me a cigarette," I said boldly.

When I inhaled the cigarette, I immediately started to choke and felt nauseous. My head started spinning, so I leaned over and laid my head on the armrest of the couch. Not cool at all.

"Don't be a wimp," she said.

"Get me a piece of bread. That will help settle my upset tummy. And for your information, I'm not wimping out. I just need to let this bread settle first before I take another drag," I said, trying to ward off her belittling accusations.

There was no need to worry about supply; we had bags of cigarettes to last a season.

A few minutes later, I was ready for more. I was determined not to be labeled a poop-butt, sissy —— or even a wimp for that matter, so I struggled but finally finished that darn cigarette. As an eight-year-old, my need for approval and acceptance had hit its peak. More so, the thought of being labeled "cool" outweighed any immediate negative effects from smoking.

I started paying close attention to movies that portrayed the attractive actress who played that certain kind of elegant, classy quality—painted lengthy fingernails as she held a cigarette with her legs crossed. This only reinforced Teri's smoking lesson weeks earlier.

Not only was smoking cool, it was flat-out sophisticated, I thought.

Even the daily exposure to the nicotine-stained teeth of the clan didn't penetrate the deception that smoking was glamorous. I continued to smoke and didn't recognize the flat-out lies that Hollywood portrayed, which fooled everybody.

It was only a matter of time that my third-grade teacher called my mother and expressed her suspicion that I was smoking because she smelled cigarette smoke particularly in the early-morning hours. When Mother confronted me, I said, "No way. Where did you get that stupid idea?"

"Your teacher called and told me that she smells cigarette smoke on you."

"Of course, she does. Everyone that comes into this house smokes. No wonder why I smell like smoke," I snapped back.

How could she disagree with that?

I became an expert at hiding my addiction and protecting my newly found "cool" image, or at least I thought so. She knew I was lying even if there was some truth to my comeback.

"I guess I'm going to tell your father [Rob] about this one," she said with a stern look on her face.

The threats didn't even scare me anymore; hardened heart had set in. Besides, Rob's discipline was unpredictable. When I thought I should be in trouble, I wasn't, just like the "playing doctor" episode and vice versa. The waiting game was upon me.

He didn't say a word about Mother's news. In fact, I thought that maybe she had forgotten to tell him. He sat on this information until he was ready to use it to his advantage and satisfy his own selfish desires.

Two weeks later, that time arrived.

Lisa and I glanced over Mother's shadow in the bathroom hidden behind the misty haze with the door slightly cracked open. As the grayish fog slowly rolled into the hallway, the steam started to evaporate from the mirror. She waved her arms rapidly to shoo the vapor trail along, then darted into her bedroom. When she pranced out, she wore a stunning miniskirt fitted snuggly around her hips and a chiffon blouse with multicolored circles. Ruffled hanging sleeves dangled around her wrists, and a pair of white shiny patent-leather go-go boots up to her knees. She stood in the hallway, placed her right arm on the entryway slab, and slightly bent her knee forward. She looked like a replica of Sally Fields fitted for fashion week on the *Rowan & Martin's Laugh-In* show as a guest star. This was mother's Kodak moment as she displayed her eye-catching, dazzling debut along with a puffiness of pride.

She looked so happy for a change.

Moments later, we heard the crackling electrical sound as she pointed the blow-dryer's tip toward the oversized pink plastic rollers for quickening the drying process. Then she removed the hair rollers and began to tease the top of her hair with a comb to add fullness for a trendy minipompadour look, then tucked the elastic neon-yellow headband behind her ears (Lisa and I understood why she did that; we had baby-fine hair too). The bathroom basin was covered with cosmetics. She leaned closer to the mirror with her mouth open and stroked her eyelashes. We got a kick out of how she made silly lip movements after she applied the tangerine-orange lipstick. This habit had always been the final stamp of approval in her eyes. She was officially presentable for the "nightlife" with her girlfriends.

They're going to be jealous, she seemed to think.

However, we did know that her absence would hold a different meaning for us.

"Oh no, Lorrie, she's going out again. We can't let her go," Lisa said in a panic state.

"Lisa, you can't stop her. You always try, but it doesn't work, remember?"

"I'm going to this time. You watch," she fired back.

I snickered because I knew what she was up to but thought it was a waste of time. *Good luck.*

She jumped up and darted to our mother's legs. She looked outrageously ridiculous in that she was much taller now, so the "monk move" was pretty much impossible. Instead, she sat her bottom on the bathroom floor, pressed her full-body weight as hard as she could, and wrapped her arms around those go-go boots and pleaded with her, "Please, please don't go. Don't leave us here," Lisa begged.

I shook my head because even though this might have worked in the past, there was no way it was going to work tonight—not after all the effort Mother put into her appearance.

"I'm only going to be gone for a couple hours. You'll be fine here with your sister," she tried to reassure us.

I gave Lisa a "here we go again" grin like, *I told you so*, which only added fuel to her frustration.

"Shut up, stupid," she told me, then tightened her lips.

Later that night, Lisa fell asleep on the light-pink satin material daybed that was positioned under the large living-room window while watching television. When I was going to bed, she said, "I'm going to stay right here by the front door when Mommy comes home."

Instead of waking up to Mother's stumbling footsteps, she awoke to Rob touching her inappropriately.

"Leave me alone," she screamed as loud as she could, kicking and screaming, pushing his hands away from her.

"Shut up, you sniveling little c——!" he screamed.

Lisa flat-out refused to shut up and continued fighting him off. In retaliation, he lifted his leg and shoved it full force into Lisa's back. She then flew several feet across the hardwood floor, almost reaching our bedroom door.

She never talked about it until decades later.

Lisa showed her bravery that night, something I never had the courage to do. I wish she would have talked to me about that night but didn't.

Rather shortly, Rob figured out that he lost at his own game after Lisa refused to be the little pawn in his perverted world; he quickly shifted his focus off her and onto me. I then became the next pawn in his game of master manipulation, terror, and bribery, strategizing every opportunity to take advantage of my youth and rob my innocence.

It was Saturday afternoon, and I was physically drained from all the household duties, scrubbing on my hands and knees, although feeling a sense of accomplishment that the house was spick-and-span. The strong ammonia smell mixed with Sanka coffee aroma coming from the kitchen area lingered throughout the house added to my satisfaction. The atmosphere was fresh and clean.

Lisa had finished her chores and snuck over to Savannah's house to play. Obviously, Savannah decided to keep the racial threats to herself. Lisa called it God.

Mother had her own agenda with the long grocery list as she carried sales newspaper and cut-up coupons to the can-food store to "get the best go for the dough" (in her own words) and beat the food-stamp stampede of welfare folks.

Rob lay on the brown beat-up couch covered in cat/dog hair and smelled like musty, stale cigarette smoke mixed with hemp odor that probably had seeped into the walls during the clan gatherings. I heard the sound of the sports commentator coming from the garage when I heard a different tone to Rob's voice.

"Lorrie, bring me a cup of coffee," as if I reenlisted for slave duty with a twist. His voice sounded a little unusual, uncharacteristic from the slave-driven demands I was used to hearing. Although his words were demanding, his tone wasn't as abrasive, which instantly brought a sense of relief, like I wasn't in trouble for a change. When I handed him the cup of hot coffee, he said, "You look tired. Come take a nap right here," and patted his hand on the couch next to his stomach. I didn't argue. I was like a robot to any of his demands.

"I don't want you falling off the couch," he said, then grabbed my hips and scooted me closer to him. I squinted my eyes shut and clenched my teeth together because my body was touching his nasty jeans, but I remained silent.

Sports entertainment was dreadfully boring and didn't spark an interest in my attention span, so I dozed off relatively easily, mostly because I was worn out from working nonstop around the house. Without going into descriptive detail here, let's just say his behavior was extremely inappropriate. He whispered in my ear, "You know what happens to a snitch, right? By the way, your mother told me you're smoking," he shockingly said out of the blue. I had been waiting for this conversation to be brought up eventually, but not in this context by no means.

Those conflicting thoughts were scattered like my neurons firing triple speed. The dizziness from the confusion and multiple questions rushed through my mind that my body became stiff. I began to get very confused. *What is he doing to me? Why is this happening? This is bad*, repeated over and over in my head. I became overwhelmed. All of a sudden, I jumped up and rattled on, "I have to go to the bathroom," bolting so fast that he didn't have time to grab me.

"Okay," he responded like nothing even happened.

I had a difficult time as I tried to make sense of it all and sat on the toilet baffled and disoriented. Those uncomfortable questions were seemingly too difficult for me to comprehend at that moment, so I concluded, *It wasn't real.*

As time went on, it became increasingly impossible to deny the molestations. He purposely created an agenda that required Mother to leave the house and insisted that I had housework to do. I strangely looked at my mother as she walked out the door. I wanted to tell her but didn't know how. How could I tell her that her husband sexual assaulted me? How could I hurt her so badly? What would he do if I told? Would she even believe me? Probably not.

Bottom line: I couldn't. I chickened out *again*.

Suddenly I heard the voice, and I knew. "Lorrie, get me a cup of coffee," really meant it was time for something else. Especially midmornings, Rob was in a position to repeat the act again and again when Mother was away. As I brought in the cup of coffee, he said, "Put that on the nightstand and get over here."

When Rob couldn't get my mother to leave for whatever reason, he suddenly had somewhere to go and chose several different locations so she would not get suspicious.

"I have to go to the store. Lorrie, you come with me," he said.

Lisa stood right by my side and begged, "I want to go. I want to go with you guys." She knew and tried to protect me in her own way.

"No, n—— lover, you didn't finish cleaning the bathroom, or I don't hang out with n—— lovers," Rob yelled.

"It's not my turn to clean the bathroom. I did it yesterday," Lisa said.

"And you'll do it again today, so get a move on it," he demanded.

If it wasn't the bathroom, he made up a chore at the spur of the moment to prevent her from even asking. Eventually, she got smart and gave up because she didn't want another chore.

We pulled into a large shopping center that was similar to the local supermarket parking lot where the "goodie box" was located. Instead of driving into the parking stall, he turned the wheel and drove toward the outer perimeter, completely away from the to-and-fro shoppers. He then threw the gear into park, leaned underneath his seat, and showed me that handgun for the first time and reiterated his infamous question, "You know what happens to a snitch, right?"

I nodded quickly, my eyes glued to the gun.

"Good," he said.

Those constant questions circled around in my head. *What if he kills me? What if Mother doesn't believe me? How can I tell her and hurt her so badly? Will she blame me? Will she hate me?*

I concluded that this was my entire fault because I couldn't stop it. This conclusion had embedded its way into my subconscious, which would silence me for years to come.

I wasn't a snitch, but I was a chicken.

In an attempt to escape my reality, I shifted my thinking and stared at the pack of cigarettes right before me. "Give me a cigarette," I demanded. For that brief moment, I felt empowered to tell him what to do for a change as I witnessed him reach for the red pack of Pall Malls and politely handed me the nonfiltered cigarette.

When we arrived back home, I darted for the shower because I felt dirty and shameful for not standing up to him. While in the shower, I began to inflict self-injury and self-mutilation to punish myself for his behavior.

One summer morning, chaos broke out when my mother woke in a state of panic and hungover from the night before. She frantically searched high and low for her teeth. Apparently, she had a blackout and couldn't remember what happened to her dentures.

"Lorrie and Lisa. My teeth are missing. Please help me look," as she threw her hands up in the air.

"Oh my gosh," I told Lisa. "We have to find her teeth. She'll look like a grandma if we don't find them." I looked at Lisa with her mouth wide open from shock.

"Shut up, Lorrie! That's mean," she said, protecting our mother as usual.

It became obvious that our mother's appearance changed dramatically overnight with her droopy-face look. She didn't resemble Sally Fields without her teeth. I couldn't help but think we had to do something before school started, which was a month away. I didn't want our classmates to see her like that, make fun of her, or say, "Is that your grandma?" Embarrassment quickly set in.

We searched thoroughly throughout the house: underneath beds, in closets, behind furniture, in between couch cushions. It was nowhere to be found.

"Maybe you took them out last night when you were out and left them somewhere," I suggested.

"No, I know my teeth were in my mouth when I got home," she insisted. "But I'm not sure if I hid them somewhere because he [Rob] was in a bad mood."

That sounded crazy to me, but I didn't want to make things worse than they already were. *Find the teeth now and ask questions later.*

I heard Mother whining, "Oh no, I can't afford new teeth." Then she raised her voice, "I tell you what, whoever finds my teeth will get twenty dollars."

"Twenty dollars?" we asked again to make sure we had heard her correctly (twenty dollars was a lot of dough to us).

"Yes, twenty dollars," she confirmed.

Boy, that was an incentive for sure. Lisa and I were on a serious mission to find those teeth. We were driven for many reasons: to preserve her appearance, save her and us from embarrassing moments, and get bunches and bunches of candy—*thousands*, we thought.

A month had gone by; our mother's teeth were nowhere to be found.

"Did anyone find the teeth today?" became a broken record.

We searched tirelessly day in and day out, which reminded me of *the hunt* with a twist. Finally, after three months well into the new school year, we had completely given up and concluded that Rob had thrown them into the garbage, but we had no way to prove it.

Another season flew by. As I cleaned the garage-converted family room and swept the cobwebs that seemed to grow like wildfire behind the entrance door, I noticed a work boot wedged into the concrete corner, missing its mate. I picked up the dusty, holey, beat-up old work boot that was stashed among other debris and almost slung it out of the side door and onto the pavement. For some oddball reason, I stuck my hand inside the boot. Lo and behold, I was holding mother's twenty-dollar choppers right before my eyes. I started screaming with excitement, darting through the garage door, "I found them! I found them!"

"Found what, Lorrie? What did you find?" she yelled back.

I dashed through the dining-room area while everyone swooped together around me. I felt like a hero as I held the missing teeth up in the air and twirled. Whoever was in the house that day, the excitement was infectious and outweighed the twenty-dollar reward by far. Without a conscious effort, all of us gathered in a ring-around-the-rosy circle, doing the twirl dance, jumping up and down, and singing songs of joy.

I had made Mother so happy that day. Those final, long-awaited words departed from her mouth, "Oh, I can feel like a woman again," she said happily, smiling.

I started screaming, "Put them on, put them on!" I was anxious to see her new look since, honestly, we had forgotten what she had looked like with teeth.

Lisa looked at me and said, "Ooh, ooh. They need to be washed."

Mother looked at us like, *Of course, sillies*, and ran into the bathroom.

After it was all said and done, Mother admitted that she and Rob had got into a scuffle that particular night, and she took them out because she was afraid that he would bust her mouth open.

That didn't surprise me. But how they landed in the boot was always questionable.

Chapter Reflection

This was a very difficult piece to write, as you can only imagine. These particular incidents drove the title of this book. Reflecting back, I see how he planned in advance his many moves to please his convoluted selfish desires and prey on the vulnerable. I sacrificed my innocence for his perversion. How dare I take on responsibility for his actions and blame myself? I was only an eight-year-old child and scared to death of this man. No wonder why I didn't like coffee for years. Makes sense.

THE PAWN

> *Instead of shame and dishonor, you will enjoy a double share of honor. You will possess a double portion of prosperity in your hand. (Isaiah 61:7 NLT)*

Also, gazing back, undoubtedly there was a greater purpose stirring within me rather than merely the competitive spirit. Inwardly, I felt powerless, fearful, and defeated, but I couldn't put a name on it at the time. I would ask myself often, how could I possibly go up against him? Since he overpowered me in the real world, beating him at chess was my opportunity to regain my dignity—in a silly kind of way, I guess. However, I never won.

As I reflect on smoking at such a young age, I'm saddened by the need I felt to be accepted. I was willing to do anything to be cool. We were all deceived back then—lies, lies, and more lies. It's not so cool to have a hole in your neck or an oxygen tank on your back. I am proud to say that after forty-five years of smoking, I'm now nicotine free. I have a funny story to share about this; I chuckle at God's sense of humor. I had been struggling for years to quit smoking for many reasons. I tried patches and pills, which worked, but I always started again. I tried smoking cessation, *no butts*, and my favorite: Nicorette gum. I was addicted to chewing the gum relentlessly, even slept with it at night. I would smoke cigarettes and chew gum at the same time. I have to say that I must have looked ridiculous chewing that gum like I was a spun-out maniac. I'm sure my coworkers could vouch for that. My goal was to soak up every iota of nicotine because it was just as pricey as smoking; therefore, I did not want to waste my money.

Then it dawned on me: it might help prevent lung cancer; however, I might end up with stomach cancer trying to prevent lung cancer—vicious cycle. (I don't really know that, but that's what my head was telling me.) Besides, there was a traumatic event that stirred the urgency (which will be revealed later on in the book). God finally put it in my ear with His small, still voice, *Listen, Lorrie, it's time. You have to quit.* I remember trying to negotiate with God, sitting in the Walmart parking lot. "Okay, after this one last package, I'll quit. I promise." In the checkout line waiting for my turn, the person on the other aisle must have accidentally tripped and bumped into the racks on the opposite side. Tons of regular chewing gum fell all over the conveyer belt right before my eyes. I was stunned. "No, you just didn't!" as I looked up. Even after that, I still bought the Nicorette. However, I kept my promise—that was the last package I bought since. I switched over to regular chewing gum. God knew; it worked.

Vicious Violence

When the girls came to visit that summer, Sarah, our younger sister, pleaded for Lisa to pierce her ears too. "I want my ears pierced just like you, sis," she said (apparently, we must have made a big deal about it). This was all it took for an immediate response to relieve a four-year-old's distress. Soon after, Lisa calculated ideas to accomplish the mission. Sarah's whiny, harpy voice continued daily. By the third day, Lisa unexpectedly spotted a capped hypodermic needle in a shoebox while she had dug in the hallway closet—of course, completely unaware of its purpose.

"Today is the day Sarah's ears get pierced," she said underneath her breath. Lisa was so excited to find an object that would actually get the job done that she darted up to Sarah and screamed, "I found something! I found something! Get ready."

She galloped to the icebox and snatched ice cubes from the tray, then sifted through the junk drawer, pilfering through the mess for a spool of thread. With all the items in her hand, she was ready for action as she headed into the bathroom and ordered Sarah to sit on the toilet seat. She first put the ice cube on Sarah's earlobe to numb it before she punctured the hole in the middle of the lobe then slid the thread through. Just before she began to proceed with the other ear, a large hand gripped Lisa's hair upward, and her feet suddenly lifted and dangled off the floor. Rob's earsplitting voice blasted, "What in the —— do you think you're doing?" His temper exploded while I watched the vein emerge from his neck and the blood surge directly to his beet-red face, as if the devil himself entered the bathroom.

This time was different. Instead of ordering her to find the belt, he yanked the extension cord from the wall with one hand and pulled her pants down with the other. I heard the horror in Lisa's scream with every wail as her face cheeks puffed up like a chipmunk from holding her breath, her eyes pressed tightly shut while her butt cheeks tightened stiffly to lighten the powerful blow. My hand automatically covered my ears because I couldn't bear the sound of Lisa's agony. I watched her skin split open as the blood began to seep from her bottom. That still didn't stop him. With every intense blow, I felt my own bottom tighten and held my own breath as if I was in the process of getting beat too. It didn't matter how many times I witnessed Lisa's beatings; it didn't get any easier to watch, and vice versa.

As time went on, Rob developed other twisted ways of punishment that caught us by surprise.

What kid doesn't get excited when they hear those words, "Go watch TV"? Those particular words held a completely different meaning for us, not the traditional cartoon downtime. Whenever Rob demanded, "Go watch TV," Lisa and I were commanded to stand in the corner military-style, shoulders up, arms pressed firmly to our sides, heads held steady, bodies upright (slouching for leg support was absolutely forbidden). After the first hour, every minute seemed like an hour, and it was only a matter of time that our weaknesses would show. If our legs buckled or we showed any movement whatsoever, he slung the bullwhip from the couch and snapped our nearest body part. Sometimes he missed, but the crackling echo sound that rippled through the living room startled us to pieces.

However, some evenings, we received the benefit of listening to Sonny and Cher cracking jokes on TV, the audience laughing while the married couple continued attacking each other's character and afterward singing, "Babe, I got you, babe" in the background. And all the while, Rob nicely kicked back on the couch, bare feet propped up on the coffee table, surrounded by beer cans with the bullwhip gripped in his right hand on the armrest. He drooled over Cher's trim physique as she wore a fancy glittery evening gown and her to-die-for, gorgeous hair draped midway to her stomach.

Suddenly Rob cracked open another beer and slurred, "Babe, I want you, babe."

He passed out while we stood and stared at the walls; snores followed soon after. To keep our minds occupied, we created our own television show from the skip-trowel, putty-looking mass on the walls. These patterns enabled us to visualize several patterns, shapes of animals, little creatures, etc. to pass time and engage our imaginations. "Go watch TV" literally meant a two to three-hour dry-wall episode for us, depending on how much he had to drink and how long he fell asleep. Sometimes our mother trampled around noisily on purpose to wake him up so he'd let us out of the corner. When she'd try to intervene verbally by saying, "Rob, you're being too hard on the girls," he'd make us stay in the corner longer. So she gave up trying.

Even though he plucked away at our soul, he couldn't rob our imaginations and creativity. And for that, we had satisfaction.

One particular evening around that time period, when evening time rolled around, Rob turned on the *Sonny & Cher* show as he was in the habit of doing and began the same ol', same ol' routine: gawking over Cher's body and making inappropriate innuendoes. You'd think on that particular day (their anniversary) he would have been more discreet or skipped the show altogether if he couldn't hold this tongue. His behavior must have upset Mother because she walked up to the television and flipped the channel to the *Tom Jones* show in attempt to give him a taste of his own medicine. We all knew Mother had the hots for the Welsh singer. It appeared they had some sort of jealousy rivalry brewing for some time, but this particular day, it escalated into fury.

Mother's actions infuriated Rob. "How dare you disrespect me, ———." Within seconds, his temper explosively erupted like a volcano while he doubled up his fists and raised his hands to a boxing position. "You love Tom Jones, do you? Well, you'll never watch that Tom Jones in the house ever again!" he screamed as he pushed his fists closer to her eyes. In a fit of rage, he walked up to the television set, turned around, and put his boot heel through the screen—just like a madman. Glass instantly shattered all over the floor. While in the midst of bickering, he threw her to the floor blanketed with glass. He snapped. Suddenly he jumped on top of her and held her throat tightly with her head smashed into the pieces of glass.

Lisa and I jumped on his back and managed to grab him around his neck in our attempt, we felt, to save her life. He slightly loosened his grip after weepy gurgling sounds and Mother's face obviously headed toward discoloration.

She managed to squeak out, "The girls are watching…the girls are watching." That comment startled him. Mother was smart, even in the moment of panic. If he was going to kill her, he needed to consider who was watching.

As he snapped back into reality, he let go completely and began to sling Lisa and me off his back. We slid across the hardwood floor. Mother lay there lifeless for a moment, then rose up wobbly, obviously disoriented from the lack of oxygen, disgruntled and distraught from being pummeled like a football player.

Rob glared at us, gritted his teeth, and calmly said without moving his lips, "You two little ——, get your —— in your room for disrespecting me too."

Lisa and I looked at each other wide-eyed like, *No problem*. We were grateful to have that option instead of a whipping.

He stood there like a beast with a mangled porcupine-shaped goatee sprung in every direction from the scuffle. He wasn't finished with her yet. While the argument continued behind our closed door, Lisa and I had our ears sealed to the bedroom door just in case; however, he had latched the hook on the outer door to keep us locked in. Our fists banged on the door to distract him, to no avail.

Creepy silence remained. Not soon enough, we heard Mother yell, "Okay, okay," like she had surrendered to his demands. Lisa and I sighed with relief like a punctured balloon.

"That was stupid. Now neither one of them get to watch their shows," I blurted sarcastically off the cuff. I knew Lisa wanted to laugh but couldn't due to the drama that just happened.

The following few days were intense in terms of tension. Lisa and I tried to remain invisible when Rob was around and extra sensitive to Mom's needs when he was gone. Any requests she made was done without bickering or resistance on our parts whatsoever.

Lisa tried to revive a positive outlook (regardless what our reality was) by singing her favorite new song that moved across the airwaves directly into her heart and over to mine. On our way to school, we held hands, and she began to sing with an angelic tone, "O-o-h Child" by the Five Stairsteps. Optimism took root because normally she couldn't carry a tune, but something in particular about this song had special meaning to her, just like "Tears of a Clown" had for me. The lyrics spoke of a "someday" when things would be better and brighter. Her face beamed with hope as I listened. Lisa was convinced that this was God's song to us and served as a reminder that someday we'd be okay.

"That's our song, Lorrie," she'd say every time it played on the radio. Goose bumps popped up every time. In fact, at times, tears rolled down my cheeks because I wanted to believe in something greater. Was there anyone out there that could see what was happening? However, I was smart enough to know if that was true, then why didn't it stop? *We must be bad. We must deserve it.*

I quickly composed myself before we reached school grounds so I didn't look wimpy. When we arrived, she headed in one direction and I in another.

Focusing on classwork was a constant struggle. It was pretty obvious that my attention level depreciated since I had to repeat the reading instructions over and over to make any sense. Sometimes I would stare at the wall, not hearing anything the teacher said. I was consumed with worry.

Is Mom okay? Is he hurting her? was what I concentrated on. I made it worse for myself, but I couldn't stop it. In fact, I couldn't wait for the end of the day to have a cigarette, quiet the voices, and hear Lisa sing our song. By not knowing the answers to my inner questions, anxiety started to build. My feet nervously shook, creating a distraction from the other students as the desk legs clunked on the tile floor. Mrs. Sanders sat at her desk, head down, grading papers with her glasses propped on the lower portion of her nose like a librarian. Without moving her head, her eyeballs met mine. This was my warning to settle down, which worked for a while; then the process started all over again—and again.

I had already developed a nervous disorder. Go figure.

Although I struggled academically, I excelled athletically with my ability to run (thanks to the bulls). My confidence grew when I outran the boys and was voted the fastest runner in school and when I was the first one picked by kickball team captain. Sometimes there were pleasurable moments like these.

Within a week's time, it happened. Lisa burst through the bedroom and practically slung the door into the wall as I lay on the floor contemplating running away, weighing the pros and cons yet always siding with the cowardly part of myself and the fear of the unknown. When I thought about the consequences the last time I ran away, I totally dismissed the idea altogether.

Lisa's face illuminated with joy as if an angel appeared right before me. She started singing our song. "Things just got brighter," she sang. I knew by the sound of her voice and her body language that something wonderful had just happened.

"What? What?" I eagerly asked.

Her lips reached her earlobes; then she couldn't hold back any longer. "You're not going to believe this. Rob's back in the clinker—but this time, he's gone for a year." She was shaking with excitement and threw her hands up in the air.

Wow! One whole year sounded like an eternity for us. Better yet, I overheard Mom telling one of her girlfriends that his past had caught up with him from another county and that he was going to be transferred to Marsh Creek Detention Facility in Clayton, which meant he was far, far away from us.

As time went on without Rob, Lisa and I began to venture out into the neighborhood, making up for lost time, living out our carefree childhood excursions and enjoying some freedom once again.

Chapter Reflection

Looking back at the "corner" punishment, how fortunate we were to have those skip-trowel/dry-wall patterns rather than the traditional flat walls. I think we would have gone stir crazy standing there for hours on end. I can see how God helped to keep our minds occupied on something positive and creative rather than wasting our minds and fretting over our corner confinement.

In addition, the violent episodes impacted my perception of life on many different levels throughout my lifetime. First, growing up witnessing domestic violence was the norm for me. I would find myself hooking up with men who had those abusive tendencies and didn't think there was anything wrong with it when the cycle repeated itself within my own household. I accepted the fact that if I didn't behave appropriately according to my man, I needed to also accept my good butt whooping. That was my truth, period. Please keep in mind that part of this book was written years ago. Today I am over that mindset. There is no way I'll ever put up with anyone treating me any less than the woman I am today: a child of God and a survivor who deserves love and respect.

I vividly remember promising myself that I would never get married—ever! My thought process was basically a question: why on earth would anyone want to get married? In my mind, marriage meant losing yourself; becoming a worthless slave; being subjected to endless ridicule, vulgar insults, abuse, both verbally and physically; powerlessness; suffering in silence; and subjecting your children to all the above. In one sentence, the marriage idea could be a death sentence of my soul. This is really a shame that any young person would feel this way. God created marriage so the two would become one, not as a prison sentence. I'm grateful today that I don't view marriage as the plague. I am now married to a wonderful man who is learning about God's love too, treats me like a queen, is a team player and supportive, and loves me unconditionally. I finally got it right.

Furthermore, many abused victims blame themselves as I did and resort to self-destructive behavior early on, sabotage, drug addiction, built-up anger, self-mutilation, acting out, and the list goes on and on. Luckily, nowadays, we have the "Me Too" movement, our outcry that "time's up"—no more silence—bringing attention to the injustice and abuse of women and children. It's about time, especially for my generation that was notorious about keeping secrets and our mouths glued shut out of fear. No more! Our voices will be heard.

While writing this, it dawned on me: *How can I work for an employer whose primary mission is to release inmates from custody while growing up? Rob's incarceration was the only solution that saved our butts. Literally. How many children out there count on incarceration for protection because their parents fail to do so? How could I not take this personally?* The struggle is profound. I was completely baffled and ashamed that I had forgotten where I came from and who I've become—a traitor, so to speak—to keep a roof over our heads and food on the table. As I continued to grapple with this insight and feeling deeply depressed about my revelation, I confided with a trustworthy colleague who viewed my situation differently through her own eyes. She responded something along the lines of, "Not everyone is guilty, Lorrie. In fact, we ensure due process and attempt to hold law enforcement accountable to prevent abuse of power." Yes, this was her viewpoint, as an African American on the undeniable influx of mass incarceration amongst her race that I witness on a daily basis.

Overall, her response helped me see another piece to the puzzle that jolted my perception—somewhat. Yes, I too can identify with abuse of power as a child, not by law enforcement per se but within my own household—a so-called parent. It's like a balancing act for me: I can see both sides and have strong opinions on both sides of the issue. I took it a step further and replayed those times when I was falsely accused, as in the banana-peel episode, or of taking my school pictures to school that Nana planted as evidence to prove my defiance. The fact that I was wrongly accused of acts I did not commit and harshly punished as a result of those false accusations, I personally identified with the injustice and wished I had someone to stand up to my defense. There was absolutely no way to defend myself even though I tried, to no avail.

I despised authority on so many levels and engraved into my mind that injustice is prevalent even at an early age. Although I couldn't name it, I felt it. It's one thing to get punished for an actual wrongdoing but completely ludicrous to get punished for someone else's lie. Therefore, I remind myself that the job is important to combat those injustices for so many who cannot defend themselves because authority figures are untruthful at times, based on my own experience. Not true for everybody, I realize. The struggle lessens.

Dragon Wagon

What! A new addition? Not too long after Rob's jailhouse departure, Mom hooked up with a Sugar Daddy, or (more like) he found a hot mama, considering his age—probably a little of both. His name was Stan. Lisa and I referred to him as "Stan the other man."

He was definitely older in years in comparison to Mom. In fact, he almost looked like someone's grandpa with a tanned, sun-weathered face and deep wrinkles—half carpenter, half cowboy. He had reddish-blond hair and a long shabby beard like Abe Lincoln, and he liked to "soak up the sauce" (drank a lot of beer), according to Mom's figure of speech. In no time, Mom joined in.

This hookup was somewhat confusing to me because Mom was still receiving jail mail from Rob on a regular basis and taking his collect calls, and as far as I knew, they were still married and not going to separate—not yet anyway. I'd hear her conversing on the phone saying, "I love you, can't wait until you come home," and the like. We were hoping that would change. We started rooting for Stan to be her permanent man.

Aside from the constant drinking, Stan appeared to be a good man, not mean-spirited like what we were used to, and obviously cared about us as a whole and our basic needs. Since we were without transportation, he showed his generosity and purchased the family a light-yellow station wagon, later nicknamed "Dragon Wagon." You'll later find out why. When he pulled up in the driveway, I'll never forget the look on Mom's face when he said, "Now you can go and see your girls." He was referring to Shelly and Sarah.

Even though they didn't appear to be a good matchup appearance-wise, he made Mom smile.

Stan was a pleasurable man. He had a youthful, playful spirit especially when he was drinking—a happy drunk. Instead of playing chess like Rob, he got on the floor, opened up the Game of Life, put our cars on start, and say, "Lorrie, you're blue. Spin the wheel."

"Lisa, you're red, you're next."

Wow, good times—playing the Game of Life instead of dealing with the game of life.

Even though I enjoyed the challenge of chess with Rob, just playing a simple board game was less stressful. To my surprise, I didn't have the competitive drive to win.

Dragon Wagon was our temporary ticket out of the ghetto, especially during summer months. Lisa and I lit up when we heard Stan's voice. "You girls, go get your mother and get in the wagon. We're going somewhere." He took us to American River, on hiking trips, seashell searching on various sightseeing excursions while he and Mom popped open another beer can.

His spontaneity outweighed the obvious drunkenness, for the time being anyway; and like any addiction, it progressed to where Dragon Wagon served another purpose other than transportation.

We ended up at a run-down bar on Tennessee Street during trips to visit Mom's friend from high school in Vallejo—Mom and Stan dancing it up inside the bar and us frustrated outside sitting in the wagon for hours. We were petrified as we witnessed the drunkards stumble onto the sidewalk and stare and point their fingers at us parked on the main street. Whereas when it was raining, we felt safer due to the fogged-up windows and the spectators' inability to see us.

Lisa and my perception changed; rooting for Stan quickly turned into a boot for the man. Little did we know that our wishes would turn into a worse nightmare later.

Twice a month was bittersweet as I got older. I was grateful to finally get the cabinets stocked with food (thanks to the government) but resentful at the same time. Although hunger pangs were temporarily relieved, there was a price to pay to get our needs met always.

THE PAWN

Bimonthly, our family's so-called Mother's Day, Mom was consumed with grocery shopping to stock the bare cupboards once the mailman arrived. First stop, we headed for the long food-stamp line at the post office. It looked like a bread line during a recession, which took hours prior to even getting to the store. Being the oldest, of course, it was my responsibility for overseeing car duties (while Mom was shopping), holding down the ruckus, intervening during sibling rivalry times, and soothing the irritation that had been building during those scorching summer temperatures—that is, until I lost it, feeding into my own frustration and reaching the boiling point, hot as the sweltering pavement beneath us.

During those peak August hours, it felt like we were actually sitting in the Mojave Desert. The heat's intensity magnified by the minute while our eyes stayed glued to the entrance door, hoping and praying that she was the next person we'd see pushing the shopping cart toward our car. As more time went by, our sighs got louder and louder, sometimes kicking the dashboard out of anger with my sisters. Supposedly being the one in control, I was worse than my younger siblings in controlling my frustration at times. It seemed as though hours had gone by—and I mean *hours*. We pictured her nonchalantly strolling from aisle to aisle, stop and go, trying to locate items on her coupons in a nicely air-conditioned building while her children sweat profusely, miserably uncomfortable, and seconds away from a heatstroke waiting for her return. Then something occurred to me—no wonder why we named that station wagon what we did. We were burning up in there. *That is how Dragon Wagon's name was birthed. Nailed it.*

Christmas shopping was a struggle too, but instead of the heat, it was the damp, cold weather. I remember pulling into the shopping center parking lot around midday, and Mom didn't return until the sunset. We'd blow smoke rings from our breath for entertainment and bet on whose smoke rings would last the longest. Guess who had more experience?

When the girls were down during vacation, Dragon Wagon looked like hydraulics had been installed due to the movement of five bodies jumping, hopping from one seat to another, fighting, and screaming with frustration. Bad shocks, maybe? Nevertheless, onlookers walked by, shook their heads like they wanted to say something, but minded their own business—that was the norm in those days. It's a miracle that no one called the cops on us. *Oh no! Not another outing with Mom. But honestly, I should have been grateful for that privilege rather than Rob being home. Period.*

It's Saturday morning once again. We all piled in Dragon Wagon headed down Interstate 80 toward San Francisco for that dreadful two-and-a-half-hour drive that made me sick to my stomach. Mom had a way of distracting my car sickness as I watched her head swaying back and forth to the beat of "Treat Her Like a Lady" by the Cornelius Brothers and Sister Rose playing on the radio while she turned it up louder through the semiblown speakers.

"Ooh, I love this song," she blurted out. She liked to change the words from *sentimental* to *Sacramento*. It just fit.

Other than Rob, our family had a deep appreciation for "soul music" and its ability to set the body in motion for the family groove instantly—a time to escape and forget about our problems. In no time, we all looked like beep-bopping bobbleheads trucking down the highway. We took advantage of our soul-time freedom together because Rob didn't allow soul music in our home. In fact, he would probably smash the radio like he did the TV if he ever found out.

I could see Mom's eyes in the rear-view mirror. Brewing anticipation with an eagerness to see Rob for those long-awaited visiting hours was obvious in her big brown eyes. In addition to the lingering stale cigarette smoke, there was a sense of nervous energy that filled the car when the music stopped, and the giggles died down, which meant we were getting closer to the destination.

The "Welcome to Clayton" sign, surrounded by a variety of trees and dead grass saturated with water from the winter rain starving for rejuvenation, meant we were almost there.

Upon our arrival, something out of the ordinary was happening. Cars in front of us were turned away by security as we witnessed their U-turns. Disappointment was obvious, followed by tears and frowns.

We pulled up to the security booth.

"Inmate's name please?" the man in a uniform asked.

Mom responded with his name.

The guard quickly flipped through some paperwork. "Ma'am, I cannot let you in. He's not allowed any visitors due to a disciplinary action taken, and he's on the list."

"What happened?"

"Several inmates were caught over on the female side, and he was one of them."

"But I came all the way from Sacramento," Mom pleaded, shooting for a little sympathy.

"I'm sorry, I cannot allow any visitor in for this inmate," he said with a stern tone.

"When can he have visitors?" she asks.

"I'm not sure. You'll have to call in and check in with the front desk."

There was dead silence that lingered for miles, completely the opposite from moments ago. No music.

Then out of nowhere, Mom said, "Hey, I've got an idea. Since we're up here anyway, let's go see Grandma."

Finally, she's thinking. Now that's something to sing about, I thought.

Lisa winked at me, and I knew she was thinking the same thing. We couldn't hold back our excitement any longer. Our arms raised up in the air, and we screamed, "Grandma, here we come!"

It had been a long, long time with many changes we'd soon find out about. Of course, Mom already knew, but we didn't. We were approaching San Pablo Avenue, just about to turn the corner, when Mom pointed to a white house with baby-blue trim and said, "That's where Grandma lives, but she's over here."

We pulled into the Eagles' Hall parking lot, some sort of veterans' hangout or senior-citizen club that was conveniently located kitty-corner across an alley from Grandma's house.

When we walked through the door, it smelled funky: a combination of cheap flowery fragrances all mixed together, just like the familiar smell in Newberry's cosmetic section. There was a thick gray cloud of cigarette smoke, and there was booze and Willie Nelson playing on the jukebox. I noticed the cloud lose its strength as it moved up toward the window behind the bartender area. Nothing else mattered when I laid eyes on Grandma sitting on the barstool as if she was the only one in the room. Bear hugs, bear hugs—smooches, smooches. Immediately she shuffled through her purse to see what goodies she could find. Of course, it had been a while.

The bartender interrupted quickly and distracted us, with good reason. "What would you two young ladies like this afternoon?" she asked.

"Shirley Temples with a cherry on top," Lisa and I responded in unison.

Good memories.

Chapter Reflection

While leaving us with a babysitter would have been preferable, I can empathize with her reasoning for leaving us in the car. Back then, it was acceptable. Stepping in her shoes for a moment, it would have been impossible for her to stay focused on grocery shopping, especially with coupons, while all of us wild children ran around the store, grabbed food items, and threw goodies into the cart. I mean, I could just imagine how unruly our behavior would have been. Starving children in a grocery store? No way. But as a child, every moment probably felt like five—just like in the corner, which made it intolerable. I wanted to escape.

As an adult, I acknowledge that whenever I felt any type of pain, I wanted to run or escape, whether physically or emotionally. I would self-sabotage and wanted to literally hurt myself. Based on my history, this kind of behavior was my norm. I hated myself regardless—horrible person or not. Thank God for His forgiveness and mercy for me today.

THE PAWN

O Lord, you are so good, so ready to forgive, so full of unfailing love for all who ask for your help. (Psalm 86:5)

*****

Friday, December 1, the phone rang. Dustin had been in the hospital exactly two weeks now. My heart raced. The thought occurred to me, *It's either good news or bad news.* My hands trembled like they normally do in an instant with the uncertainty of who's on the other line.

"Hi, may I please speak to Lorrie?"

"Speaking," I said.

After a brief pause, the person on the other line said, "This is Dr. Owens," with deep sincerity.

I could tell by the sound of his voice that something wasn't right. I held my breath for a second.

"I need to let you know that Dustin's condition has progressively worsened overnight, and we need to meet to discuss his prognosis. Do you think Wednesday will work for you and your partner?" he asked.

"Well, if his condition is getting worse, why not today?" I responded in a harsh tone. "And don't you think it's best that he be transferred to Children's Hospital like I've been saying all along?" I said with a matter-of fact tone.

"Unfortunately, I'm on call the next few days, so my schedule is unpredictable, making it virtually impossible to schedule any meetings. Besides, I still want time to consult with some of my colleagues and have them present if possible. In response to your second question, those are some of the options I would like to discuss with you at the meeting. Will that date work for the both of you?"

"I guess it will have to be Wednesday then, huh? Where? What time?" I asked snappily.

"Neonatal Unit, conference room, about 11:00 a.m. I look forward to seeing you both there," he said with a slight nervousness in his voice.

This was the call I had been dreading. My hope was getting that call: "You can pick him up now—he's ready to come home." But somewhere deep down, I knew I was in denial.

I hung up the phone, walked to Dustin's room, and shut the door. I plunged my forehead into the door, beating myself up in a weird kind of way by knocking my head in a forward motion and asking myself why. *How could I have been so self-centered to do this to my baby? This is all my fault.*

Closing the door was my way of shutting out the truth so I didn't have to look at my reality. It was too painful to see myself as I really was: a monster.

I lingered around like a zombie for the rest of the day until Jason returned home from work. We decided to take a drive to visit Dustin and maybe prove the doctor wrong.

No music. Dead silence. The drive to the hospital felt slow motion even though we were going the speed limit. All I could do was stare at the fruitless fields.

Upon arrival, my hands started trembling as all the visual memories of this nightmarish building came racing back. Dizziness set in. I took a minute to get out of the truck and sighed.

As we walked into the Critical Care Unit, all the nurses stopped what they were doing and stared, presenting a flat-affect look. More dead silence.

Drawing back Dustin's hospital bed curtain, I understood why this unit felt like a cemetery. He had a little Santa hat propped on his swollen head, his face covered with red blotches, tubes inserted everywhere, his body severely bruised from all the needle pokes. His chest pulsated uncontrollably from the breathing machine. He looked like he had gained weight, not from the nutritional standpoint but from massive fluid buildup. I didn't even recognize him; his face was distorted, grossly discolored.

"He looks like he's dying. Oh my goodness, Jason, our baby's dying!" I shouted and dove headfirst into his chest. I was overwhelmed with sadness and sobbed on his shoulder. Then it hit me. I couldn't help but think about his comment when I was rushed to the hospital, wishing that the baby and I would die. A deep disgust overwhelmed me, and I pushed him away. I didn't want him to touch me. Half of his wish was coming true before our very eyes.

I couldn't take it. Watching my baby suffocate was taking its toll on my emotions. All of a sudden, the monitors started beeping, red lights flashing like an ambulance was in the room. My body started shaking because I was unsure of what was happening. I was scared. The nurses rushed in trying to console me and advised that his heart rate was accelerating due to the excitement, which wasn't in his best interest, and suggested that I settle down. My ability for calmness wouldn't even register; I was incapable. Obviously, I was making the situation worse. The intensity of my own guilt was unbearable as I watched the nurses frantically grapple with the machinery; then eventually they stopped the noise. The presence of the nurses magnified my shame—not by what they said but how they looked at me. Pitiful. I gently squeezed his little hand, gave him a kiss on his forehead, and told him that Mommy would be back.

The ride home was ten times longer than getting there. I felt like a sitting dead woman—speechless, lifeless, numb. In a weird kind of way, I wanted to do drugs. *How can I think of such a thing when my baby is suffering because of my addiction? I must be a horrible person.*

I guess I had to see for myself. I hated to admit that the doctor was right, and Dustin wasn't getting any better, which hurt to the core of my being. At least I wasn't in denial anymore, and my hopes for his survival were diminishing by the minute. I couldn't help but think, *What does that really mean? Am I going to jail? Am I going to be charged with murder? What's going to happen to Nicole?* All those questions were racing through my head, and I wanted to use drugs even more—but instead I went to bed in hopes that his condition would improve by the time I woke up. Checkout.

I pretty much slept until Wednesday's appointment, severely depressed. Jason took the day off from work so we both could be there. Deep down, I despised him for not supporting me during a time when I needed him the most. He continued to use drugs while I had to remain in my own body, feeling extremely uncomfortable in my own skin and not wanting to feel. He called me jealous. I called him an insensitive, selfish pig. Most of the time, I kept my mouth shut (which was hard to do), or it would have become a blown-up, knock-down, drag-out fistfight. We were growing apart by the day.

When we arrived up at the Critical Care Unit conference room, I was expecting an entourage of medical staff, but that wasn't the case. One of the nurses guided us into the smaller waiting room. Maybe the conference room was occupied.

Dr. Owens sat there alone with his legs crossed, I guess waiting for our arrival. Hmm, that was weird. I thought he said he wanted his colleagues to be here.

"Please have a seat," he politely suggested, pointing to the chairs directly across from him. "I brought you both in here today to go over Dustin's prognosis, and unfortunately, I have bad news, I'm sorry to say."

"I know he's not doing well after visiting him. He actually looks like he's going to die," I sadly pointed out.

Somber silence remained for a moment; one could hear a pin drop.

The doctor cleared his throat, trying to fight his emotion. The intellect soon followed. "First of all, your son has viral meningitis. Despite all the antiviral medication, his condition is rapidly worsening," he said, tapping his foot. "We are trying different medications, and our hopes are that he will improve. However, if he doesn't, there are three possibilities that may occur."

I sat in a hunched position with my hands folded in between my legs midway on the chair. "What's that?" I asked, hoping there was something positive out of the three.

"Well, there's a possibility he may become blind, have brain damage, or cerebral palsy, which will require a lot of attention. And... unfortunately, the worst-case scenario is that he could die as a result of having this condition."

Jason and I were stunned when he said the *d* word.

The ride home was déjà vu of the two days prior. The doctor confirmed my greatest fears about our son's devastating condition, future disabilities, or possible death. By his facial expressions, his obvious lack of confidence in my parenting ability if my son were to survive was evident, no doubt.

Leader of the Pack

Rob's bust in the clinker obviously stirred an awakening in Mom's heart. Besides, the visit with Grandma might have enlightened her to take a second look spiritually.

She was willing to jump at the opportunity despite Rob's unspiritual influence and ruthless authority. Deep down, she knew something had to change. Up until then, we were taught how to cheat, lie, steal; inappropriateness; criminal activity, violence, drug use; who the "pigs" were; and that snitches die. So her attempt to introduce us to her Catholic roots was rather ridiculous and too late, in my opinion. This remedy for redemption was sending us to catechism class with a stranger we had never seen before. In my mind, Mom was the one who needed deliverance and should go with us. She didn't.

Nancy was her name—a tall, slender redheaded woman with a pixie-type hairdo, fair-skinned, and naturally toned. She pulled up in a four-door faded maroon vehicle every Saturday and honked. I'd be ready to go, not because I was excited to learn about God but for the frequent stops we made to the ice-cream shop after class. During class time, my thoughts were preoccupied by two banana slices resting on the side of an oval bowl, a scoop of vanilla ice cream plopped in the middle covered in rich, thick chocolate syrup, sprinkled with nuts and topped with a cherry. My mouth watered entertaining the vision, waiting anxiously for those departing words, "See you next week, class," chiming in my ear. This recipe was more appealing than any spiritual bread message. If Mom asked me what I had learned, I would have said, "Banana splits are yummy." She never asked.

Nancy's ice-cream incentive worked. Over time, I was not totally shut off from the spiritual transformation. Mostly, I wanted forgiveness (not for anyone else but for myself), though I would never forgive Nana.

Springtime was the season that Lisa and I would receive our first communion, which symbolized we had achieved some spiritual growth. However, confession had to occur before I would be able make that walk down the aisle and receive communion. I had to forget about the banana splits and focus on memorizing the Our Father and Hail Mary prayers. I was stunned when the priest ordered me to repeat a hundred Hail Marys after I admitted wishing people would die. I couldn't see his facial expression behind the curtain, but I visualized his eyes bulging wide open after I said I wanted to kill Nana when I got big. That must have been pretty shocking coming from a nine-year-old child. I'm sure he had heard worse in his vocation, right? He also added several repetitions for my ongoing five-finger discount problem. (I was a slick thief by then). I couldn't help but to think, *If I continue to snitch on myself, I'll be praying for days and miss the ceremony.* I shut up.

The best part of the communion (besides me being center of attention for a day) was witnessing Balloon Grandma's pride sitting in the audience (our number one cheerleader). She was obviously overjoyed that her grandchildren accomplished that important step by carrying on the family tradition. I didn't want to disappoint her. She was not only my grandmother but, then, my godmother. Afterward, they celebrated our milestone. We were fitted in fancy white dresses, laced veil headdresses, holding our Bibles while the relatives clicked their Polaroid cameras, encouraging us to smile. It was a good day.

I wish I could say that my character was totally transformed and all my defects had disappeared. Don't get me wrong. I did change for a while with Nancy's support, but I guess my heart wasn't in the right place to begin with. It was all about my sweet tooth instead of learning about God.

Soon Rob was back at home. Nancy vanished from our lives, and the familiar clan scene resumed in no time. Within months, like the ol' saying goes, "Monkey see, monkey do." I became exactly what I hated. I soon developed my own gang, riding beat-up bicycles rather than motorcycles. I thought I was "big and bad." One member of our minigang was Kelly, a cute blonde blue-eyed classmate who lived around the corner. From her outer appearance, she looked like a typical all-American kid. However, she developed a little thuggish behavior from her so-called past. Her father was a reformed dude who turned his life around. He resorted to other tendencies instead. His obesity required XXXL overalls. I don't recall seeing him wear anything else. Whatever works.

Included in our little gang was Little Lucy. She was a small-boned, scrawny girl who compensated for her puny size with her quick-wit, troublemaking, feisty, take-no-crap attitude. Mischief was a bonus. Also involved (tagalong was more like it) was her little sister, Clumsy Julie—a shy girl in the awkward growing stage who wore thick bifocals that covered most of her face. She had long stringy hair that dropped into her eyes to cover those big glasses. Undoubtedly, that contributed to her gawkiness.

There also was Tracy, Little Lucy's best friend, who was a bit chubbier than the rest of us but also had extreme antagonistic behavior. That was a plus. It took no time for Lisa to get involved. I, being the oldest, had gained recognition for being the leader of the pack, or so I thought.

Leading the way, we were running amuck, creating havoc up and down Woodland Street, scouting our territory looking for trouble. The classic wet-toilet-paper attack, egg hits, and ding-dong ditch were the primary instigations around our neighborhood. It's funny. I would have to manipulate Kelly to go steal items for attack since we seldom had anything at our house (food, toilet paper, etc.) that was beneficial. Even if we did have food, it was idiotic to consider wasting it.

Showtime! We'd hide in the bushes and crack up when the neighbors exerted their sourpuss grins, cursing and grumbling about the inconvenience as they hosed down their vehicles to remove the hardened splattered egg. We'd pedal down the street the next day playing dumb. A couple people gave us the finger when we rolled by, yelling, "Don't let me catch you." We'd laugh.

We'd ride to our hideaway tent made from blankets with short wooden sticks used as stakes pounded in four corners. We inserted a long pole in the middle from the inside for breathing room. We'd brainstorm other ways to distract from the boredom.

"Guess what happened at my house last night?" Kelly blurted out.

"What now?" Tracy responded, her voice sounding as if anything was possible at Little Lucy's house.

"You know that stupid, nosey neighbor that lives next door to us?"

"Yeah," we all said in unison.

"He called the cops on my sister last night for having a party, said we were making too much noise," she said. "Teri was playing that new song from Janis Joplin, 'Somebody to Love,' full blast, but he could have told us to turn it down, or he could have put some dang earplugs on."

That was all that needed to be said. Next target?

We all looked at each other wide-eyed. Mr. Fletcher was in for a special surprise. Not toilet paper or eggs but dog duke for the snitch.

Neighbors were hot on our tails. We had to escape the radar and explore other areas outside our norm a few miles away, especially after almost getting my little butt whooped recently by a boy that I was antagonizing for years. He was fed up.

About a mile away, the nearest mom-and-pop minimart was located through an industrial park that was desolate during nonwork hours. The area was surrounded by vacant parking lots and dingy faded gray dumpsters. Across a main intersection, we bypassed an elderly independent living community of "flashers."

In my view at the time, Sacramento was not only the capital of California but also the capital of weirdoes, perverts, and predators lusting after children to satisfy their twisted way of thinking.

Of course, I know this behavior is not limited to Sacramento. This is widespread—anywhere, anytime. It's that my perception was reinforced one blistering hot summer day heading home from the community pool. The gang and I gallivanted through the industrial park when a dusty off-white two-door sedan rolled upon us. An ugly older white man, midforties, with dirty sandy-blond hair and an overgrown multicolored mustache approached us, looking a bit frazzled as if he was lost. That was easy to do. He slowed down and, with his head tilted slightly out of the window, asked, "Hey, does anyone know where Montgomery Street is?" (or whatever street he said).

I stopped and attempted to point him in the right direction while the gang continued to walk on.

Not paying any attention, I noticed several boxes in the back seat with blankets, disheveled clothing, along with toiletries loosely hanging out as if he lived in his car. As my eyes surveyed the back seat, suddenly he reached out of the window and grabbed my arm with one hand and opened the car door with the other. I was too quick for him to shove me into his car, and I yanked my arm away in desperation and screamed for help. Meanwhile, the gang ran like a herd of cattle instead of coming to my rescue. I managed to escape his grip by slamming his wrists into the car door and jetted off, bypassing those slowpokes. On my way passing them up, I yelled, "Thanks a lot, you chickens. That guy almost kidnapped me back there!"

I then realized that I was the leader of the poop-butt, sissy —— gang. Pathetic.

Just as the season changed, so did our lives. As a few autumn leaves fell from the barren trees, our hopes for freedom disintegrated from thin air. We knew the time had arrived when Stan the other man looked at us with puppy-dog eyes, gave us a farewell hug, momentarily stood at the front door with a suitcase in his hand, and waved goodbye. We never saw him again. Even though Stan was gone, his memory rolled on—Dragon Wagon.

Our silly juvenile gangbanging efforts carried on for a while but diminished when Rob's jail cell reopened, and he arrived back home. Lisa and I were soon summoned back to active slave duty, and our outdoorsy lifestyle was over. The reformed new man Rob put a damper on our schemes—except one. A couple of Mom's best friends, actually the parents of Tracy and Lucy, devised a plan to rob

Joan's ex-fling's house in attempt to retaliate against him for some reason and recruited us since we had a reputation for sticky fingers. We were given permission to carry out a robbery while they kept the ex-boyfriend distracted in the other room.

Joan convinced us that we would not get into trouble by saying, "Don't worry about getting caught. Guarantee you, Ernie will be soaking up the suds." She mimicked his drinking patterns by pretending to gulp down an imaginary can of beer in a fast motion.

"He won't realize that anything's missing. Just load up whatever you can find," Sherry told us.

Ernie was already buzzed upon arrival, still standing but wavering no doubt, with watery, bloodshot eyes. The house smelled like a bachelor's party pad—sour beer and stale cigarettes. An unexplainable heaviness also lingered. Beer tops popping, chatter turned into mumbo jumbo before dusk hit. Voices mushroomed as they sat around the small oval wooden kitchen table crammed against the wall. Ernie's words became more slurred, and soon after stumbling footsteps emerged in his attempt to dance to "I Can See Clearly Now" by Johnny Nash that was playing in the background.

Preoccupied, you could say, mingling with the gals and the rhythm of the music distracting enough that he didn't have a clue what was about to happen. Joan was right. I chuckled because of the song.

Mom's other friend, Sherry, gave us the go-ahead nod to proceed with the plan. It was on. Within an hour, we had wiped out a huge amount of his belongings including jewelry, antiques, collectibles, and expensive knickknacks and then loaded the items in the car—lickety-split.

When the alcohol wore off, Ernie must have been shocked by our low-down, scandalous thievery. It was obvious he had been robbed blind. It didn't take long for the shocking news to get back to Mom.

She was disgusted that we were involved in taking advantage of a vulnerable man who was still mourning his wife's death after a tragic accident. Apparently, some years earlier, his wife had died in his arms after being run down by a drunk driver after leaving a nightclub. He always blamed himself, according to Mom. After that, his children were sent to a foster home. His lost his entire family and was overly burdened with guilt and couldn't seem to pull it together.

No wonder why he drank.

After hearing his sad story, I was ashamed for my involvement. Condemnation ruled in Mom's eyes. I knew she wanted to beat us.

"How could you both do such a thing?" She pointed her finger at me as if she was holding me responsible for the idea. "Just wait until your father hears about this one." She was leaving the beating up to Rob.

"Lisa, how were we supposed to know about Ernie's life? She is acting like this is our idea. She needs to blame her friends for that, not us."

Turned out, Rob blamed Mom's friends instead of us. For once, he got it right.

Our family dynamics had been out of balance with Rob's transformation, but it didn't take long for that familiar dysfunction to maneuver its way back in. Soon we were dangling from thick strings like puppets again. Rob was again at the top of the pyramid controlling our every movement, so to speak. He had our lives spinning around in circles: from the invasion of the clan, a part-time motorcycle maintenance chop shop in our living room, late-night parties, to the "get me a cup of coffee" routine, n—— lover innuendoes, and "what happens to a snitch" theory. Unfortunately, the awful beatings were the norm again. Most of the time, the garage (his playhouse) looked like a bottle-recycle joint. Soggy cigarettes butts mixed with stale smoke and contaminated blue-jean funk lingered. Rob soon wanted Mom to participate in encounters that were against her moral compass and values. We didn't know what that meant at the time, but whatever it meant, she was appalled.

A taste of freedom stripped away—yet again. I wanted to run away and tell someone, but the more I thought about it, the more scared I got. It worked. The dying-snitch brainwash theory worked.

"Praaaay, Lisa, pray," I whined.

It worked. This time, it wasn't the clinker who sent him away; it was another woman. (Yay! Hopefully he was never coming back!)

Sleazy B——

Before we had the chance to pick up where we had left off with our neighborhood monkey business, things were about to change dramatically. Mom was holding an extra envelope beside the usual Mother's Day government check. She waved the envelope at us with excitement in her eyes and said, "Finally!" We thought she was referring to the welfare money; we were always waiting for the mailman like he was Santa Claus.

Apparently, it was a notification from a new government program that offered affordable housing for low-income families.

"We're leaving this place for good," she shouted and then snickered.

"You mean we're really moving from Woodland Street?" We kept in mind that we'd moved several times before but had remained on the same street.

"We're getting the heck out of here," she hollered exuberantly.

Lickety-split. Within a month, Mom found us another place to live.

This was our ticket out of the ghetto and leaving the past behind—without Rob. Even though it was a new start, there was a sadness saying goodbye to Woodland Street for good.

We piled in Dragon Wagon and headed east toward a small city outside of Sacramento approximately thirteen miles called Rancho Cordova. As we pulled up toward our new suburb community, I noticed a cheerful couple gripped onto the leashes of their Alaskan Malamutes. They were smiling at the admirers, obviously proud of their show-dog ownership and enjoying the springtime weather as we drove past.

This was unreal—a new environment, neighbors-walking-the-dog kind of day, which reminded me of Grandma's house.

"Wow, this place even has sidewalks," I noted. "Must be moving up."

We pulled up and stopped in front of an off-white modern-looking L-shaped house. There was a flower bed filled with colorful petunias sprouting from the ground just below the front bedroom window. I was relieved that I saw the garage detached kitty-corner from the dwelling—just in case Rob returned. We just never knew.

Our first day of school was interesting from the setting to the instruction, very different from what we were used to in the ghetto. How would we fit in?

We lived on the other side of the main freeway, and the only entryway for walkers was via an overpass. Our new school was oddly structured, oval-shaped, and the building's sheet metal glared from its rooftop. It looked like the school had solar panels before they existed. I had never seen anything like it. From a distance, it looked as if a UFO had landed in the middle of a barren field, out in the middle of nowhere, especially the view from the overpass. Quite bizarre yet fascinating.

The brown building had windows surrounding the outer exterior, creating a certain beam of brightness when the sun reflected off the spotless windows. The interior had its own uniqueness. There were no doors for entry into the classrooms, and it looked like a huge maze—interesting atmosphere for any child. If it was too noisy from the other classes, the teachers had the option of closing the partitions, which looked like a giant accordion, for privacy. I was fascinated and had a hard time believing that was actual school. What a trip! But honestly, I still was homesick for Woodland Street and being away from the childhood gang.

Weekday mornings, Lisa and I strolled through the bypass, flashed our peace signs toward the cars down below during morning commute, and persuaded the truckers to honk their horns, recalling the good old times with Uncle Allen. Things couldn't have been better.

Lisa wasted no time gaining popularity with her cuteness, her rosy-red cheeks, and her ability to make friends with little effort. For me, not so easy.

The highlights of our weekends were a combination of the milkman stopping in front of our house and let us choose anything on the menu until payday and the privilege of petting the neighborhood snow-white Samoyed dogs—eventually getting to walk the dogs. Of course, the mailman was a given, as it always had been.

We were on top of the world.

A couple months later, returning home after school, Lisa and I heard a loud scream that sounded familiar.

"You —— —— [terrible name-calling vulgarities]. Who gave you permission to sell my Harley?"

Lisa and I looked at each other astounded.

"Oh my goodness, he's back!"

When we opened the front door, there was complete silence—not typical at all. That was quite unusual because, normally, he (Rob) didn't care who was witnessing his tyrannical behavior. Before we dropped our backpacks on the floor, Rob bolted around the corner waving two dollar bills. Lisa and I could tell he wasn't in the mood for introductions (nor were we), so we stood in the doorway, paralyzed.

"I want you guys to go the store right now. Buy yourselves something," he demanded. "And don't come back for a while." Bribery or not, we didn't question his authority—even still.

We left the house scared for our mother, not knowing what to do.

"He is going to beat her when we're gone," I predicted.

On the way to the store, Lisa said, "I've got an idea. Let's take a shortcut so that we can get back there as soon as we can, so maybe we can stop it."

Wishful thinking.

We did just that. We completely ignored his demand to stay away and returned fairly quickly after spending his money on candy. However, in the short time we were gone, it seemed the situation had escalated, which was no surprise. He was repeating the same question over and over about the bike's whereabouts, but we couldn't hear our mother's response, like maybe he was covering her mouth.

Here we go again. As we approached the hall entryway, our mother was plastered to the hallway wall with both feet off the floor, hanging by Rob's hands. Her face was turning blue from lack of oxygen. There was our answer; that's why she was unable to speak.

We hammered our fists on his back, terrified that he was about to murder our mother. In the midst of our screaming, he came to his senses, loosened his grip, and let go of her neck. We watched her body drop to the floor, and she deeply inhaled for a breath of air.

After catching her breath, she screeched loudly, "I had to hide it somewhere because of welfare. I had your friend hold it for you until you got out." Her elbows tightly gripped around her head.

He suddenly fired back on a rampage, "He's not my friend anymore. I can't stand that —— ——."

"How was I supposed to know that?" Mother responded. "The last time I knew, you guys were friends, and I trusted him to take care of the bike."

"He's bragging around town that he bought my bike." Then his jaw muscles began to pulsate with each word, as if he was ready to explode again.

Time didn't come soon enough when he stormed out of the house, cursing obscenities, then slammed the door behind him. The last words we heard were, "I should kill you, sleazy b——."

Shortly thereafter, Mom took a couple of heavy, deep breaths and settled down. Silence again—then *wham!* A revelation hit.

"He almost killed me over a —— motorcycle. Can you believe that?" she stated, then looked up to the ceiling. I think she was questioning her own head because she wasn't looking at us for an answer.

Lisa and I nodded in absolute agreement anyway, reassuring her that she was most definitely on the right track.

She sighed for a moment. "Well, that's it! No more. It's all over," she screamed. However, Lisa and I were a bit surprised; we thought it was already over when we moved from Woodland Street. Maybe this was her validation that she did the right thing in the first place.

She walked over to the door, opened it, and then slammed it as if she just had thrown him out. Lisa and I liked that.

"Goodbye, —— ——!" she yelled, repeating the same vulgarities as he did.

We liked that too. We hoped that she never forgot that day.

Still Rob periodically showed up unannounced, grabbed some of his belongings, and continued to use the garage for personal storage, obviously still flexing his power and control, doing whatever he wanted, whenever he wanted. Of course, it was his way of keeping tabs on our situation, mainly Mom. During his revolving-door process, Rob dropped off a new addition to our family. Sleazy B——, he named her. She was a golden-brown Great Dane that looked grossly malnourished. Her rib cage protruded outwardly, and she appeared extraordinarily jumpy about her new surroundings. Or maybe she was just skittish beforehand. Who knows? Rob knew our mother was a pushover for stray animals; however, he took it upon himself to drop her off without permission. Not that Mom had any say-so anyhow.

Who names their dog Sleazy B——?

He chained her to the front patio faucet near the front door. Great. Flashback trauma from the Blackie (dog at Nana's) era awaits me and Lisa. More so me than Lisa. In fact, Lisa had to remind me, "At least the dog's chained up, so we won't get bit." Lisa was acting like the older sibling, as usual.

Life was starting to look on the bright side again. Rob was showing up less and less. Good for us, but not for Sleazy B——, with her natural protective instincts. When Rob finally popped in, she growled at him. He snapped.

"——, I saved your life. Now you're going to growl at me! I'll knock your teeth out." He shoved his boot into her rib cage. Luckily, she had put on some pounds to cushion her bones somewhat. She still dropped to the concrete and yelped for mercy, trying to protect herself the best she could confined to the chain around her.

From thereon after, every time he saw the dog, he kicked her as a reminder of her past disrespect.

"——, you'll never forget me now, will you?" he mocked as if she could respond.

I guess she got the message; she never growled at him again.

Nylon Man

The separation was getting to Mom, and soon she'd be out mingling in the nightlife to escape the loneliness—understandably. Even though Rob's sighting was less and less, the pain of him dropping by with another woman waiting in the car seemed to be wearing Mom down emotionally. Lisa and I were latching on to the long-overdue positive changes around us (mainly Rob's absence); however, we were in for another surprise: Mom's passion for dancing. We loved the fact that Mom was slowly healing from her horrific marriage, but her absence became more and more frequent, mainly at night.

One night while she was getting dolled up, Lisa ran up to her, screaming frantically, "There's a man outside looking through the window. Don't leave us here alone. I'm scared."

Apparently, the bright moonlight had created a silhouette of a tall, slender manly figure behind the sheets dangling from the clothesline, which frightened her.

Mom thought Lisa was using one of her manipulative tactics to persuade her to stay home that particular night. She looked at her with her eyebrows raised. "Lisa," she said, "you're seeing things. There's nobody out there. The dog didn't even bark."

"But I saw a man through the sliding glass window, I swear! He was standing behind the clothesline," Lisa exclaimed.

"Lorrie, did you see or hear anything?" Mom asked me.

Totally oblivious to what was going on, I responded truthfully and said, "No."

I looked at Lisa. Those natural rosy-red cheeks had disappeared and now looked as though she had seen a ghost. I knew she wasn't lying. As I continued to observe her pale face, I quickly changed my tune.

"Ummm…yes. I did see something," I responded a few seconds later.

Mom rolled her eyes again in a precarious fashion, brows raised backed with a tight-lipped smirk. She wasn't buying it and somehow knew I was lying, as she always knew. Overlooking Lisa's panicked plea, Mom must have thought we were in cahoots to keep her from leaving. It didn't work. She left the house that night, but locked all the windows and doors, attempting to reassure us that we'd be safe and she wouldn't be too long.

We knew she wasn't being truthful—not the way she was dressed up.

Lisa had an undeniably disappointment in her eyes. The tears rolled down her cheeks.

"I guess I blew it, huh?" I whispered.

"I don't think it really mattered anyway," Lisa sobbed. "She was going to go out no matter what."

After her departure, Lisa started freaking me out. "Did you hear that? Someone is out there," she said, notably extra sensitive to any noise, including house creaks, the wind blowing, or the dog's chain moving across the concrete pavement.

Soon we both were jumping out of our skins, petrified at the slightest sound multiplied by ten.

"Let's get out of here!" I demanded. Without hesitation, I swooped our baby sister Mary, and we ran frantically out the door. We were so frightened that I don't think we locked the door behind us.

We ran across the street to the neighbors who had let us walk their dogs in the past. We pleaded for her to let us stay there until our mother returned. She must have seen the fright in our eyes and welcomed us with open arms.

The kindhearted neighbor offered us something to drink and comforted us with her soft-spoken, reaffirming words. "You're safe now."

Lisa tried to forget about the Peeping Tom and acted like it never happened because the thought of our mother leaving us alone was too painful to believe. I believed it.

One day out of the blue, Rob showed up with his new girlfriend looking quite mysterious, as if he'd seen a ghost.

"Get your sisters' things together. You are coming to stay with me for a while. Something has happened to your mother. Don't ask any questions. Just do it," he demanded.

Although I wanted to know what had happened to Mom, I did not question his authority. I felt as if I was just punched in the pit of my stomach, holding my breath involuntarily, perplexed and scared.

We arrived at an unfamiliar apartment. We (sisters and I) were ordered to sit on the couch, and all the while, he and his buddies were in the kitchen drinking and carrying on (same ol' motorcycle crosstalk) as if nothing happened. Thereafter, there was whispering, silence, whispering silence. Whispering was never in his character; therefore, we knew something serious had happened. As the drinking *continued*, the whispers became louder and louder. My ears were glued to every detail in attempt to gather enough information to draw my own conclusion.

Then I heard the unthinkable right out of Rob's mouth. "Apparently, Jenny was in a motorcycle accident and flew a hundred feet, splitting her head wide open. She's now in ICU with a head injury."

I could not believe my ears. *Is Mom going to die?* Trying to hold back the tears in order to protect our youngest sister from the awful news was impossible. In addition, I was trying to hide the fact we were sniveling and being nosey. Lisa and I took turns wiping our eyes dry, but our noses grew beet red—a total giveaway. All we could do for comfort was to hold each other's hands and squeeze, reminding ourselves to breathe. It was apparent that we would be staying there for who knows how long, I thought.

The fear of unknown was the hardest. While we were constantly worried if Mom was going to live or die, the party carried on as usual—celebrating their existence, drinking, skinny-dipping in the apartment pool with a total disregard for our feelings. Nothing new.

Then something unusual happened. To my amazement, right before my eyes, I witnessed the impossible. Rob was snitched on, and no one died. At least, as far as I knew. Apparently, a neighbor called the police and complained about the noise and exposed bodies in the complex's pool. When the police arrived, Rob was handcuffed and arrested. Before the police questioned us, Rob conveyed that he was caretaking until our mom got out of the hospital, and we did not live there.

This was our ticket out *again*. Incarceration always had a way of saving our butts (time after time).

After a few phone calls from the police, we found out Mom was at her girlfriend's house recuperating from the surgery, still in bad shape but wanted us with her. Arriving home, Mom looked to me like she was released from the hospital too early. Her head was wrapped in mesh-like gauze with white adhesive tape to cover up the stitches from the deep gash on her forehead. I could tell she was in pain. Although apprehensive about hurting her, we ran up and gave her a hug anyway to show our gratitude that she survived and that she was loved. *Relieved* is the best way to describe our emotions.

After Mom's concussion symptoms faded and she appeared healed (at least on the outside), our childish behavior resumed, and we were back to kids' stuff—admiring the neighborhood dogs, looking forward to the milkman, and swimming at the pool. I even broke my arm falling out of a tree.

I took a trip to the Sierra Nevada's for a one-week camping outing through a scholarship program for needy children. The worst part about the trip was craving for a cigarette *all the time*. Homesick for a cigarette at ten years old. *Ridiculous.*

When Aunt Sally came to visit, she would bribe me with money not to smoke, but I was a slave to nicotine, and the bribe would serve one purpose: purchase more cigarettes. I would accept Auntie's money, write a permission slip, sign my mother's name, and buy my own cigarettes. This was acceptable back in those days. A ten-year-old could purchase tobacco products with a note. Imagine that.

During this process, I became a forgery expert (Mother's signature), which came in handy later for writing my absence notes from school. I was on the path to destruction, sabotage, and ignorance.

One day coming home from the pool, we discovered Sleazy B—— was gone, missing. Nobody knew anything. I was going over many possibilities. Maybe she broke the chain and ran away, or maybe Rob picked her up then killed her, or maybe she died from starvation and was taken to the pound. It remained a mystery. Although, I did have my suspicions.

Lisa had gone to Grandma's without me that summer. Then about three weeks later, "Peeping Tom" struck again. This time, he did more than peeping. Even though I was disappointed about missing out at Grandma's, I was looking forward to the upcoming doctor's appointment to get my cast removed. I was relieved that I could scratch my arm without a knife or swim without that ridiculous rainbow-bread plastic bag wrapped around my cast with a rubber band cutting off the circulation of my forearm (creative inventions in order to go swimming).

June 28, 1973, the temperatures were scalding hot during the day, then dropped into the nineties that summer night. It was such a time when something spine-chilling happened.

I thought I was having a nightmare, but then I realized it wasn't a sleeping nightmare—it was a living nightmare. My body froze, paralyzed as I couldn't believe this was happening. With my eyes closed tightly, my thoughts were racing, my heart palpitating from anxiety and perplexity.

Oh my God, his hands are all over me—everywhere.

I remained silent for a second and pretended to be asleep, then courageously opened my eyes, petrified.

Directly in front of me, I saw a manly figure, his body halfway in the window, his lanky arms reaching over my bed that was located directly underneath the bedroom window.

The moonlight was shining brightly behind him, and he appeared to have nylon-looking material over his face, so his features remained unrecognizable and distorted. My body began to tremble uncontrollably. He must have realized that my eyes were larger than silver dollars, petrified with fear, as I started to squeal.

That startled him, or something did. Then I heard heavy footsteps running against the pavement, echoing from a distance, then quickly fading away. He was gone. I lay there in my bed contemplating what to do next since obviously Mom was still asleep. I was confused and wondering if this was a nightmare and was shaking my head about what to do next.

I need to tell Mom. But what if she doesn't believe me? I questioned. *I know. I'll leave my underpants down—then she'll believe me.*

I ran into her bedroom, screaming hysterically to wake her up, "Mom, there was someone in my window!" I yelled with pressured speech.

"Lorrie, you're having a nightmare," she said, her voice still groggy as if she was half-asleep.

I continued to repeat myself over and over while shaking her to alertness. She jumped out of her bed, shocked that this was a reality. She stormed down the hallway with her hand on her disheveled hair. She stood in my bedroom doorway and stared for a moment. It was as if time stood still in a creepy, weird kind of way, living-nightmare-like.

"I know I shut that window before I went to bed, so I know you're telling the truth," Mom stated.

I took a deep sigh of relief to hear those words. *She believes me.*

As she scrambled toward the telephone, she picked up a frying pan from the stovetop for protection and called 911. When the police arrived, they proceeded with their routine questioning, which made me extremely uncomfortable, having to verbalize the exact details about the sexual assault and having to rewind the last hour. However, one descriptive comment I made raised a few eyebrows during his questioning. One officer excused himself and brought my mother to the side for more questioning. I could hear his deep voice transmitting across the kitchen area.

"Pardon me for asking, ma'am, but what was that word she was referring to?" He was looking rather puzzled, seeking an explanation with a raised eyebrow.

My mother rolled her eyes. It was obvious by her red face that she was absolutely mortified explaining my vocabulary at ten years of age and what body part I was referring to (Gramp's language).

"Oh my goodness," my mother responded.

Shortly afterward, I heard whispers that I could not interpret, but I know what was said even if I did actually hear the verbal response.

"I never quite heard of that expression before," the officer commented, still somewhat bewildered, slightly shaking his head.

I heard another man yell from a distance, which echoed down the hallway and coming from the outside.

"Hey, I found something out here. Come here, guys, and bring the camera."

Right below my bedroom window was a flashlight lying on the ground, which was apparently left behind by the perpetrator. I saw the man take pictures of the evidence, then place the item in a plastic bag to be tested for fingerprints. My mother had a suspicious gaze in her eyes as if she was doing her own detective work during this process, her eyes fixated on the evidence: the yellow flashlight.

"That flashlight looks familiar," she said. "But, of course, there are hundreds of those flashlights around these days," she added, trying to dismiss her suspicions, then mumbled a few words under her breath. Then she paused for a moment and continued picking up where she had left off. "Ummm....it just seems mighty strange that the dog disappears, her sister that sleeps in the same room is currently away, and now this happens. Whoever did this had too much information and was more than a random episode," she said, adding her thoughts into the investigation.

I couldn't help but notice that she had selectively forgotten to tell them about Lisa witnessing the man in the backyard, probably because she had originally dismissed the seriousness of the former possibility of Peeping Tom and didn't follow through with a complaint that night. Wow! The fact that she tied our missing dog into this situation was a good assumption that I did not piece together. In hindsight, she was absolutely right. If our dog was present, she would have surely deterred and/or prevented that from happening altogether. *Well, maybe this scenario, but who knows?*

The officers finished up their questioning, carefully shut the window, and indicated that a professional would be out first thing in the morning to take fingerprints, reinforcing further instruction:

"Do not touch the window." They reassured us that they would continue to circulate the neighborhood looking for the suspect and for us not to worry and try to get some sleep.

That didn't help. I was creeped out, as I'm sure Mom was too.

A couple of men arrived early in the morning and brushed an ashy black substance onto the window frame with a paintbrush-looking item. We all stood nearby waiting with our fingers crossed in hopes they would get the evidence they needed to catch the weirdo. Suddenly their faces displayed an emotion with wrinkled chins and a "darn" smirk that we didn't want to witness: disappointment at its core.

"The problem here is, there are too many fingerprints overlapping one another that it is virtually impossible to get even one valid fingerprint," one man said. The tones of their voices signified that they were just as letdown as we were and worried that there was a sexual predator still on the loose. They continued to reassure us that they would pass on the information and do whatever they could to protect us, including interviewing the neighbors for possible leads. A revelation occurred to me that day. Police were no longer considered "pigs" in my view but rather heroes trying to catch the bad guy on my behalf.

When Lisa returned home from her visit about a week later, she noticed some of the leftover ashes on the windowpane instantly. I mean, how could you miss it? After she was told what happened, she blurted out in hysterics, "See! I told you I saw a man looking through the window that night, and you didn't believe me." Then she placed her right hand over her forehead, like, *Golly*. That was a jaw-dropping statement.

Mother stood there speechless, probably flabbergasted that Lisa was right and she had disregarded any potential danger. It must have been a relief for Lisa to know that she wasn't hallucinating or losing her mind, but again maybe she wished that she wasn't right in the first place.

The atmosphere had a lingering negative energy of paranoia, trepidation, and discomfort that surrounded us for weeks following that creepy night. Mother thought it would be worth the financial sacrifice to keep the lights on all night in hopes to deter any potential risk, which felt right at the time. However, Lisa and I were always "future tripping" (I don't know if that was even a word back then)—although, for good reason, based on past experiences when the bills were not paid, which happened quite frequency (rather typical struggles of any welfare recipient trying to make ends meet). We liked her idea in an attempt to keep us safe for the time being. In addition, with Nylon Man still at large and police patrolling our neighborhood on a regular basis, this eased our fears somewhat. Even though mother's nightlife excursions tapered off a bit, at least she found a babysitter to take care of us, not at our house but in another location when she had an upcoming date.

As months came and went, Nylon Man remained a mystery, along with our missing dog. We could not shake the future possibilities of what-if and constantly living in fear.

It was time to move on and leave that place and the awful memory that came with it behind. So, we did.

Chapter Reflection

I've concluded that leaving children alone was really no big deal during this era. The neighbor did not panic that we were left unattended or scold our mother upon her return or call the police. I guess this mindset was a part of the "it takes a village to raise a child" theory. She took care of us as if we were her long-lost children even though she barely knew us. In fact, I didn't even remember her name. Apparently, she stayed awake most of the night awaiting mother's return, then carried us back home. I don't remember if Mom got mad at us for running to the neighbor's house or not. If this situation were to happen nowadays, the police would have been called immediately. Surely, Child Protective Services would have been involved with the possibility of removal from our mother's care.

A part of me wishes that some sort of intervention had taken place to protect us. Then on the other hand, I would have worried too much about Mom's well-being. Obviously, we loved our mother. What I've learned from my past is that children love their parents regardless of what they might have done in the past and will always try to cover for them. Children love unconditionally. I wish I could say that remained true throughout my lifetime, but it most definitely did not. I had deep-rooted hatred, rage, and resentment toward my parents as an adult. In fact, I blamed them for all my bad choices, which left me unaccountable for my consequences and imprisoned within my own body. That was until the day I acknowledged the truth about myself and took responsibility for my actions.

As I was nearing completion of this book, mid-May 2018, my phone lit up with "Sis" displayed on the screen. I was surprised since Lisa rarely calls me during workdays unless it's something rather important, so I answered without hesitation. She was inquiring if I saw on the local news that the serial killer who was recently discovered was actually in Rancho Cordova right around the same time period that the "nylon man" incident occurred. She encouraged me to call the police to see if they had any DNA on the item that was found in my case. I was both hesitant and doubtful. However, Lisa's questioning did stir my curiosity about our new technology with DNA evidence and the possibility of finally getting some closure of this unsolved mystery. Even though I do not think the killer was the perpetrator in my case, I do have my suspicions of the culprit. For some odd reason within myself, I felt some resistance picking up the phone—almost like it doesn't matter anyway. Sitting at the dining-room table with my hand on my forehead, I stared at the phone. Then all of a sudden, it occurred to me that it *did* matter because *I matter*!

Going deeper within myself, I realized that over the years, this was never talked about, almost like it never happened—just forget it. But I never had the ability to completely forget. Something would trigger me, like Halloween or sometimes when I put a pair of nylons on. I never said anything, just shoved it down like everything else in my past. No more. I picked up that phone and called the police department. The lady on the other end was very short and rude; she cut me off and referred me to the Sheriff's Sexual Assault Unit. I was glad I didn't have to deal with her awful customer service, especially considering how vulnerable I was initiating this step in the first place.

I called the other department. Immediately, the voice on the receiving end sounded like an angel (maybe she was an angel). Just by the sound of her soft-spoken voice, my anxiety dissipated quickly, and I was able to communicate with clarity and ease. She listened with concern and compassion, validating my every word and assuring me that she would do everything in her power to locate my file, but there were some challenges ahead since the case was so old. Before hanging up, she mentioned it may take some time to search the archives and any possible upcoming challenges with conversion between city and county timelines. When I ended that call, something unusual swept over me, something invigorating and liberating that happened within my being. Regardless of the outcome for some long-awaited resolution, or if it remained an unsolved mystery, I've learned some valuable lessons within myself—my own truth:

- I had the courage to stand up for myself when no one else did.
- I'm not a victim. I am a victorious survivor, and I'm not staying silent anymore.
- I have a voice—and a loud one at that! Rather than the degrading label *loudmouth* being a hindrance from many opportunities, having made me shameful almost for decades, it's going to be an attribute that I will be most proud of. It's funny, different people have asked me multiple times in the past, "Why are you so loud?" My response would be, "Because no one ever bothered to hear me as a child." They shut their mouths.

A few months later, I received a call from a sergeant of that department who compassionately reiterated that too much time had passed, and all the files had been purged or destroyed. That didn't surprise me since it had been more than forty years, but it was helpful to hear directly from the source. I let him know that I appreciated the effort on my behalf and especially a returned phone call, which meant that someone cared enough to listen and investigate.

June 25, 2019, ironically the day before submitting my edited manuscript, I received a call from a retired Sacramento sheriff that currently works as a reserve officer investigating cold cases. Apparently, he had been assigned to the 1972–1973 Cordova cat burglar unsolved crimes during that time period, which might have been linked to another high-profile case. For the record, his investigation has been completed. He stated my incident happened 1973 (that's how I got the exact date). They were able to locate my police report after all these years since it had not been destroyed as previously indicated. It just so happens that my case was one of twenty-eight crimes committed in those surrounding areas. He mentioned that this particular area was the "epicenter and focal point" of multiple documented crimes. I told him I had my suspicions who I thought the culprit was all these years. He reassured me that my suspicions were wrong, and he was convinced the perpetrator was the "cat burglar," which had been documented at the bottom of my incident report.

I was utterly shell-shocked because I had never heard of such a person in my entire lifetime. But on the other hand, I believe without a television, of course, we'd were oblivious to what was happening around us. (Well, Lisa and I had a small TV in our bedroom, but we sure were not interested in news.) Yet again, Mom might have protected us after all by not divulging any information she possibly had at that time. Unsure. I have to say, I am relieved that the heavy burden has been lifted and the perpetrator wasn't the person I assumed it was. My healing journey continues.

> *And you will know the truth, and the truth will set you free. (John 8:32 NLV)*

> *Fear not, for I am with you; do not be dismayed for I am your God. I will strengthen you. Yes, I will help you. I will uphold you with my righteous right hand. (Isaiah 41:10)*

> *You have given me your shield of victory. Your right hand supports me; your help has made me great. (Psalm 18:35)*

The Fight Within

Soon we'd be on the road again. This time, our destination was back to familiar Woodland Street so that Mom could be next to her longtime buddies, the other two musketeers, Sherry and Joan. It made perfect sense that Mom would choose a duplex directly next door to Joan for security purposes. Joan had the take-no-crap attitude and was the leader of fortitude and hustle out of the three. Nevertheless, we were delighted with Mom's choice. Also, to be back in the hood around our old friends was a huge bonus. However, soon Mom's habit and pattern of going out resurrected in full swing, and we were left alone again. It seemed as though her head injury had caused serious short-term memory loss about Nylon Man. But at least we felt safer in our old neighborhood. It seemed her nightlife escapades were totally understandable, considering the traveling news of Rob's remarriage (completely unlawful since they [Mom and Rob] had never divorced); nevertheless, Lisa and I were elated, singing praises, that he had moved on so quickly. It was utmost relief.

Now that Rob's revolving door seized after his remarriage, unfortunately our own household became a revolving door with different men coming and going without notice. On one occasion, I was rudely awakened by a clumsy bearded old man with rancid breath on top of me, smelling like a combination of sour beer and rotten tooth decay. This heightened my emotional distress from Nylon Man all over again. Apparently, Mom said he was just drunk, tripped, and accidentally fell over and passed out. I do agree with her analogy because he did not attempt to touch me inappropriately, thank God.

Nonetheless, this isolated incident triggered the fear and trepidation I had experienced months prior.

To get away from the house as much as possible, I started hanging out at Judy and Ricky's house; they were also known as Judy and Needle Rick (because he was known to "shoot up" drugs, I guess). But I was too young to interpret what that meant. Besides, there were many weird nicknames in that culture. They lived across the vacant field to the left and not only fed my cravings for cigarettes but would eventually introduce me to tiny aspirin-like tablets that had an engraved cross in the dead center of the white pills. They referred to those as "beanies" or "crosstops." Once ingested, the potency flared within minutes, which didn't take long for a petite, scrawny ten-year-old. The effects surged through my body instantaneously: my head tingled mysteriously like my hair follicles were dancing in different directions, my energy-level skyrocketed, and my heart started beating a mile a minute. The scary part is that these effects didn't frighten me. It was the beginning of the end of self-control and the beginning of a long road of addiction and chasing that high. I didn't have a clue what would lie ahead for years to come after taking my first pill. In my immature, ignorant brain, I thought I had found the solid answer to all my problems.

It was all wishful thinking and downright lies. While under the influence, I was compelled to compulsively clean everything in sight, which was a major plus in Judy's eyes, being a mother of an energetic, vivacious toddler and miserably pregnant with her second child, struggling to keep up with the tedious household duties in her third trimester. I was heaven-sent for her inner desire to keep up. My personal goal was to be over there any chance I got, my driving force for more pills. Moreover, the convenience of proximity matched the intense cravings. Every time I even looked at their surroundings, it immediately triggered cravings for more and more—that fast. As young as I was, I was aware on a deeper level that I was being used as a gopher to meet her needs, but I didn't care. Use me, I was used to it. At the same time, I felt in control because I was the one using her to meet my own needs—on multiple levels. It was a win-win relationship in my mind.

I soon became known as the "cleanup girl" of the neighborhood, and that title carried an open-door policy—it not only supplied my addiction around the neighborhood but uprooted prior negative nicknames such as Garbage Can, Pissy Pot, and Loudmouth and placed me in a more affirmative role that implanted positive reinforcement for me to continue the behavior, nonetheless. My next stop was Karen's. She was a single mother who lived across the street from Judy and kitty-corner from us to the right. She had five small children ranging from five downward to diapers. She was struggling to keep up with motherhood, rightfully so for anyone under that amount of stress. Let's just say, there was a lot of work to do. If there weren't mundane chores to be done (which was rare), I found options—anything other than going home to my own pithole environment. I would rather be cleaning up someone else's garbage rather than my own household filth—maybe because it was expected of me and not appreciated. "Welfare child" and "cleanup slave-girl" were my identity, either way I looked at it, but still I'd rather choose some sort of appreciation even if payment was drugs, coupled with stroking my ego. I'll take it. I just couldn't put a label on my motives at that age. It just *was*.

Around the same time I was feeding my addiction and staying away as much as possible, Lisa was going through her own health dilemma, which went unnoticeable for far too long. She started complaining nonstop that her throat hurt while she cuffed her jaws in her hands, especially after she ate something. I tried to offer suggestions to ease her mind, which were useless. Day after day, Lisa's complaints continued with no response from Mom for a doctor's visit. For some reason, Mom did not like taking any of us to the doctors. I couldn't understand why that was so. Then one unusual day, none of us could ignore the urgency of Lisa's condition. She had an enormous knot the size of a golf ball growing in her throat. When she tilted her head, the knot protruded to the point that I ran screaming for Mom to take her to the doctor.

"Oh my goodness, look at Lisa's throat," I said, putting great emphasis on "my goodness" with an overly dramatic tone that demanded immediate attention.

Mom instantly placed her hands over her mouth, breathing heavily through her fingers as she stared at the knot bulging in Lisa's throat. She stared for a moment and must have realized that this problem was not going away on its own. In fact, it absolutely required a doctor's immediate evaluation.

"*Oh my goodness* is right. That looks like a tumor," she said with pressured speech.

"What's a tumor?" we asked.

"Oh, never mind!" she said and grabbed her purse off the coffee table and rushed Lisa to the nearest hospital. It seemed like every minute was an hour, waiting anxiously for their return while I sat rocking on the couch craving a cigarette. When they arrived back home, Mom appeared to be somewhat relieved. Apparently, the doctor felt Lisa had some sort of gland infection and prescribed a medication that would help reduce the swelling. Although the medication was yellowish liquid that looked like lemon pudding, apparently it didn't taste like it according to Lisa's facial expressions. Nevertheless, we were quite relieved, trusting that doctors knew what they were talking about.

Over time, rather than witnessing the medicine working and shrinking the so-called tumor, it was growing at a rapid rate. The ultimate failure occurred right before our eyes. Lisa was complaining about her throat hurting more frequently. Mom was waiting for an appointment with a specialist, which took time, especially since we were Medi-Cal recipients. By the looks of it, Lisa was at the mercy of the system. The odds were on her side because she was a nine-year-old child, so she was placed at the top of the list. Lisa was assigned to a specialist in San Francisco and was later diagnosed with thyroid cancer. Apparently, this diagnosis was very rare in children, or so it had been said during the early 1970s.

That awful news was one of the scariest times of my life. Well, one of them, but it was up there. I had experienced some terrifying, unthinkable challenges in my life up to that point, but the thought of my sister dying was beyond my comprehension. *How can I live if my sister dies?* The answer was—I couldn't. We had experienced everything together—the good, the bad, and the ugly (mostly ugly). We survived together, not apart. We were tough, so surely she could survive cancer. The fear of the unknown was terrifying.

As if matters couldn't get any worse, Rob and his new wife moved right next door to Karen's, supposedly to keep an eye on us. Not surprising. Mom soon moved on as well, and finally the revolving door was meant for one man only. She started dating that guy Ernie, the one we had burglarized, but he never held that against us. Maybe he knew we had been coached, so it was a topic that was never brought up, almost as if it never happened. Apparently, Mom and Ernie were making plans to get out of Sacramento and move back to the Bay Area so that Mom could be closer to her family. Most importantly, to get us completely far away from Sacramento as possible, mainly from Rob. Little did I know at the time, Mom and Ernie were mapping out their own plans that would change our lives entirely. In the meantime, my drug-seeking behavior had escalated to whoever had pills. Mom was getting suspicious due to my bizarre behavior, which only reinforced her decision to get her family out of the contaminated area—for multiple reasons. I don't know if Mom had a clue or not; she just knew something wasn't right.

One fall weekend day, while running amuck and seeking my day-to-day hustle for any possible drug consumption and/or satisfy a nicotine craving, my family drove up to a trio of houses and ordered me into a giant moving truck, stating, "Come on, we're moving." I couldn't believe my ears. I was in complete denial and refused to leave. I mean, my drug days were coming to a halt right before me, and that was difficult to accept. My immediate excuse was, I didn't have time to say goodbye to my best friend or anyone I cared about. I continued to refuse and was shouting out of the window, "I'm not going anywhere, and I am capable of taking care of myself."

As I look back at this, it's totally ridiculous coming from (by that time) a twelve-year-old, smart-alecky, self-centered brat.

As I became more and more combative, they became more and more persistent and threatening. "I mean it, we're about to leave you behind if you don't get in this truck now."

Lisa started screaming, "Come on, Lorrie, I don't want to go without you."

That's all it took—Lisa's voice. Once I heard Lisa's plea, I ran out of the house without saying goodbye and jumped into the truck. I had a stronger bond with Lisa than any drug craving I had ever experienced. It was a good thing she was there to set me straight, or I may have run away or who knows what.

On the road again—this time, surprisingly enough, back to Rodeo Projects, right back to the pre-Rob marital disaster and before the agonizing nightmare even started or the inconvenient relocation to Ohio. What a terrible waste of time—one person's decision determined a cesspool of meaningless deprivation on our quality of life, literally. However, there was an exception to this: two out of five sisters wouldn't have been born—the only good thing that came out of this unfortunate so-called marriage. Nonetheless, on the flip side, two out of five were still gone living with Nana, as if this was the norm for the past six years. There was no denying that Lisa and I felt the unspoken emptiness about their absence. We were not a complete family unit without them all under our roof, period. I had to just put this out of mind because the what-if's were too much for any twelve-year-old to bear, which was my painful reality. To forget was my coping mechanism that serviced me well in my youth. Understandable. At that time, in our present circumstances, I never knew if we'd all be reunited with our two siblings again permanently or not. It's crazy how life could come full circle, and we'd possibly have the slightest chance to start all over again—I mean for real. Was it a new beginning or just another way of carrying on the same ol', same ol'? Only time would tell.

*****

Fifteen days had passed since Dustin was born and hospitalized. It seemed he had taken a turn for the worst according to my visual observations from our visit a couple days prior. After that visit, I was too ashamed to show face at the hospital, knowing that they probably blamed me too. Quite frankly, I felt unwelcomed, judged, and ridiculed. I didn't need any additional negative projections added to what I had already felt. It was ridiculous for anyone to punish me more than I did myself. The truth—I was a coward.

After our hospital visit, I witnessed Dustin increasingly deteriorating at a rapid pace. His facial features were almost unrecognizable from water retention. I was trying to prepare myself for the worst but hoping for a miracle. But deep down, I knew. The next couple of days were mentally and emotionally unbearable. I was in a zombie-like state, unable to muster any cognitive functioning or articulate any type of sentences for communication with anyone. I was there, but no one was home. I sat on the awful-looking orange couch, chain-smoking with a blank stare, eyes glued to the TV. I could not tell you what on earth I was watching, only seeking to distract my deepest fears from becoming a reality with all the noise—and I kept increasing the volume louder and louder.

Day 18, December 5, 1988, I was still on the couch, and the telephone rang. My heart dropped. I knew this was the call that I had been dreading. I didn't want to answer, but I knew I had to. It was a struggle getting off the couch since I had been sitting in the same position for a couple days. I didn't want to hear the truth, but I had to face it. Running away was no longer an option.

Lorrie, get up! I screamed at myself to move my bottom.

I slowly walked toward the old-fashioned yellow telephone sitting on a small oval table next to the refrigerator, hoping it would stop ringing. Everything was moving in slow motion that day. The receiver felt like a ten-pound weight, and my body was lifeless and lethargic.

"Lorrie?" a male's voice questioned.

"Yes," I responded. I recognized the doctor's voice.

"I am sorry to notify you that your son has passed away this morning," the doctor said in a delayed, soft-spoken tone.

My heart dropped as the overflowing tears swelled underneath my eyelids, and I bent my index finger tightly over my lips to prevent screaming at the top of my lungs. I knew the news was coming based on the baby's appearance, but I didn't want to accept it.

Now I had no choice. That was such an overwhelming, sad day for all of us. A lingering heaviness draped over the entire household that was indescribable. Then shortly thereafter, the grieving emotion flooded our minds and turned into uncontrollable sobs after the devastating news was delivered. I was emotionally depleted.

The following weekday, Maria did notify me to express her deepest condolences and tried to console my emotions the best she could, although unsuccessfully.

"Lorrie, you'll be pleased to know that we're closing your case. The department feels you were not responsible for your son's death according to the medical reports, so case closed."

I needed to hear that and was relieved that Nicole was not in jeopardy, nor were any type of criminal charges to be filed against me in the days ahead. However, those facts didn't take away the pain and the endless guilt I would carry for years to come. I sincerely thanked her for breaking my silence, her seamless compassion, and her kind nature, which provided me a safe environment without judgment and opened the ongoing dialogue between us. I concluded that her departure was bittersweet—grateful that my case was closed but saddened our relationship was coming to an end as well. What she didn't know was, she had brought to my dining-room table earlier in the month was much more valuable than just merely a job. It was human kindness and understanding at the deepest level. It can show up anywhere at any time when you least expect it. I was very fortunate to have had her in my corner.

Chapter Reflection

I know my son is in God's loving care, and he's in a much better place than I could have ever provided for him. I was not equipped (mentally, emotionally, physically) to care for my (possibly) special-needs child, and God knew that. Moreover, the baby's father murdered my oldest daughter's (Nicole) father four months later, which would have left both children fatherless—not to mention the painful reality among the siblings growing up—unconceivable circumstances. My hope is that I will one day get to hold him in my arms, show him the love he should have received from me, and have an opportunity to share my deepest regrets. He's in good hands. Amen.

The eternal God is your refuge, and underneath are the everlasting arms. (Deuteronomy 33:27)

We Are Family

We pulled up around sunset on Trigger Court and gazed at our new environment, which was parallel to the other end of the projects that we previously lived several years prior. Basically, everything looked the same, no matter where you lived in the projects: similar-looking complexes with the signature touch that defined our hood, those familiar oil refinery metal barrels in one's eye view as I looked out of my two-story bedroom window after scurrying around and deciding whose room was whose. It wasn't that difficult to figure out since there were only three bedrooms anyway, and Mom was the final decision-maker.

After settling in our new environment, something awful happened within a month of our arrival. Our poodle, Harley, was hit by a car and killed. This was my first encounter with death, which was overly debilitating to me personally. I was devastated and overwhelmed with deep sorrow and unbearable grief. I sobbed relentlessly for three days, unable to attend school and unable to deaden the pain with drugs. This was a situation that I could not evade; the thoughts came rushing in uncontrollably even though I was a master of avoidance, or so I thought. Over time, each day got easier and easier to function. Even though the pain remained, it was manageable.

The first six months, we were in transition: starting a new school, making new friends, while Mom had her own agenda to fulfill. Unbeknownst to me at that time, apparently Mom had many conversations with Gramps and Nana regarding taking physical custody of her two girls with the least interruption since she was now in a better position to care for her own children. They counteracted with threats and stated they would do whatever in their power to prevent the girls from returning to Mom's care. Completely oblivious to her scheme, Mom rocked our world, for the better. I did notice an intense glare in her eyes like she had been strategizing her perfect move for some time. The day that changed our lives couldn't have come soon enough. May 12, 1975, Mom made the gutsiest move probably in her lifetime, despite her fear of retaliation. While we were attending school, she took a trip to the girls' school and kidnapped her children back. We came home from school that day overwhelmed with joy that Mom finally grew a spine.

We overheard her speaking to our grandmother, "Yes, I barged directly into their classrooms without permission, grabbed their hands, and told them, 'You're coming with me.' Shelly's teacher had the nerve to tell me, 'Ma'am, you're not allowed to just take her out of class without notifying the front office.' I told her, 'Oh yeah? I'm her mother!'" I guess she told them.

Within a month of getting the girls back, she came into the house and sat on the couch with a cigarette in one hand and a piece of mail in the other. I could see her hands trembling as she opened the piece of mail from an attorney in Oakland. It must have ignited her anger because suddenly she blurted in her forceful voice, "They have the nerve to call me an unfit mother when they have raised a heathen for a son." Then she shouted at the top of her lungs, "THE WAR IS ON!" With the court date approaching, she leaned on Legal Aid for counsel to help the needy since she was unable to afford an attorney. Thank God for county resources.

Well, Mom was correct with the war thing. She was being terrorized with threats and worried about our safety constantly. One day in particular, the telephone rang, and a raspy voice said, "I want you to know, we'll do whatever it takes to win this case. By the way, I'll let your husband take care of you." *Click*. Mom recognized Gramp's familiar voice.

There was no denying that we all feared for our lives, just knowing that this family had the means to carry out their threats. What was new? We always lived in fear basically our whole lives with that twisted family. The tension was building, and the fear of the unknown was overwhelming even though Mom tried her best to hide it.

To make matters worse, eleven-year-old Lisa was battling cancer at the same time all of this was going on. We went back and forth to San Francisco for the surgery to remove her thyroid and then chemo treatments. These were all overwhelming circumstances for all of us. It just dawned on me: no wonder why we all have anxiety disorders. It all makes total sense with all the stress and strain we had endured over the years. Just sayin'.

I was on the brink of a nervous breakdown myself—not sure if Lisa was going to die, and the possibility of Mom losing custody of our three younger siblings, and/or Mom dying too. I was a mess emotionally. I'm sure Mom felt the same way or even worse, knowing there was a direct threat on her life.

She received a notice that the judge had ordered all of us to speak with an advocate before she went back to court in August and that we might have to see the judge in the near future. She was trying to get us prepared for the future court proceedings. We did meet with an advocate from the probation department shortly after Mom's warning. I was honest with the gentleman about all my experiences I had with that family up to that point, but by the facial expressions on his face, I could tell he didn't believe me. He probably felt I was making up stuff to persuade a decision in Mom's favor. It was unfortunate that he didn't believe me and ask more questions or at least refer me to a counselor.

That day arrived on August 26, the day that Mom had warned us about. Apparently, this was that pivotal hearing that may determine our family's fate. I remember that day as if it was yesterday. On the way to Martinez (the county seat), which may have been twelve miles out, not a word was spoken by any of us—very unusual—despite all of us children crammed tightly into the car. The only sound we could hear were outside disturbances, along with the striking of matches. Mom chain-smoked all the way to the courthouse. I guess we all knew the stress she was under, just an unspoken knowingness. I caught a glimpse of terror in her eyes from the rear-view mirror, which scared the heck out of me. It was hard to grasp the many emotions I saw in her eyes that day—too many to count. But that certain glare, in particular, I could quickly pick up on.

Upon arrival, after climbing many stairs into the main courthouse and into the elevator, we arrived on the second floor. There were the petitioners (Nana and Gramps) with their entourage of support and potential witnesses to testify against Mom as an unfit mother standing along the corridor. This scenario was so warped that I could not believe my eyes. Hypocrites! How dare these people point their fingers at Mom when, in fact, they caused more damage to me personally: they chemically fried me with HEET, forced us to eat hot peppers, beat us, lied against us, and on and on. Not to mention, those so-called witnesses who supplied me with pills molested me, hurled verbal insults at me, and all the physiological irreparable damage that was hammered on us as children. *How despicable*. I sat there stunned because I experienced the truth. I mean, Mom wasn't perfect by any means, but the accusations against her were preposterous. Her fault might have been failure to protect in the past and neglect, but she was not a monster and was showing the utmost courage to finally stand up for us. She would have never tortured her children in the manner these petitioners did, standing before us self-righteously in the hallway, waiting to present their case before the judge. They would just lie through their teeth.

Mom pointed to the bench for us to take a seat on while she went through the courtroom door. I sat there nervously tapping my foot as a distraction while noticing that the tile floor looked like our apartment floors in the projects—I guess anything to distract me from looking at our opponents, filling in a noticeably awkward moment. Turning my head behind me, mainly for avoidance, I glimpsed at an empty corkboard with graffiti carvings of children's artwork, I guess. Quickly, I moved toward the colorful paintings and attempted to escape the possibility of doom and gloom approaching. I couldn't go there. I noticed sad faces coming out of nearby courtrooms, which was not encouraging at all. Nerves instantly set in. We all sat on that hardwood bench smashed closely together, each of us squeezing the other's hands down the line, until the door finally opened.

Mom's attorney peeked his head outside the door and stated, "Girls, come on in and take a seat in the front row so the judge can see all of you."

The judge looked at us with a poker face for a few seconds; then he looked downwardly at something, more than likely, the advocate's report and recommendation. "Hello, girls, do you know why you're here today?" he questioned.

"Yes," we all said in unison.

"Well, it's up to me to decide what's in your best interest and to make the right decision on placement or where you all will live. Do you understand that?" he asked.

"Yes," we said.

"Are you happy being with your mother?" he inquired, getting straight to the point.

"Yes!" we said as we nodded to reinforce our position.

"Is this where you want to live?"

"Yes!"

He then nodded to the left toward the door, signaling for the bailiff to guide us out of the courtroom. While we were headed out, Mom headed in.

We were directed back to the bench until Mom came out of court showing no emotion. We nervously followed behind her out of the courthouse into the car.

She then explained when we were in a safe place. "We have to wait for the final decision. In the meantime, you girls stay with me." Then she gave an ear-to-ear smile—a hopeful expression. This was, indeed, a good indicator to keep our fingers crossed.

Thereafter, the focus to be readjusted to Lisa's health condition. Her doctor visits to San Francisco were becoming less and less frequent, which was a good sign of improvement. Her facial coloring was coming back, and it seemed she was returning to her normal self, returning to school and participating in everyday kids' activities. I was overjoyed that I was getting my sis back, but there were three sisters who were still in limbo that left us uneasy.

September 20, 1976, Mom barged up to Lisa and me, waving the envelope from Contra Costa County Superior Court, screaming, "Girls! Girls! We won! We won!"

I stood there for a moment, too stunned to process if I had heard her correctly. Then I joined in on the celebration of hollering for joy and jumping up and down—our victory was here!

We all huddled in a ring-around-the-rosy kind of circle and started singing the new hit single by Sister Sledge, declaring that we are family. I mean, these lyrics rang true to the core and couldn't have hit the airways at a better time. To this day, this song has a deep-rooted meaning of our family's exceptional victory and demonstrated Mom's extraordinary bravery and courage to stand up for what's right despite the debilitating fear she had on all levels, even risking her life.

On that day, September 20, 1975, Mom's reputation skyrocketed from zero to hero. Yes, you could say this was the year of redemption.

In addition, thanks to the amazing, brilliant doctors in San Francisco, Lisa conquered cancer.

*****

I recently asked Lisa how she knew there was a God at such a young age. She responded, "I just knew God was with us, even if it didn't appear that way." In addition, unlike me, catechism made a lasting impression on her and sparked her interest in learning about Jesus. But more so, it had to have been when she was sick with cancer that she had an inner "divine confirmation" from God, fighting for her life. Wow, sometimes children just know that they know. It's called *faith*.

> *Faith shows the reality of what we hope for; it is the evidence of things we cannot see. (Hebrews 11:1 NLT)*

Decades later…

Recovery Process
&
Spiritual Journey

The Experience

This might appear risky, but I need to address my resentments toward God over the years. Having my childhood upbringing, the only possibility that made any sense to me was, "There must not be a God." This perception was much easier to fathom rather than all the other possibilities floating through my brain. Such as, if there was such an actual God, why did He allow me to have gone through such horrific, inhumane treatment and abandonment from people who were supposed to love and protect me? He left me to the wolves to be devoured. If He was all so powerful, He could have stopped the torture if He truly wanted to. More so, if there was truly a God, then He hated me. It was much easier to not believe rather than continually be looked upon with hatred. For the record, I believed both simultaneously when it was convenient for me or depended upon what mood I was in at the time, especially under the influence.

I was very confused. At times, I was a blatant God hater because in my mind He hated me, so naturally I hated Him in return. Then I was an atheist and could not wrap my head around that a loving God existed and wanted what's best for me since I had experienced the complete opposite. My limited thinking was, that might be true for other people but wasn't true for me. I was unlovable. Growing up, I thought Lisa was out of her mind when she would refer to God. I would shut down her faith or have something negative to say and profusely cursed her God. I blamed everyone for my drug use, including God. My single-minded excuse would always be, "If you had a childhood like mine, you'd be a drug addict too." That was my justifiable right, or so I thought. I refused to take responsibility for my addiction; that's why I stayed in that lifestyle for so long. My heart was made of stone by hardened scars over the years, incapable of receiving any type of love—only abuse and self-destruction that was familiar and accepted. So sick but so true.

Then one day the unexpected happened, and everything changed. I've never been the same since. The day that changed my life forever, although not instantly like it should have.

The murder trial was getting underway within a couple of weeks, and tension around the household was an understatement. The thought of my daughter and I having to relive and account for every detail on April 17, 1989, was overwhelming and quite disturbing to recall as direct witnesses. I was a nervous wreck anticipating what was ahead for both of us and fear of the unknown, so I did more and more drugs to escape the inevitable.

I remember I was babysitting my daughter's cousin on that particular day, an adorable-looking four-year-old who reminded me of my sister Shelly when she was small. Her behavior was like a little mischievous rascal: coloring on the walls, running all over the house, wouldn't listen, a total disobedient brat in my eyes. I didn't believe in disciplining other people's children, so I did the best I could to manage that difficult situation by cleaning the walls, picking up toys, and yelling a lot. Upon the family's return, I went overboard complaining that she was out of control, and they needed to do something to make her behave, or else I would never babysit again.

The aunt's response was something like, children often cope with stress differently; and considering the circumstances that the entire family was dealing with, she thought that the child's behavior was rather expected, and everyone was doing the best they could. It's not what she said, per se, but how she said it that made me receptive enough to acknowledge. She wasn't defensive by lashing out but delivered a soft-spoken, evenly toned response that was quite pleasant to counteract my obvious disapproval and criticism. I looked at her wide-eyed and agreed that my own daughter's behavior was erratic and unstable during that time as well. *Who was I to judge?*

At that moment, I took a good look at myself, and I didn't like what I saw.

After their departure, I anxiously got into the shower. For some reason, I felt dirty and cruel for voicing my opinion; I felt uncompassionate and hypocritical. In a hypothetical kind of way, I needed to wash myself clean of the yucky, unpleasant feeling that consumed me.

In the shower, I heard God's powerful voice outlining everything I had ever done, said, or acted that was judgmental and hypocritical. Now we're talking about thirty years of Lorrie's crap, so this process took longer than I was ready for. I was screaming, "No, God, no!" I shook my head in disbelief. I huddled in the corner on one leg (almost in a standing fetal position) with my head buried in the corner of the shower, deeply ashamed of who I was and how blinded I had been, yet still screaming at the top of my lungs. There was no reprieve. The visions kept coming and coming, and by that time, I was bouncing off all four walls of the shower like a lunatic. This revelation hurt me to my deepest core and had triggered all the suppressed childhood trauma. I fell out of the shower and lay bare naked on the blue bathroom carpet in a convulsive state with the shower still running. I could feel my little six-year-old legs coming out of my body, kicking for relief, along with other terrible things that I was too young to describe and visions of vomiting up who knows what.

The unbearable pain in my heart repeatedly stabbed, and my arms were laid out side to side, suddenly crucified with Jesus. I couldn't handle the pain any longer, and I gave up. I spiritually died. Before death, I heard the voice, *Forgive them, Father, for they know not what they do.* As wretched as I was, He still chose to die for me. Shortly afterward, my heart burst open with an overwhelming joy as I saw radiant light zooming downwardly between a gigantic open gate—heaven perhaps. The uncontrollable tears of overflowing joy streamed down my face with an expression of utmost relief. *I'm sure.*

I was born again, but didn't know it at the time because I had no spiritual knowledge of God or the Bible. In fact, I was spiritually illiterate. I thought I was hallucinating from all the stress. My significant other at the time shook me to snap out of it, telling me I had a nervous breakdown and suggested that I don't think about what just happened and go to bed, and I would be better in morning. I dismissed everything that happened that night because I thought I had a neurotic episode, which was common in our family makeup, and there was the fact that I was only two days clean from substances. I never told a soul about that night because I thought I lost my mind, and I didn't want people to think I was crazy, so I remained silent. Besides, I was a veteran at holding secrets. I forgot to mention that Lisa had moved to Tennessee two years prior, so I didn't have her to lean on at that time anymore.

I should have changed overnight and became a saint, but I didn't believe. However, I was definitely not same person. I didn't want to hurt myself anymore, and the conflict was on to quit using drugs. I was waging a war within myself of what was right and wrong. It was a constant battle with my flesh and the Holy Spirit. I still felt like I was going crazy because I wanted to do well, but I fell hard—a lot. Most of my life after that experience has been off and on, on and off the spiritual path, running away from God, scared to dissect the meaning of that experience, or acting like it had never happened. *How can I possibly forget it?* That experience is engraved in my soul. It's who I am. I thank God for His merciful grace and His refusal to give up on me when I felt unworthy, undeserving, and pitifully shameful. Bottom line: He is a faithful God, and He keeps His promises even though I didn't deserve it. His unfailing love reigns.

I finally got the answer to my long-awaited question. I heard this recently, and I grabbed it for my own personal truth: *my pain has a purpose, and my test has a testimony.* (Actually, I think I heard this from Joyce Meyer. Man, I love her.) Here's another one of those profound statements that I cling to daily as a reminder of the swirl of goodness in the end—that's hope. It is one of those spiritual affirmations that sinks deeply into my soul.

God allowed me to go through everything for a reason: to be used for good, not harm. I finally believe that. God gave me a purpose to share my story with the world. So I am.

He has commanded me, "Now go and get my children." I will.

Chapter Reflection

Revisiting this once-in-a-lifetime experience, I was given a new heart in exchange for my battered, scarred, rock-hard one, although I didn't realize that at the time. I want to point out that all of us may have had spiritual experiences that differ from one another but are valid nonetheless and may not require that type of intensity as mine. In my case, I think my heart was so hard from all the severe abuse at such a young age. Therefore, any life-changing outcome required intrusive force to transform me from the inside out. There was no other way. I see that now. Even after that experience, it had taken me years to believe (shameful to admit).

> *I will give you a new heart and put a new spirit in you; I will remove from you your heart of stone and give you a heart of flesh. (Ezekiel 36:26 NIV)*

The Letter from God

Prior to my recovery journey, I was sitting Indian-style, my boney legs underneath the coffee table, nervously flapping my knees onto the worn-out shag carpet, contemplating suicide. *How will I do it? I asked myself. Pill overdose? But I don't have any pills. Throw myself in front of a BART train? But I don't have a car to get there. Carbon-monoxide poisoning, maybe? Hmmm. No car, no garage, out of the question. I could take a bus to BART...or perhaps slit my wrist? But I hate the sight of blood.* Then reality crept in. *How can I do this to my daughter? Both parents dead. How selfish of me! But I'm a terrible mother anyway. She'd be better off without me*, I reminded myself.

Feeling hopeless and defeated that "once an addict, always an addict," as they say, I couldn't stop using despite countless attempts to do so. I was beyond disgusted with myself and who I had become—a lowlife dope fiend, a pitiful waste of human life. This addiction left me worthless and madly suicidal.

How can I continue to use drugs after my baby died? What kind of person does that?

The more questions I asked myself, the more drugs I did in an effort to escape the hard-core reality. Then *zap*—the more suicidal I became! It was a chain reaction, day in, day out—that is, unless I was drugless or in a sleepy comatose state for days at a time. Then I'd wake up, disappointed that I had opened my eyes, and I was still breathing.

It should have been me that died and not him. Why did God let me live?

An overwhelming urge overtook me, which was unexplainable at the time, and disrupted my suicidal ideation to develop an actual plan and carry it out. It suddenly dawned on me to search for that rather small, four-inch box titled Gospel Gems that my boyfriend brought home from a dumpster-diving mission the night before and which I had previously rummaged through upon arrival that night. The highlight of our lives was "hitting the jackpot" with other people's junk becoming our treasure. You know, goodie box in childhood turned into "treasure chest" in adulthood. But in reality, it's called dumpster diving. The free rewards: clothes that fit, size 8 shoes, costume jewelry, household items, and small appliances. All these were deeply appreciated, unless infested with cockroaches—disgusting but worth the risk.

Profusely sweating and highly irritated from drug withdrawal, I located the square box in the hefty garbage bag that was buried at the bottom of several miscellaneous items. I cuffed the box in between both hands and stared at it for a moment. "Open it," I heard a gentle whisper within my head.

Inside were about fifty plus multicolored, half-inch cards with typed scriptures, as well as words of positive affirmations and popular quotes from who knows who. I randomly pulled out seven cards and laid them in order, one beneath the other. Shockingly, it was a perfectly structured letter I assumed to be directly from God. It got my attention.

> **But now, this is what the Lord says – he who created you, O Jacob, he who formed you, O Israel, Fear not, for I have redeemed you; I have called you by name, you are mine. (Isaiah 43:1)**
>
> **I will instruct and teach you in the way you shall go; I will counsel and watch over you. (Psalms 37:8)**

> **And I will do whatever you ask in my name so that the Son may bring glory to the Father. You may ask me for anything in my name, and I will do it. (John 14:13-14)**
>
> **Consider him who endured such opposition from sinful men, so that you will not grow weary and lose heart. (Hebrews 12:3)**
>
> **And whatever you do, whether in word or deed, do it all in the name of the Lord Jesus, giving thanks to God the Father through him. (Colossians 3:17)**
>
> **Faith is the pledge and forerunner of the coming answer (Andrew Murray)**
>
> **Therefore, since we have been justified through faith, we have peace with God through our Lord Jesus Christ, through whom we have gained access by faith into this grace in which we now stand. And we rejoice in the hope of the glory of God. (Romans 5:1)**

For whatever reason, I knew this letter was extremely important, so I wrote this down several times, memorized every word, and tucked this deeply within my heart. I didn't know it at the time, but God knew I would someday share his letter with the world. Yes, even in my pitiful state, God was preparing me to do something purposeful in the future. That night, however, I didn't have a clue.

Although not instantly, I'd soon be on my way to a new life but had a long road ahead of me. Looking back at this, my residence would burn down years later; and if I hadn't engraved this on my heart, the letter would have gone up in flames like everything else I owned.

A wise spiritual woman told me recently, "It's not just about you, Lorrie." She was absolutely right. This is not only my letter; it's our letter—the oppressed, battered, beaten, abused, drug-addicted, broken, or anyone who feels that undeniable rejection. It's not a coincidence that you're reading this book. God desires to use our stories (testimonies) for His glory.

> *"For I know the plans I have for you," declares the Lord, "plans to prosper you and not harm you, plans to give you hope and a future." (Jeremiah 29:11 NIV)*

My falling hard a lot journey...

Long Road to Recovery

I wish I could share that after my spiritual experience, I was changed overnight (like I should have), but unfortunately, that is not my story. Remember, I thought I had a nervous breakdown, so I had denied His power out of ignorance and tried my best to forget about the experience that I didn't understand and continued on the same old self-destructive, violent, druggie behavior. However, something was incredibly different after that experience: the intensive war fuming within my soul. Many times, I wanted to do good (Holy Spirit), and again there was the physiological reaction to cravings (flesh) that desired what I had been accustomed to for years—intense cravings for drugs. There's a scripture about this: "For I do not do the good I want to do, but the evil I do not want to do—this I keep on doing" (Romans 7:19 NIV).

Boy, can I relate to that scripture. I know that this scripture is not limited to just drugs (actually, anything evil). However, in my life, that is what rang true for me during that time period.

Surprisingly, I had a deep inner desire to quit. I didn't want to hurt myself anymore—out of guilt, escapism, or justification due to my childhood trauma—or feel devastating guilt when I was under the influence due to my child's death. At times, the addiction overpowered my inner desire for help. My problem was, I didn't know how to abstain due to a lack of knowledge and being saturated in the drug-infested zone, uninformed about resources available in the community and being biblically illiterate and, of course, flat-out selfish. *All of the above.* I vividly remember when I was under the influence that I hated being in my own skin, completely different than the pre-experience high times in the past. So in reality, I could not forget about the experience I had in the shower that night. It changed me forever, although not instantly—but it did change my perspective dramatically. Remember, I mentioned in the beginning of the book, I am a slow learner, so it had taken me a while (years) to put the pieces of the puzzle together (I guess I'm *extremely* slow).

Then there is Liz. You know that saying, "people come into your life for a reason, a season, or a lifetime." Well, this friendship is for a *lifetime* to me. There is an amazing backstory about our relationship that I can only sum up as "predestined" by God.

> *And those he predestined, he called; those he called, he also justified; those he justified, he also glorified.* (Romans 8:30 NIV)

I met Liz in Rodeo about the same time our mother was fighting for custody for the girls (my sisters). Apparently, Liz had lived in Sacramento (we had attended the same middle school) before we moved to Rodeo; I just had never met her in Sacramento. Liz would often visit her father, who lived in the Rodeo Projects, during the summertime or holiday vacations. Liz and I connected instantly. We didn't know why; we just did. When we'd see each other, we'd jump on each other (I mean literally), extremely exuberant, overjoyed with excitement—like Lisa and I would.

One day she came to the house to hang out. My mother looked at her curiously, stared for a moment, and asked her, "By chance, is your mother's name Eloise?"

Liz responded, "Yes," puzzled that my mother would ask her that question. I guess there was an undeniable resemblance, so my mother had to ask the question. Liz resembled her mother: a beautiful Latina with big brown eyes, thick black hair midway down her back, and she had signature dimples that, when she smiled, were a dead giveaway (it couldn't go unnoticed).

Mother went on to explain that she and Liz's mother were good friends in high school in Richmond and were pregnant at the same time. In fact, my mother would babysit Liz as a baby. Moreover, we would play together as infants. Hearing about that past connection only made our bond stronger. It gets better. Back in Sacramento, Liz went to her friend Renee's house. Well, remember Renee—my best friend in the world whom I previously spoke about? Apparently, Liz and Renee became friends after my departure from Sacramento, or maybe before (I'm unsure). Liz went into Renee's room, and shockingly she saw a school picture of me inserted into the crack of the dresser mirror. Liz pointed at my picture and said, "Hey, I know that girl!"

Renee responded, "You do? She's my best friend Lorrie, who moved away."

"Yeah, she lives in Rodeo near my father's house," Liz told her.

"No way," Renee responded.

They planned a sneak-surprise attack to come visit me. When they did so, I could not believe my eyes. I mean, what were the chances of that happening? It's not that my residence was in a nearby Bay Area town; we're talking about a sixty-five-mile difference here. Mind-blowing. But again, I thought it was a weird small-world coincidence.

To make a long story short, I moved in with Liz in adulthood, who introduced me to God's Word and taught me how to pray and fellowship with believers who exemplified unwavering faith. More importantly, I saw her conviction with my own two eyes, her complete lifestyle transformation. She was a real-life, living example of what God could do in a person's life. I mean, she tried to help me see my brokenness, my need for God, and turn my life over to Him. Unfortunately, I wasn't ready. I was making progress but slipping into old habits that would not be tolerated and were in conflict with her new way of life. Totally understandable. I love her to pieces and always will. Moving forward, I mean backward, I returned to the old lifestyle that was familiar to me.

I failed to mention my violent tendencies, the rage, and the continued escalation of domestic-violence episodes which would explode quite frequently in my household. Fast-forward months later, a terrible incident brought me to my senses *and* to my knees—

depleted and begging for mercy. In one of my violent rages, I threw a knife at my now ex-husband and accidentally almost hit our four-year-old son at the time. That was my wake-up call. This took me to a bottom below my bottom, if that makes any sense. I had already felt responsible for the death of one child; now I was inches away from repeating another devastation. I was at the end of myself.

After our breakup, a new acquaintance at that time (future boyfriend) suggested a substance-abuse treatment program. I jumped at the opportunity and even excelled. Shortly after I was discharged from the program, I ended up hanging around old friends and using again. But at least that time, I was determined to get it right, and I had the confidence that it was possible because I was successful in the past. I wish I could say that I got it right away, but I did not (of course not). Honestly, to respect the anonymity of the 12-step program, let me just say that I diligently followed the suggestions wholeheartedly and *beyond*, tailored to my own specific issues because I needed all the help I could get.

After I achieved that one year (which actually took me three years to get a solid consecutive one-year abstinence chip), I got medication for depression and anxiety (yep, not afraid to admit it), meditation tapes for managing stress, church fellowship, and God's Word. Oh yeah, and exercise. Let's just say I was trying to live a well-balanced life. By then, I was pregnant with my fourth child and determined to deliver a clean/sober baby. And that I did. I started attending school to become an alcohol and drug counselor, became addicted to education, received an AODS certification, and went on to achieve an AA degree (took me seven years to walk across the stage). I worked in the field for eight years and have been substance-free for numerous years.

Today I have absolutely no desire to use drugs whatsoever. I thank God that I do not have to suffer any longer with that horrible fight within and that I have been completely delivered from that druggie lifestyle. Long story short, God's love is relentless. I ran from Him for years, and He still chose to come after me with His unfailing love. Today, instead of running away from Him, I run to Him. His amazing grace is sufficient for me.

Chapter Reflection

I have no doubt that Liz was deliberately put into my life very early on because later on in life, she would be very influential in introducing me to God. Years later in her life, she had become a disciple of Jesus Christ, (SF Church of Christ); she still is to this day.

God tried to save me from myself again and again, but I was too stubborn to listen. I walked away from His will for my life. I could have saved myself tremendous agony if I would have submitted in the first place. But then again, considering my history, I had a problem submitting to anyone. Unfortunately, I dug a deeper hole for myself that could have been avoided altogether.

> *Long ago, the Lord said to Israel: "I have loved you, my people, with an everlasting love. With unfailing love, I have drawn you to myself." (Jeremiah 31:3 NTL)*

Forgiveness

As I stared at my computer at work, somewhat in a daze, my phone lit up, displaying "Sis" calling in. *It's about that time*, I thought to myself. Lisa has been taking care of Mom for the past two years since her significant other passed away. Besides, with Mom's reoccurring falls and considering all her ongoing health problems, it was imperative that she not live alone. Despite In-Home Care Supportive Services visiting on a daily basis, it wasn't enough.

I have been Lisa's mental-health lifeline whenever she needed a break or when she was ready to drop her basket, so to speak. We have a long history of nervous disorders in our genealogy. I call it the "family curse."

"Lorrie, can you come and get Mom? I need a break." I could hear the desperation in my sister's voice.

I was willing to help her out in any way I could—not for Mom's sake but for Lisa's, sadly to admit. I stopped writing this book since I became second-in-command as Lisa's support system. Maybe I was a bit resentful because my aspiration had to be put on hold indefinitely. But on the other hand, I didn't want to publish this book as long as Mother was alive anyway. My true desire was to preserve any dignity she had left. I couldn't bear to hurt her any longer considering what she went though as a child, harboring the family secrets and holding the dirty laundry from her own childhood, as well as the hatred she experienced from me throughout the years.

In my heart of hearts, I wanted to care for her to the best of my ability without letting the deeply rooted hurt and unresolved anger possibly affect my ability to properly meet her needs. Rather, I wanted to love unconditionally.

I had to consciously forget my childhood and love her as if nothing ever happened. And I did just that. I cooked breakfast so that her medication wouldn't upset her stomach, gave her showers, dyed and curled her hair, took her shopping while listening to Motown beep-bopping around, and connected with extended family and friends. More importantly, I kissed her on the forehead before work and told her "I love you." That worked for a while—that is, until I was triggered, like the mention of my stepfather's name or a nightmare I might have had the night before.

Shamefully, one night, in a drunken state, all the negative emotions came uncontrollably rushing out of my mouth as if I totally dismissed my inner desires for the latter (like I've said, I'm not perfect and don't claim to be).

I confronted her in the kitchen and demanded some answers. "Why didn't you love me?" I lashed out. "How could you allow me to be tortured and not protect me? For heaven's sake, I was only six years old!"

The questions were coming out so fast that I didn't give her time to respond. Her mouth dropped open. She looked shocked and overwhelmed, as if she couldn't believe this was happening, as was I. She remained silent, broke eye contact, and looked down to the floor, but at least she was hearing me out.

I wanted her to grasp that her lack of intervention caused me a lifetime of physical and emotional damage, which is irreparable. I wanted her to tell me that she was a bad mother to validate my views and, most importantly, that she was sorry. Because she didn't respond to my inner wishes, I attacked her verbally, stating, "I hate you." It was my typical childish tantrum response when I didn't get my way. She started crying and went downstairs as if she was the victim, making me the "bad guy" for expressing my feelings.

I realized at that moment that I would never hear an apology; in fact, she was incapable of accepting responsibility for her past mistakes, or maybe it was too overwhelming for her—but I had to forgive her anyway. Forgiveness is a choice.

If you forgive those who sin against you, your heavenly Father will forgive you. But if you refuse to forgive others, your Father will not forgive your sins. (Matthew 6:14–15 NLT)

Bottom line: I need to forgive if I wanted to be forgiven. Reflecting and looking within, I too was a terrible mother, ingesting drugs while pregnant, which might have contributed to my son's misdiagnosis. I too failed to protect my daughter by the awful choices with men that have affected her for a lifetime—forever fatherless, for which I feel responsible. I too was full of secrets, lies, and deceit, leading my youngest daughter to believe her biological father was someone he wasn't. In addition, I demonstrated fistfighting and spewing out vulgar insults in my relationships with men, showing my children that this was normal behavior, carrying on the chain of ugliness and violence, and the list goes on and on.

The painful reality—I was no better, by far. Then it hit me: I needed to forgive so that I can forgive myself, in order to receive the ultimate forgiveness which only comes from God. While wrestling with the insightful revelation and feeling the heaviness of my feet, I made a conscious decision to walk down those stairs, look my mother straight in the eye, and say, "I love you, and I forgive you." And I meant it. She locked eyes with me and responded, "I love you too."

There is one decision I regret that night. I wish I would have taken it a step further and told her what my oldest daughter, Nicole, told me repeatedly: "Mom, I give you permission to forgive yourself." That was a powerful statement of mercy by my daughter, considering all the turmoil I had put her through over the years. Just because my mother didn't voice *sorry* doesn't mean she didn't *feel* sorry. Her body language told me that. Now it's too late.

Several months later, February 24, 2017, the dreadful anticipated call came in from the hospital staff that made our hearts sink. The doom and gloom were upon us. The medical team set up a meeting with all five sisters to come to some sort of agreement to either move forward with a trachea insertion or order "do not resuscitate/comfort care" on our mother's behalf. Although two rigorous attempts were made to intubate, her health had been declining without any long-term success in sight. The hospital staff was pressuring us to come up with a resolution that we could all agree on. Easier said than done. The notion of intubation for a third time was unforeseeable among all of us due to the harsh invasion into her already brittle lungs. Two out of five siblings would not consider anything other than "bringing her home," nor accept the reality of her frail condition. However, Shelly (middle sister) said it bluntly, "She is wasting away before our eyes, and we have to do something."

That was the most difficult decision that we as a family had to encounter. It left us all devastated. Basically, the thought of "putting the nails in her coffin" was an overwhelming and daunting task to wrap our heads around. It was clear to us that she did not want a tracheotomy, and the fact that residing in a rest home was one of her deepest fears left us with only one other option. The dire decision was made, but not accepted lightly without opposition among the siblings.

I remember that day as if it was yesterday. It literally felt like an elephant was sitting on my chest—the heaviness in my soul was an understatement, and the size of my budging eyelids matched the outer with the inner. Lisa's spiritual goal was to reconnect Mom to her Catholic roots and requested the on-call priest to perform Mom's last rites in preparation to meet her Maker. Lisa did this not only for Mom's benefit but for our comfort as well; just knowing our Mom would be okay was at the forefront of her intentions. Lisa's broken heart was authenticated by her facial expressions showing her powerlessness and her wrestle with God, pleading for mercy on our mother's behalf. She elaborated how Mom was labeled a divorcee, ostracized and shunned from her Catholic faith (which was her view in the 1960s) when our father divorced her without her consent—double the rejection, hurt, and dismal despair on multiple levels. Lisa could not shake our mother's abandonment as she hovered over her bedside with compassion, love, and deep devotion in her eyes. She had to intervene somehow. She tied ruby-red ribbons around our mother's silver bedrail to represent the blood of Jesus, along with a purple feathered scarf to represent Jesus's garment and a neon-orange ribbon to represent her favorite color. She stuck multicolored butterflies on the hospital windowpane to resemble her flight to heaven and primped her fragile face with her signature orange lipstick and a matching hair tie to manage her mangled bedhead hair to present her as a gift to God.

According to Shelly, the priest had come by for a five-minute visit the day before without Lisa's knowledge. Lisa requested a revisit of last rites in the presence of us five girls for some type of spiritual relief. Shortly thereafter, there was an unexpected brief encounter in the hallway with the priest, where he pointed out that he'd already visited our mother's room and that he had several other individuals in the same condition; but if he had time, he would return. This statement didn't fly well with some of my siblings and annoyingly rubbed them the wrong way—to the max, to be exact.

"Thanks, but no thanks. I will do this myself," Lisa said after his departure, walking toward the other corridor. "Lorrie, if he comes back while we're gone, tell him we don't want to take any more of his time," she added at bit sarcastically but sternly. So I did exactly what I was told and relayed that message to the priest when he did return about a half hour later.

Both Lisa and Mary (the youngest sister) went on a mission and returned a couple hours later. They arrived back at the hospital with several items in baskets: unleavened bread, wine, tiny clear cups, family photos, our grandmother's rosary, her Catholic Bible that had been in the family for centuries, heirlooms such as a cross that had been passed down throughout generations, organic frankincense oil, and other miscellaneous trinkets of special meaning.

Lisa then told us, "Mom hasn't had communion for decades, so today will be that day."

We all knew where she was coming from and didn't hesitate to honor her wishes. Tears filled our sorrowful eyes while she was speaking. We knew her purpose was to intercede for our Mom's inner desires, although she did sound off her rocker at times; we just rolled with it.

She instructed all of us to hang up our family photos around the interior walls of her room and place some of the heirlooms around Mom's head and her body as a symbol of honor. They then anointed her forehead with the frankincense oil in a symbol of a cross with her fingertips, then rubbed her hands and feet with a portion as well. Lisa knew what she had to do to prepare herself, as if she had done this before. She excused herself in an attempt to get spiritually ready by going into a quiet room nearby, praying for God's guidance, and marking parts of the Bible that would be used. Patience was inevitable since this process had no time limit, other than Mother passing away. She would be ready when she was ready, and no one bothered her.

Lisa returned to the room with an unspoken glow as if she had a meeting with God. All sisters and some grandchildren gathered around Mother's hospital bed, holding hands as each of us read a scripture from the Bible directed by Lisa's instructions. My youngest daughter, Serena, read most of the scriptures because she was blessed with her soft-spoken tone and angelic voice, which was music to our ears and brought a bit of peace in the midst of an unbearable emotional storm.

We then jumped in to help prep the communion and facilitate the process—Mom first. Lisa carefully soaked the unleavened bread in the wine to soften so Mom wouldn't choke, then used the mouth-moistened sponge to rub throughout her inner cheeks, being extra cautious not to dislodge her breathing tube. We followed suit and concluded with more biblical verses and hymns.

Mom had finally received that long-awaited communion that she never felt worthy of receiving, thanks to our sister Lisa.

I'll never forget Lisa's answer to my question after our family ceremony.

"Lisa, how on earth did you know how to do all that?" I asked.

"Lorrie, I've been looking at those pictures in that Bible for years on our coffee table. God had been preparing me as I knew I would someday possibly have to do this," she responded in a matter-of-fact tone with a slight jerk of her shoulders like, *So be it.*

I was speechless and concluded that I witnessed God's mercy and grace that day.

All five sisters gathered around Mother's hospital bed, holding hands and singing our hearts out in unison to "I'll Always Love My Mama" by the Intruders and, of course, "We Are family," two nights before she took her last breath. We know she heard us. In fact, maybe the entire ICU unit heard us, considering the Bluetooth speaker was fully charged. Music always had a way of getting us through the hardest of times, and this situation was no different. Our motto: *She brought us up with music; therefore, we'll take her out with music.* We were appreciative that the hospital tolerated our way of saying goodbye.

The gratitude I felt to be a of that moment with a sincere heart of forgiveness and love is priceless and will be forever treasured. I was in it, heart and soul.

Mother passed away two days later on my youngest daughter, Serena's, birthday. Lisa wrapped her head in a cloth-wrap like Mother Teresa's, topped with a bright-orange signature hair bow on the side, as they took her body out of the hospital. Shortly after, Lisa was clearing out Mother's belongings from the hospital room and fumbling with the radio, trying to turn it off, and ironically, the song "I Just Called to Say I Love You" by Stevie Wonder started playing. Lisa wept as she listened to those powerful lyrics and recognized that was Mom's way of saying goodbye as well. Impeccable timing at its finest. I guess she had the final say: she brought us up with music, and she'll be the one taking us out with music, not the other way around.

One early morning eight months after Mom's passing, I sat at the dining table and examined my past behavior after a spiritual tug to do so, just out of the blue. I guess God wanted me to get a glimpse through His eyes rather than my limited, tainted view. I thought I had completely forgiven my mother, but apparently, I had some unresolved issues secretly tucked away in my heart. An overwhelming sadness rushed in my soul. After further reflection, I admitted to myself that I have a deep regret that I wasn't more empathetic toward my mother over the years, unable to look past my own pain and consider all those challenges that she had to endure, to see the hidden wounds of her heart rather than my own hurts and battle scars. More than likely, she was an abused child as well. Although I don't know the exact details, I do remember her saying that her father warned her, "If you leave, you are not welcome back, ever." She never had a soft place to fall when a crisis hit.

Repeating Lisa's words in my head, Mom had felt ostracized from her Catholic faith due to a divorce by my biological father, which wasn't her choosing—double the rejection. Not only by her spouse but by God—at least in her mind. She was looked upon with ridicule and disgust by the norms of society during that time period. She had been outcast by many and subjected to horrible name-calling, vile remarks, feelings of unworthiness, and unspeakable shame. In addition, she had carried an "unwanted" spirit within her soul since birth. Her father repeatedly reminded her about his disappointment that she wasn't born a boy, so of course, she had her own insecurities to battle, as well as a deep seed of unworthiness that she secretly tried to hide.

When I was abused, she was only twenty-six years old—still a very young adult, with a lack of employment skills and stuck out in the middle of a secluded area with nowhere to go. Today I look at my own twenty-six-year-old son and can't help but think, *It must have been extremely hurtful for her to be unable to protect me.* Maybe she really wanted to, but she was scared—and rightfully so. She was a victim too, having been bullied and abused verbally as well. Fact: she was unable to even protect herself, let alone her children. She had fallen into the trap of brainwash and deceit, with four children and one on the way at such a young age. Not to mention the spiritual, moral code to stay married no matter what was embedded into her soul, more so with the second husband.

In addition, she had mental health barriers like nervous breakdowns and depression with no treatments available like we have today. There were no medication options, no other treatment alternatives. She didn't have the knowledge that we luckily have today, only the stigma and unspeakable embarrassment that had been attached to the disorder. She suffered in silence too, just like I did. I would do anything to rewind history and repeat the night I sat on my son's bed and forgave her. I would take it a step further by acknowledging her struggles and meeting her at a place of compassion, honestly voicing my newly found insight directly to her—face-to-face, eye-to-eye. I would top it off with the biggest hug of all. I need to forgive myself for being so self-centered, unable to put myself in her shoes with no understanding of all her circumstances. Now there are no shoes to fill.

Like Lisa reflectively pointed out to me recently, "She just wanted to be loved, just like everybody else."

During funeral preparations, Lisa made it very clear that since Mom never had a real wedding dress either, on her final resting day, she would get that special dress that she always wanted and deserved. She did.

Mom, it was impossible for you to rest here on earth with all your inner turmoil. I sincerely hope you rest in peace. I love you. Please forgive me.

Moving through the forgiveness process, I must address my biological father. Even though he has never harmed me sexually or physically, the emotional wound of abandonment left a firmly embedded scar of unworthiness and low self-esteem that made me believe I didn't matter and I was unlovable. Moreover, his refusal to pay child support instilled in me that I was unimportant, inasmuch as letting the government take care of my sister and me, which should not have been the taxpayers' responsibility. I don't think he realized that his lack of concern imprinted a lasting impression of no value and left us as bottom-feeders of society. The most damaging lie was that if my own parents didn't love me, then how on earth could God love me?

The reality is, in adulthood, it makes sense why I'm always trying to prove myself, convince myself that I am somebody, that I am important, seeking approval from others and getting hurt when I'm not appreciated. In my heart, I still feel defective, broken, and confused at times, but I'm slowly recovering from the lie and going through the healing process. Yes, even after all these years. That's why it makes total sense that what damage is planted at such a young age, it takes a lifetime to uproot. *Thank God for His Word, His Promises.*

The truth be known that while writing this, I realize that I am important in my Heavenly Father's eyes—always have been and always will be. It's unfortunate that it has taken so long to really believe it. But like they say, better late than never, right?

Coward, I used to call him, mainly because he didn't show his face, regardless if my stepfather was a dangerous lunatic, which might have caused an outright war. If he had checked on our well-being, he might have gotten a clue of what was happening to his children and perhaps even made an attempt to protect us. Or maybe not. I'll never know.

As a young adult (about midtwenties), I was tired of being unimportant—rather, nonexistent—during his whirlwind of multiple marriages, too busy and self-centered seeking happiness for himself while his children suffered beyond belief. I resented him for not being available, for wasted dreams of being "daddy's little girl," instead growing up as a poverty-stricken slave and a daughter of a welfare recipient. That was my identity, period. I guess you could say I had resentments—big time.

While writing this, I made a reflection of my "snapping" point when I was at an incredibly vulnerable state during my midlife crisis. I called him begging for his participation in counseling with me in hopes that he would validate my hurt and pain, only to be rejected again by him flat-out refusing to even consider my plea. I vividly remember that day as if it were yesterday. His response was the epitome of ultimate rejection, which sent me into a destructive spiral of rage and fury. I slammed the phone down. *I'll show him*, I thought. I stomped into the living room and punched and shattered the entire sliding glass door. I'm extremely fortunate the thick curtains were closed that day; otherwise, I might have lost my arm and wouldn't be writing this right now.

All the hurt that was built up in me came out in an uncontrollably violent and threatening manner. I wanted him to hurt as bad as I was hurting. Anything important to him, I wanted to destroy. I made that very clear. I immediately called him back. I threatened his wife and told her she'd "better watch her back" because I was about to smear her face into the BART pavement, and I knew where to find her. I called his home and threatened to have all my druggie, thug-life friends rob his home and take away everything that was of any value to him. The crazy part—I left those threats on his voicemail like a dummy, not thinking about any legal consequence that could have occurred from the evidence I left behind. I didn't care. I told him I was changing my birth name because I no longer wanted a name that he had chosen, and in fact, having his last name was a disgrace. As a result of my pain, I used more and more drugs to numb all those negative emotions. I didn't want to feel any longer. I'm not using this as an excuse; it's just the way I coped with anything in my life up to that point: happy, sad, angry, lonely, tired—you name it.

As years passed, he did make multiple attempts to reconnect, mainly during the holiday season. He'd ask, "What do you want for Christmas?" My response was always, "Nothing," before slamming the phone down.

He didn't give up. This gave me a sense that maybe he cared after all, and I eventually took him up on his offer and gave him a Christmas wish list for the children and myself. I came to realize that this was his way to try to make up for his absence over the years, or maybe I was just clinging to optimism. Nevertheless, his persistent efforts opened a door back into my life. In turn, he got a glimpse into my so-called relationship that was in a broken state as well as my mental-health instability.

The turning point in our estranged father-daughter relationship was in the midst of my marital dilemma due to my husband's continued drug use and denial to get help after I had gotten clean. At that time, I became a drug counselor for a perinatal substance abuse program for pregnant women, which I thought was my life purpose after getting certified. This was the only way (in my mind) I could remotely give back, make amends for my own mistakes, and attempt to make a difference somehow. I was preaching the importance of a clean/sober environment, only to come home to a drug-infested homelife. I was living a lie. I was sick and tired of leaving for work with unknown males lying on my couch after tweaking all night. The last straw was my husband's unwise decisions that could have had major legal consequences in our future. This was absurd and a slap in my face for what I was trying to accomplish for our family and our children: a new way of life. Not to mention, he was putting us in legal jeopardy and possible removal of our children. As painful as it was, I had to make a decision to either go back to that lifestyle or get a divorce. I filed for a restraining order, and it was granted a few days later; then the divorce followed shortly. Ironically, it was granted on Valentine's Day. *What a trip!*

My father became my backbone; he supported me emotionally while I transitioned through my divorce in attempt to have a better life. Shortly thereafter, I was laid off from the county, which left me devastated. I was going through a divorce, without purpose, a single parent, and broke. Then and there, God resparked the vision to rewrite my life story again and turn all the negative aspects into something hopeful, therefore creating an entirely different purpose.

I would call my father and read him what I had written. He listened patiently, acknowledged my pain, and made comments that I was a good writer. Today my father and I have a wonderful relationship. I call him "Poparuski," and I can hear the satisfaction in his voice with a subtle giggle. He admits he was a "terrible" father, and I agree with him. I have forgiven him wholeheartedly, communicate with him regularly, and love him dearly. My family and I have holiday gatherings to which he and his wife are invited every year. Yes, the same wife I had threatened years ago forgives me as well. Oh, and by the way, he finally got it right and has been married for more than thirty years, to date.

I'm amazed after all these years to realize how God moved and answered the desires of my heart without me even realizing it—until now.

Revelation: I received my counseling sessions after all—for free.

This might appear irrelevant, but it's pertinent to my healing process, so my hope is that you understand where I'm going with this toward the end. Economically, I purchased a larger container of body wash (approximately sixteen ounces) a few months back. Shortly afterward, I accidentally dropped it onto the tub and broke the nozzle, so I had been transferring the liquid in a smaller dispenser in the meantime.

During my rewrite, it was suggested by my writers' small group for me be more descriptive of the HEET experience, I've been brokenhearted, extremely anxious, and encountering crushing heart pressure and palpations (not sure if I had been experiencing symptoms of a heart attack or if it was severe anxiety). I've been asking God to please protect my heart, not only physically but more so in a spiritual sense. I do not want to become outrageously angry (like in the past), nor self-sabotage by drug use to escape the reality of brutality and wickedness that was inflicted on me as a six-year-old child; nor did I want my heart to become hardened to protect itself from the intense pain. I would rather feel the pain, no matter how gut-wrenching, so that I can heal to gain wholeness, love without measure, and grow spiritually as a result of the process. This hardcore reality is, I must *feel* in order to *heal*.

It would be worthwhile to mention when I initially wrote my experiences several years ago. I was emotionally detached and was having difficulty imagining this act on anyone, let alone on myself. It was as if I was writing about someone else, like Sybil, unable to connect the trauma at that time. As I look back, the disconnect to put anything on paper is totally understandable; otherwise, I may not have attempted to write in the first place. Notably, as I was going through a painful divorce as well, why the need to add such pain, right? Reflecting closely at my initial writing back then, I was emphatically and emotionally distraught when Rob made me wear a diaper and say "goo-goo, gaga" on the apartment sidewalk while he instructed Lisa to gather the neighborhood kids and classmates and pointed out I was a bed-wetting baby at the age of eight. Humiliation at its core. Needless to say, I was grateful when we moved. Believe it or not, that was harder to swallow than the HEET.

Not so now.

Fast-forward, I'm in it, feeling the insurmountable pain in my heart with the raw emotion from being shoved down for forty-eight years and having to carry that burden for decades. I was sobbing for myself, for my six-year-old inner child who was tortured beyond belief, with no explanation as to why someone could be so inhumane as to harm an innocent child in such a brutal manner. In fact, having my oldest daughter and six-year-old granddaughter live with me at the time only reinforced my painful memories and made them virtually inescapable.

On July 15, 2017, I was taking my morning shower before work. I noticed that the smaller dispenser was empty. I reached for the larger container and pulled up an applicator. My trigger:—it reminded me of the HEET applicator that was placed on my private area. I lost it at that moment and wept uncontrollably. I grabbed my heart in attempt to hold it together. I could feel the brokenness. "Why, God!" I wailed at the top of my lungs. I heard that familiar voice when I'm receptive. However, His answer was something that I didn't want to hear:

You have to forgive, Lorrie.

I started pleading, "I don't want to forgive! She tortured me!" I stomped my feet into the tub basin and shook my fist up into the air. "I don't know how!" I shouted.

I must have sounded like a crazy person that morning. Lucky for me, I was in a safe place, so I didn't have to worry about who heard me or what they thought, considering there were seven family members currently in our household. In fact, no one was around to distract me. I suppose he really wanted me to receive this message, but I didn't know where to begin.

I started searching for possibilities to get the concept from my head and into my heart. *I can picture her in my mind and say, "I forgive you," several times a day until I feel it,* I thought to myself as I continued to get ready for work.

To my dismay, walking down the stairs on my way out the door for work, I glanced up at the skylight displaying the beautiful decal of multicolored leaves that my husband installed a few years prior (which put him at risk for harming himself in the process) to distract the blinding sunlight. Shockingly, I saw Nana's profile picture in one of the tiny leaves in the upper right-hand corner. My mouth dropped open with disbelief. *I've never seen that before. Okay, I get it.* I looked at it and said, "I forgive you," with a bit of hesitation, still struck by the impeccable timing. What's mind-boggling: I was the one that initially chose the pattern. Or was I?

Every day I look at her picture and say, "I forgive you," but I really don't feel it in my heart. In fact, it stings badly for those words to exit my mouth. Then it dawned on me to call my sis Lisa because she's my witness, and she can identify with my pain. I confided in her everything I'd been going through. She validated my feelings and said, "I wouldn't know where to begin with forgiveness, but you can ask God to show you how to forgive." What a brilliant idea. How silly. It didn't occur to me to ask for God's help.

I took Lisa's advice. Before I knew it, God revealed that I don't know Nana's upbringing, and it's possible that she might have experienced the same treatment. I pondered on that idea. If that's the case, it's easier for me to forgive and mean it. *I can have compassion if she was a victim too.* If not, may God be the Judge because as far as I'm concerned, she got away with all the crimes she committed. But God knows everything, and I must believe that. I'm a work in progress and continue my forgiveness process daily until it sticks. Fact: I must forgive regardless of her circumstances—not for her sake but for mine.

I must let go, forgive, and let God handle the rest.

After pointing out my revelation to the entire household, my husband offered to climb up in that small space and color the leaf in with purple pen so that I don't have to see her image daily. "Why torture yourself anymore?" he asked. "Let me take care of it."

I told him, "I'm still working on my forgiveness process, and when the time is right, that will sound like a great idea—without removing the entire decal."

Six months into this process, I *must* be passing the test. I've looked at her image daily, and it doesn't sting anymore. I mean, I cannot miss it. Her image is there when I'm watching TV, when I'm cleaning the living room, and when I'm walking down the stairs. It's interesting that several triggers have come up recently that could have sent me over the edge. A couple of examples: I was tidying up downstairs, and there was a pile of my granddaughter's unfolded laundry lying on the couch. So I naturally started folding her clothes. I picked up a pair of her underpants and held them up in eye's view for a moment. I noticed how tiny they were and looked at the size of the underwear: size 6. I couldn't help but acknowledge and get an actual visual of how tiny I was at six years old. Rather than acting hysterical (like in the past), having hatred in my heart, ranting and raging about the injustice, I walked upstairs, looked at her picture, and said, "I forgive you." I even took it a step further and asked God to have mercy on her soul. I didn't cry, yell, or scream but rather stated it in a calmly fashion.

> *Bless those who persecute you. Don't curse them; pray that God will bless them. (Romans 12:14 NLT)*

Another situation that has come up recently is my granddaughter's school pictures. For some reason, they've been sitting on the coffee table for a month or so, but I overlooked the lesson here. It finally dawned on me that day when I was severely punished for supposedly giving my school pictures away when Nana planted them in my desk, making me look like a liar and flat-out disobedient.

Just this morning while writing this, I relived that scenario, looked at her picture, and said, "I forgive you for that too." Do I sense an art project from my husband on the horizon? I guess you can say I'm healing from the inside out. Praise God.

Continuing to move through the forgiveness process, there are multiple instances of abuse that are quite heinous and bothersome. But rather than be repetitive of what's already been shared in previous chapters, I can't help but ponder the saying by Joyce Meyer: *Hurt people, hurt people.* This is one of those true statements that jolted my perception profoundly. Some people take their prior mistreatment of themselves on the most vulnerable species: the meek, submissive women, innocent children, helpless animals, and the like. Makes perfect sense to me.

For some reason, even though the list of harsh cruelty goes on and on from my stepfather, I am reminded of the abuse I suffered at the hands of his mother. I could sympathize by just imagining what could have occurred in his own childhood and the compassion that might stem from that—just knowing that possibility. What if? Only God knows the truth. It's much easier to forgive and let go of the resentment I have clung to for years—hurting myself and others in the process by using drugs, sabotaging myself, and seeking dangerous behaviors. I've been holding on to the "victim" mentality, feeling sorry for myself, seeking sympathy from others for validation, and being stuck in the past for too long.

God has told me to *rise above* the victim role and be victorious through to the power of forgiveness. I *am*.

Lastly, I forgive *myself*, which is an essential part of this process to free myself up to accept God's forgiveness. I've come too far to go backward, so I will press forward through this painful truth. Disturbing as it might be to admit, I see all those dreadful characteristics I hated the most in others throughout my lifetime. The fact that I possess those same character flaws in myself makes me sick to my stomach.

Who would have known? This is the day that I bare my soul of truth, acknowledgement, and plea for redemption. As ironic as this may sound, today, mid-November 2017, my son would have been twenty-nine years old. As fate would have it, my expected surgery date was postponed until this week due to a coworker's prearranged vacation schedule. This gives me the chance to not only recover physically from a surgery but deal with the unshakeable emotional distress that is very difficult to describe, let alone feel. I've been carrying this burden for years, which have paralyzed me with relentless shame. By the looks of it, it seems to be the family tradition: shackled chain of shame passed down generation after generation. By no means am I disqualifying myself from accountability but knowingly admitting my own mistakes and the terrible choices I've had to live with. Even though I have tried to pay to cover up my own guilt by becoming a substance-abuse counselor, it was never enough. I've come to realize that without God, the guilt and shame have no endings—like a lifetime battery that never dies and just keeps going and going (for me, at least).

This is not only about what I've done but who I had become—heartless, selfish drug addict thinking about the next fix rather than the dire consequences I had left behind. Fortunately, I'm in the privacy of my own home and have the opportunity to unleash the burdensome guilt, a chance to weep from my gut in attempt to gain restoration and seek freedom from condemnation—once and for all. I am so tired.

I carefully relive this entire nightmare of April 1989 and look at the entire picture four months later after my son's death. The baby's father would tragically murder my oldest daughter's father in our presence. How awful would it have been for both of my children live their lives under those extreme conditions and the emotional problems that would have resulted from it, knowing one father killed the other. I can't imagine what that may have looked like and the pain it would have caused both children regularly. Let's just say, things do happen for a reason. Those powerful words that my oldest daughter told me time and time again come rushing through my mind as if she's whispering in my ear right now: "Mom, I give you permission to forgive yourself." I think I'll finally take her up on that offer. Thank you, Nicole, for those unforgettable words of mercy and forgiveness. I love you.

I forgive myself for failing to protect my unborn fetus. The fact that my baby was unable to protect himself from my drug addiction and from the pain and the suffering that occurred in utero. Looking back, I pointed my fingers at those who failed to protect me as a child—my mother, my father, and even God—when I *am* the hypocrite and did the same behavior. I acknowledge these hypocrisies within myself. I consciously forgive myself, which frees me up to receive God's love that I feel that I don't deserve but willingly accept. It is called *grace*.

I forgive myself for being a coward for not speaking up regarding the ongoing molestations by my stepfather. The fact is, Lisa had more courage to stand up and defeat him when I allowed it to happen, regardless if I was terrified. In fact, I used to refer to my biological father as a coward for not checking on our well-being, not intervening, not speaking up, and not saving us. It was I who was the coward.

In my mid-thirties, I was given a chance at redemption when my silence became loud and alive in attempt to protect my nieces and nephews. It's ironic. I do have an annoyingly loud voice today. I know why.

It was brought to my attention that Rob (stepfather) was staying with my middle sister, Shelly, after he was released from jail and was camping out in a tent in her backyard. The problem with that was, she had three young children at that time, which put her children at risk for sexual abuse. Although she was aware of his perpetration toward her older siblings, she felt that it would be unlikely to occur with his "own flesh and blood."

I had to take a stand to protect *my* flesh and blood, regardless of any potential retaliation, based on my own life experience of abuse, to prevent that from possibly happening to the next generation all over again. I called and had Shelly get him on the phone. I told him, "I remember what you did to me as a child, and I'm also aware that Shelly is *not* your biological daughter. You are putting her family in jeopardy, and I demand you leave her house immediately, or else I'm calling the police, snitching [used his own language], and having you forcefully removed."

He suggested to meet with me and discuss the matter in person. *He must have bumped his head.* That invitation was not an option and nonnegotiable. I absolutely refused and demanded he "better comply or else deal with the consequences." I vividly remember those involuntary tremors while on the phone, but my delivery was steadfast and demanding as I prayed (in my head) that my voice didn't shake like my hands.

Within thirty minutes, he was gone. There was satisfaction in my heart that I courageously stood up to the monster that I feared the most in order to protect the children. Believe me, I was terrified to death for confronting him and actually wanted to purchase a gun to protect my immediate family. I had to remind my inner child that I was grown up now and not let the fear control me. I feared retaliation against my own household but prayed to God for our protection and safety. With the little faith I had, I pleaded in desperation. I remember specifically crying out for intervention and demanded, "You need to have my back on this, God," as I shook my finger toward the sky.

The next day on my way to work, still shaken up about potential danger and a bit paranoid, I drove by a U-Haul moving truck to my right, where it was written with huge, black letters, "No Problem," and right behind me was a motorcycle in my rear-view mirror. That was my confirmation—the confident security I needed to move forward, maintain my employment without paranoia, not be paralyzed by fear, and function like a sane adult.

Shelly called me back and wanted to know what on earth I had told him that he made such an abrupt exit from her house without saying a word. I had no choice but to reveal the thirty-year-old family secret that Rob was not her biological father. We all were living a lie. It hurt me to have to be the one to divulge the truth when it was not my responsibility. However, I was put in a predicament, and she had to protect her children by knowing the truth. It was obvious that our mother was not going to ever reveal the secret. I've always resented her for that. I was disowned by my mother for sharing the truth. A couple years later, she reconsidered our relationship and thanked me for having the courage that she did not.

I forgive myself for being a liar and a hypocrite. I carried on the same lies and deceit that my mother did by having my youngest daughter believe that her biological father was someone he was not. I knew in my heart that someday I was going to be the one to reveal the secret and not anyone else. That came to pass. What I know to be true is, we are as sick as our secrets, as the 12-step program reiterates. I no longer want to be crippled by the generational secrets that have hindered our family for decades. Besides, nothing is hidden from God—nothing.

By honestly opening myself up and accepting God's forgiveness and grace, my hope is that someday I'll be reunited with Him and received with arms wide open. I am forgiven.

Happy birthday, son. I love you.

God's Love

God is creating everything new in my life.

My life today is full of epiphanies and aha moments. It appears that for every heartache I've ever experienced, God is reprogramming my mind with new experiences using the same/similar past encounters exemplifying love rather than hatred, courage rather than fear, and hope rather than despair. I do finally perceive this to be true.

> *But forget all that—it is nothing compared to what I am going to do. For I am about to do something new. See, I have already begun! Do you not see it? I will make a pathway through the wilderness. I will create rivers in the dry wasteland. (Isaiah 43:18–19 NLT)*

Yes, Lord, I see it.

He wants me to "leave the past behind" so that He can create anew. He has already done some, and those He is continually rebuilding daily. I just need to acknowledge that it's coming from God and see the love behind the experience, not brush it off as coincidence, which doesn't pose any meaning or intentional purpose. I'm open to receiving the love I never knew existed. It was always there, but I was blinded by ugliness and cruelty of my world. Now that I have purged the poison, there's room for fulfillment on a deeper level of hope, goodness, and gratitude spelled out in God's Word.

Here are a few examples:

First of all, it's fascinating at times when "someone's throwaway becomes someone else's treasure. Often there may be a story behind the find that's extraordinary. I can relate to this more often than not, especially having been a fan of the "goodie box" while growing up on welfare. Goodie box refers to the Salvation Army drop-off box. My sisters and I would shout "Goodie!" whenever our preferences were donated, so that's the name that stuck.

But this is something entirely different, not poverty-driven.

Clearing the clutter out of my garage a few weeks back, I found several of my six-year-old granddaughter's toys in a big green plastic bin that I had forgotten about. To my amazement, I pulled out a Baby Alive in tip-top condition that I had bought for her a couple of years prior.

Since that particular doll just so happened to be my number one choice from Santa that year in 1968, I thought my granddaughter would appreciate one too. The problem with that: it was fifty years ago. Yikes! The flipside was the much better quality nowadays with new technology, so it was a no-brainer to purchase. *Besides, trends/fashion have a tendency of repeating itself,* I thought to myself.

I picked her up and reflected how I earnestly yearned for that specific doll; however, I didn't receive her as a Christmas present that year. How hurtful I felt when I was tricked to tell Nana what I wanted that year from Santa upon her request just so that she could purchase a Baby Alive for her biological granddaughter, not me. I dwelled on that for a bit and shook my head regarding her cruelty at my expense, thinking that Santa loved her granddaughter more than me.

Nevertheless, I put the baby in my granddaughter's play closet, hoping to surprise her, since she hadn't seen it for at least a couple years and might have forgotten. In addition, she was too young to probably remember anyway, so it would be like brand-new.

A week or two went by. Returning home from work one evening, my granddaughter's mother, Nicole, came through the door and mentioned she was in big trouble for her rotten behavior earlier that morning by refusing to get ready for school and being overly defiant and flat-out disobedient.

She put her in time-out in the bathroom for a cool down; however, it had a completely opposite effect. My granddaughter had one of the worst meltdowns that I had ever witnessed, crying, kicking the bathroom door, shaking the doorknob, screaming, "Let me out!" Her emotional outburst escalated into the granddaddy of temper tantrums in my view. Tensions flared on both sides of the door. I just stood there wide-eyed and shocked at her behavior. When it was all said and done and tempers calmed, she was allowed out of time-out. Within a few minutes, the unexpected happened.

My granddaughter stomped up the stairs and forcefully slung Baby Alive by the hair over the railing and shouted, "Grandma, I don't want your creepy doll! I hate that doll!" she hollered.

I didn't react to her lack of gratitude attitude and thought, *Good, I want her.* In fact, I smiled and said to myself, *I finally got my doll—not from Santa but from God.* She's on my dresser now, and when I look at her, I am reminded how much God loves me. She's a prime example that God never forgets a hurt, not even fifty years later. I'm grateful that I wasn't a throwaway ("Garbage Can"). In fact, he rescued a pawn and turned me into someone that can have a positive impact; He gave me hope and a future.

Also looking back, I realize that God never left me. He was in the fire with me, and we went through the pain together. I was never alone.

Skimming through my entire life, I can count so many examples of God's presence during the difficult times. When the HEET was on, He put an angel in my life at the same time—my first-grade teacher, Mrs. Ball. She made me feel special, took interest in my abilities, pointed out what I was good at, and always had something positive to reinforce. I talked about her continuously to Lisa. Lisa couldn't wait to have her for a teacher the following year. She made going to school heaven when my life was hell. She gave me something to look forward to instead of what I was going home to. She was an example that humanity can be kind, loving, supportive, and gentle. She was put in my life when I needed those traits the most. I am forever grateful to God that she chose that profession. God bless the schoolteachers that make a difference without even knowing it—kindness rather than cruelty.

In addition, I cannot forget how He protected Lisa and me from being attacked by the cattle. We were put at risk daily never knowing if we were going to die on our way to school. But God knew. He used His power to invisibly tame the beasts regardless if Lisa had a red lunch pail. Sometime last year, my husband and I went to our recent hiking location when our hiking group was on break. Off in a distance was a herd of cattle with no fencing around the perimeter. My muscles instantly tensed as stress raided my inner being. God gave me an opportunity to face my fear, but I chickened out and pleaded for my husband turn around. Later on in the day, I regretted that decision and wished I had more courage. I hope to get another chance to tackle my fear without letting it control me.

Well, that day finally arrived: February 10, 2018. On our first hiking small group of the spring semester, I was given another chance to face my fear. But on the other hand, I didn't have a choice. We were too far into the hike to turn around.

During our climb up the mountain, I had an up-close-and-personal encounter with a herd of cattle that (similar to my past experience) hovered on both sides of the path, fenceless, and lacked boundaries that triggered my childhood phobias, like I knew it would. This time, I not only had my husband with me, but I had a few of my brothers and sisters in Christ walking alongside me that eased my fear—even if they didn't know it. It was doable. Now I can leave the traumatic bull experience in the past where it belongs and appreciate my new experience, which has been programed into my memory—*courage rather than fear.* Out of this hiking group was birthed a steep hill named in my honor called *Lorrie's Hell* because I struggled, but I conquered. Okay, okay. Maybe it wasn't a monster-type hill, but for any hiking amateur, I had my moments of giving up. I'm sure you get the picture.

More so, have you ever heard this saying? "God wants more for you than you want for yourself." I've heard this quote in the past but viewed this statement as merely a trendy cliché, especially with my struggle with low self-worth that rendered me incapable of absorbing the concept into my heart. Today I know this to be true as it has happened to me personally. Let me explain.

In 2008, when the housing crisis swept across America, for a few of us wannabes, this was an opportunity to dump the never-dreamed-of-owning-a-home mindset and turn it into a slight possibility for renewed hope for ownership. Being a California native, born and raised (most of the time) in the Bay Area, I never imagined I could minutely come close to be a recipient of the "American dream, until that economic downfall. I know it sounds cruel to capitalize on others' misfortunes, but I didn't cause the downfall. Therefore, I jumped at my shot before it was too late.

Then the unexpected happened, and I was given an opportunity of a lifetime. My credit report was atrocious after my initial divorce; however, I had maintained my employment for several years, which showed stability that worked in my favor. The home-loan procedure was a daunting, never-ending challenge of endless paperwork coupled with credit repair and maneuvering through the demanding qualification process, but I did it and was eventually approved to move forward. Then came the hard part: picking out the house. Now this process could have been much more pleasant and exciting, but at that time, the government was giving incentives that included at lump-sum cash back with a home purchase to jumpstart the economy. For the following two years, every bid I offered, an investor would come along and snatch it right from beneath me, or someone else who could afford to pay more would get the house—discouragement at its finest.

Luckily for me, I had a mentor in my corner (an esteemed colleague) who had purchased her own home and had experienced the same disappointments but came out a winner. She was a fighter. I wanted to give up countless times and settle for "it was not meant to be" for me. Mind you, I'd still have to submit monthly paperwork to maintain my eligibility, which I thought was useless and a waste of time for those two years. Nope, my mentor would not accept any excuses from me but rather would question, "What did you do today to make your dream a reality, Lorrie?" She'd look me straight in the eye with the "I'm not kidding" smirk on her face. I knew I'd better have something positive to say; if not, she'd tell me, "You better get on it, and I'll be back to hear your progress in thirty minutes." Thirty minutes! I'd scratch my head and exhale a heavy sigh.

Golly, can't even wallow in my pity party for a day.

Two years in, an offer was finally accepted, not surprisingly, after the government incentives had expired. The house was not the most appealing, eye-catching home in the neighborhood. In fact, it had a hideous baby blue paint job, a weathered-torn roof, and rather small square footage, but it did offer a decent neighborhood and short commute to work. Most importantly, it would be mine, and the exterior was repairable. Moving forward, I paid for the home inspection, gave a thirty-day notice to my current landlord, my exit date, started packing, and so on.

Lo and behold, I was unaware of all the shenanigans that laid before me: jaw-dropping soap-opera drama that if I had I known, I would not have put myself in that predicament—well, maybe. Apparently, the homeowners were going through a messy divorce because her cheating husband was having an affair with the next-door neighbor, and the court ordered the couple to sell the house during the division-of-assets process or something like that. The estranged wife apparently got out of Dodge and moved back to her homeland in Japan. Roadblock after roadblock became the norm to finalize the purchase. It got worse. Japan got plummeted by the tsunami, so mail delivery and/or communication with her was virtually impossible.

A month had passed. The seller's realtor stated she received the paperwork, would sign, and return. It lingered on and on—still nothing, nothing. I had finally given up. We sent a form notifying my intention to pull out of the contract, and it was returned immediately. This was her way of saying, "Stick it where the sun doesn't shine." Not to me but to her ex-husband. And rightfully so. However, I was caught up in someone else's bitter divorce. On one hand, I completely understood where the female was coming from, feeling sorry for her circumstances but also feeling sorry for myself: wasted time, energy, nonrefundable inspection money, and the worst: possible homelessness since I well exceeded my move-out date. I was completely devastated, exhausted from the entire emotional roller coaster, and fearful of repeating the same outcome in the future from ever trying again. Of course, there she was (coworker of mine) offering emotional support, lending a shoulder to cry on, but sternly telling me to put my "big-girl panties" on and try again. I'd routinely hear things like, "God doesn't close one door without opening another," or "God has something better planned for you—keep the faith," or "This is developing your character through perseverance," on and on from a variety of folks. Those were good words of encouragement, but it did not ease my heartache and hard-core disappointment. I could not visualize that for myself; I had absolutely no faith. I was angry, depressed, and developed an "I'll never make it" syndrome that was causing a deep wrinkle right between my eyes. That is the best description to tie those feelings together. While I was busy sulking and feeling sorry for myself, behind the scenes, the housing prices were continuing to drop at a rapid pace. With my steady income, the decline put me into a higher purchase-price bracket of potential homes, and the availability expanded. Apparently, there was more supply than demand. Could it be?

Yes, I now own a tri-level, beautiful home that is beyond my wildest dreams, not only more spacious and less expensive than the blue house but at a better location as well. It gets better. My home is in walking distance to my home church. This was my gift from God. How do I know this? Well, while I'm writing this, I look up to my right, and I see a huge cross separating our dining room from our kitchen. My message: God wanted exceedingly more for me than I felt I deserved. I would have alleviated a lot of pain and suffering and my forehead wrinkle if I would have had faith and trusted God's direction rather than fighting continuously.

I live in this place as a beautiful and incredible reminder of God's love. Oh yeah, and my endearing angel (Paige) whom He put in my path along the way to remind me to never give up on my dreams and that I am worthy to receive God's favor and goodness.

In addition, a new startling revelation I acknowledge to be powerfully mind-blowing is serving a cup of coffee. In my youth, serving a cup of coffee signified molestation at the hands of my stepfather—countless memories that became the norm of my powerlessness and his abuse of power at its core. I would cringe at the sound of his voice, saying, "Lorrie, get me a cup of coffee." I knew what was about to happen. Looking back at this, it's not surprising that waitressing was never an option for me as a career choice. However, today I serve on the hospitality team at my church, and my primary post is at the coffee station serving coffee in God's house—with an entirely new approach of God's love rather than of slave-driven fear—another prime example of Him reprogramming me on a deeper and profound level. God continues to amaze me with His IT capabilities—the Master of human information technologies instilling freedom rather than slavery.

Several months later, November 8, 2018, at work, eyes intensely focused on the computer before me that midmorning, and my personal cell phone was blowing up. Some of the numbers were unrecognizable, so I brushed it off as unwanted solicitors; I completely ignored their efforts. Shortly following, some of the sisters randomly started calling in, texting "emergency." The texts displayed, "I am worried about Shelly [middle sister] and her family!" Suddenly the catastrophe of the worst devastation appeared nonstop on several radio stations and random information coming from other people.

Scrolling through social media, one of my dear, longtime friends, frightened and petrified, posted her reality on Facebook. I could hear the explosions in the background of her video, as if she was trying to escape a war zone. She was stuck in gridlock trying to vacate the town, along with thousands of other residents—panicked and terrified.

My sister Shelly and her three adult children were residents who called Paradise, California, home. The blaze consumed the once beautiful scenery of Paradise; the entire town almost wiped out in what is now referred to as the *Camp Fire*. It was the worst wildfire in California's history. As it would be that day, Shelly had worked a graveyard shift the previous night, had her headphones in, jammies on, lying in bed, and ready to call it a night (in the day). She didn't have a clue as to what was happening as the inferno, as they say, was growing a "football field" a minute, miles up the road, headed in her direction. Luckily, her son, our family hero, was on the move, banging frantically on doors to get people out. I am very thankful that my sister, nieces, nephew, and their families made it out safely. Sadly, some were not as fortunate, God rest their souls.

A couple of her children went to their in-laws as Shelly couch-surfed temporarily from place to place. She was back to her graveyard shift several days later with a breathing mask tightly snug over her nose since the skies were filled with heavy black smoke, and specks of ash were falling around the surrounding areas into the nearby towns. She wondered what to do next.

Shelly tried to hang on to keep her employment down the hillside from the charred, smoldered debris within an eye's view. However, each day created its own challenges. Since thousands of residents were suddenly displaced, finding any type of permanent shelter was darn-near impossible.

That's where I come in. Shelly now lives with me, planted into a new community, in therapy, attending school to obtain her GED, attending church, and participating in small groups, as well as branching out in other community gatherings and activities. Her basic needs are totally provided for so that she can focus on rebuilding her life and future. I am tickled at the opportunity to help.

My point to all of this: we never know when our Lord will turn a tragedy into an opportunity for new beginnings. As for me, remember my agony decades earlier, when I was devastated that Shelly was taken away from me, and I was unable to take care of her? Well, guess what? That hurt is now history and can be forgotten.

Oh yeah, I have another amazing story that I'd like to share. It cracks me up how God works. As you well know, as I was growing up, there were plenty of shameful, revolting secrets that plagued most of my childhood (too many to count). Well, forget all that. Today our church has a special group called *Secret Sisters*. One of our very own brilliant sisters birthed this as a small group at our church. Each sister fills out a three-page "All About Me" section. Those forms are placed in envelopes and assigned a specific number. Within a couple days, each one of us picked an envelope at a prearranged gathering. For the following thirteen weeks, we were committed to pray daily, uplift, encourage, write letters, quote Scripture, exchange gifts, and attend a one-day serve-the-community event as an entire group. Furthermore, it's an opportunity to study all about her (secret sister), get to know her on a personal level, and what her prayer needs are. I mean, this commitment is taken very seriously. Now, mind you, this is a *secret*. Each one of us does not know who our sister is. After a thirteen-week period, we have a revealing party to find out who our secret sister is. The process is absolutely healing for me because it's redefining what a secret means to me from within. I no longer have to view a secret as a disgusting, degrading, or repulsive experience. Now with God's amazing IT capabilities, *secrets* have taken on an entirely new meaning for me: love, connection, togetherness, spiritual, wholesome relationships, and digging into God's Word regularly. And Shelly is participating too! *We are growing together.*

I'm in tears right now typing these words—not tears of sorrow but tears of joy.

Healing revelation: We are no longer as sick as our secrets.

Lastly, the ultimate example that I began this book with, and I'll end it with this: He plucked me out of hell because He loved me too much to leave me there. He didn't cause the pain and suffering, but He did use it for the good in my life—*heaven rather than hell.*

For so many years, a repeated question I used to ask with a heavy burdened heart was, *Why me?* Today I ask with a hopeful heart, *Why not me?*

I'm a part of the Dream Team at my church. I have to say I'm living the dream rather than living the nightmare.

> *He heals the brokenhearted and bandages their wounds. (Psalm 147:3)*

To sum up all these experiences: God has a way of bringing "beauty from the ashes" (in so many ways).

> *To all who mourn in Israel, he will give a crown of beauty for ashes, a joyous blessing instead or mourning, festive praise instead of despair, in their righteousness, they will be like great oaks that the Lord has planted for his own glory. (Isaiah 61:3, NLT)*

This is the ultimate example of, "It's never too late." What is true for me is true for everyone who believes. God can restore us. Just let Him. Glory to God through Jesus Christ, our Savior. I love what our church says: "Let's go make another story together."

For what is to come, my hope is that:

> *God will wipe away every tear from their eyes, there shall be no more death, nor sorrow, nor crying nor pain for the former things have passed away. (Revelation 21:4)*

Just to think back on September 21, 2007, I was petrified to share my story to an audience of only a few hundred that day in San Francisco, and now I'm sharing my story with the world. I am forever grateful God gave me the courage to open my mouth—one of my characteristics that I'm honored to live up to. *To God be the glory for Lorrie's completed story.*

What was intended for evil that spearheads wickedness, hatred, and self-pity, God has *WON* according to His purpose to exemplify love, peace, and forgiveness in my life.

Checkmate!

An astonishing revelation: my curse has become my blessing. But again, it's not only about me. We all have a story.

Acknowledgments

This acknowledgment expresses overwhelming gratitude and reciprocates a gift that was freely given to me. I present my story back to my Lord, Jesus Christ, with the intention to help the *broken* through His love, peace, forgiveness, along with the message of incredible hope.

In addition, I'd like to dedicate this book to my sister, Lisa Joy, who endured just as much as myself. She refused to give into the dark side of humanity but clung to the hope of possibilities though her unwavering faith growing up. Lisa, thank you for being born, enduring the unconceivable with me, and for being my hope when I had none. I can't imagine having to navigate through life without you. This is not just my story alone—it's our story together. I love you far beyond these words.

I would also like to extend my heartfelt thanks to the following people and groups:

My husband, Scott—thank you for being my committed partner and picking up the slack in so many areas. Your ongoing support freed me up to persevere, focus, and complete this twenty-year project without being consumed with the tedious day-to-day responsibilities. Thank you for being my helping hand. You are a Godsend.

To my siblings, I'm so grateful to have each one of you in my life and the love that binds us together forever. We are family.

To my amazing children—Nicole, Dustin, Thane, Serena, and Phil; stepchildren Mackenzie, Kayla, and Anthony—thank you for understanding my emotional ups and downs, loving me through the difficulties, and encouraging me through the process. I know it hasn't been easy. I love you more than words.

Thank you, my dear Laqurisha, for keeping me grounded and sharing your spiritual insight to guide me along the way. You are very special to me.

A special shout-out to the amazing graphic designer, my son, Thane. Thank you for working tirelessly perfecting the cover to my satisfaction and developing something incredibly priceless.

To my photographers Phil (front) and Nicole (back), your eye for imagery is exceptional. Thank you all for sharing in my journey and, most importantly, for being my children. This is a family affair.

To colleagues Niki, Nicole, Diana—thank you for being my literary buffers during the initial process many moons ago and your compassionate listening skills. You're amazing, ladies.

To my editor, Darla Bruno, your feedback broke my heart, but it was the best critique that made this book what it is today. Thank you for doing your job with boldness and integrity, regardless of how it was received on the other end. Now I see the blessing in the pain. Thank you.

Joyce Fox (Serena's high school teacher), thank you for being my second pair of eyes, for your proofreading skills and grammar corrections. Much appreciated.

To Benicia Writers' Group: Kristine, Judy, Susan, Vivian, and Karen. Thank you, ladies, for reinforcing that I have what it takes to be successful and inspiring me to go after it. I'll never forget you all.

To Fellowship Church, Words of the Heart small group—Andrea, Joni, Barbara—thank you for carrying my bleeding heart when the brokenness was unbearable and directing me back to God; for your fervent prayers; for reaffirming that my story matters and could ultimately be used for the good; most importantly, for guiding me through the healing process, wiping my tears on your shoulders, and inspiring me through completion to potentially impact others for God's glory. Yes, you ladies are the epitome of what our church stands for—*hope and healing* at its core. I'm forever grateful. Thank you also to our next group of ladies, Andrea, Shannise, Cynthia, Christianna, and Judi, for your continued encouragement and prayers along the way. I love you all.

Freedom Sisters, thank you for helping me dig deeper, for your compassionate listening skills, and for your loving arms that have encouraged me along the way. I love my Freedom Sisters forever.

Thank you, my Secret Sisters—a special part of my healing journey that I've previously written about. I love you, sisters.

To my dear friend Becky, who has seen me at my worst and loves me anyway. Thank you for not judging me for sobbing uncontrollably on the job, not bringing unnecessary attention to my weaknesses, and hugging me through the pain. You are a difference maker.

Dr. Castello and Dr. Keller, my deepest gratitude for repairing my long, overdue medical condition that had plagued me with the utmost shame being labeled a "Pissy Pot which negatively affected my quality of life for decades. Thank you for not giving up on me and reassuring me that I'm fixable. Mission accomplished. Today I can finally dance like *everyone's* watching and live the carefree life I used to dream of without the embarrassment and shame. You are amazing doctors.

Dr. Saffier, thank you for noticing the value in my story and giving me a platform to share with professionals who help those who still suffer, to raise awareness, and to give back to the community. Thank you for that opportunity. You're not only an amazing doctor but also a wonderful, caring human being. I can see why you have chosen that profession.

To the many, many of you who have touched my soul in one way or another over the past twenty years (too many to count), who have inspired me to keep going and never give up; who listened to my agony; and most importantly, accepted me for who I am. You know who you are.

Also, for the many naysayers—you helped me to truck on and prove you wrong, and for that, I'm thankful.

To the godly-anointed Joyce Meyer. God used you in countless ways to help me through my healing journey, not only through the Word but also those powerful one-liners that were easy to remember: "God will make a message from my mess," "There's a testimony in my test," "The only way out is through," "Hurt people hurt people," and my favorite—"purpose in my pain." You are a powerful teacher of God.

Thank you, K-LOVE, for being there each and every morning, helping to stabilize my attitude, encouraging me with positivity, and playing uplifting music that spoke directly to my heart at times—when I needed it the most during my three-hour daily commute.

To all of you who have taken the time to read my story, *we are stronger together*.

Last—but first—thank You, Lord, for dying for me when I was pitifully sick in my addiction, not worthy of Your sacrifice, and completely undeserving. I did nothing to earn such a wonderful gift. By Your grace, and Your grace alone, I can live with a purpose—to make a difference and hopefully impact others with Your ultimate love. Thank You, my Lord and Savior, Jesus Christ.